Praise for *Freedom is a 1*

'This elegant novel continues to surprise and beguile throughout, its magic unceasing until the stunning denouement.'
PATRICK MCCABE

'This gripping novel is an act of reclamation of buried lives and a livid portrait of a young woman courageously trying to make sense of a society that contains no place for her.'
DERMOT BOLGER

'Freedom Is a Land I Cannot See is an intriguing, satisfying and beautiful novel about love, loss, truth and courage.'
CIARÁN COLLINS

Love, war, loyalty, rebellion, sacrifice, passion, honor, and pain: It's all here, meted out across a heartbreaking story. This is a masterful novel that – like Rose – will never leave you.'
JULIA KELLER

Praise for *The Trout* and *Acts of Allegiance*

'Cunningham's engaging novel challenges us to create our own metaphors so we may, like the trout, raise our head above the surface towards truth.' *The Sunday Times*

'*Acts of Allegiance* is a wonderful brew of a book about politics, family, violence, love, betrayal.' JOHN BANVILLE

Peter Cunningham is from Waterford, Ireland's oldest city. His novel *The Taoiseach* was a controversial best seller; *The Sea and the Silence* won the prestigious Prix de l'Europe. *Acts of Allegiance* was nominated for the Dublin International Literary Award. In 2017 Cunningham was a nominee for the Laureate for Irish Fiction. He is a member of Aosdána, the Irish academy of arts and letters.

Also by Peter Cunningham

The Taoiseach
Capital Sins
Who Trespass Against Us
Sister Caravaggio (as editor and contributor)
The Trout
Acts of Allegiance

The Monument Series

Tapes of the River Delta
Consequences of the Heart
Love in one Edition
The Sea and the Silence

To Claudia —

Freedom is a Land
I Cannot See

Peter Cunningham

with my best wishes —

SANDSTONE PRESS

First published in Great Britain by
Sandstone Press Ltd
Dochcarty Road
Dingwall
Ross-shire
IV15 9UG
Scotland

www.sandstonepress.com

ISBN: 978-1-913207-20-5
ISBNe: 978-1-913207-21-2

Cover design by Stuart Brill
Typeset by Iolaire Typography, Newtonmore
Printed and bound by Totem, Poland

For Carol

&

For Mory Frederick McIntyre
who knew this hinterland so well

PART ONE

1

On mornings when the bay turned eggshell blue, as it must have that morning, when zephyrs of darker blue chased through the deep and a veil of speckled mist stood between Ireland's Eye and Lambay Island, my heart soared. I knew that Howth's flanks bulged like castle buttresses and that the rigid eyes of screeching gulls fixed us sternly as they swooped. Come summer, the buddleia on these high bluffs would throng with Red Monarchs blown in from Africa; but for now it was a bare, forlorn precipice sat above the sea.

'This is the life.'

He stooped to kiss me.

'Rudy ...'

'There is no one else around.'

'You should wait.'

'Shall I sing to you?'

'No!'

'I dream of Jeanie with the light brown hair ...'

I was laughing as dead ferns crumpled beneath us.

' ...I see her tripping where the bright streams play ...'

I knew the heft of him, every contour, and the smell of his clothes and pomade, and his warm face so near me, etched forever in my mind, a young man's face with a full mouth and

3

dark, dark eyes, his expression so startled as all at once the air behind him burst into fragments of light.

'I love you, Rose Raven.'

And I held him in great affection for his wisdom and diligence. He removed his glasses and kissed me deeply. As his breaths shortened and quickened, and as his weight grew, I held his face, and drove my fingers through his hair, and he thrust with sudden passion and called out, 'Oh God! Oh God! Oh God!'

2

Of course he begged me to marry him – several times a year – beginning each New Year's Eve, and on my birthday, which falls in August, and often too on summer nights of great tenderness when he sang arias. I tried to explain that I loved him too much to let him marry me; that I wanted children for him, but not my children; that I could not bear the thought of giving birth to a child I would never see.

'But there are women who will help us! My mother, or Martha. Women around here only begging for a job!'

People were often shocked when suddenly they realised. On the tram, sometimes – their intake of breath, often followed by an apology, as if they were somehow to blame, whilst simultaneously widening the space between us. Although forms or objects were not visible to me, I was by then, thanks to the surgeons, aware of certain shades and colours. Rudy said I was a butterfly.

'Did you know that although butterflies are blind, in the accepted sense, in some light they become aware of particular colours beyond the violet end of the visible spectrum?'

I sometimes wondered if I might have been better without the surgeons – better to see nothing. My children would always be shadows, my images formed by the feel of their baby skin, or from their scent and taste and sounds. Early on, when a child is born, he too can see only phantom outlines, blurred shapes – and for that short time, maybe a month, my child and I would be the same. But day by day he would grow away from me, into his sight, and his face would be just the child of my imagination. I could never see his limbs, or expressions, or how he would smile at me and change as he grew older. Even worse, because I would not be able to see him, or to recognise his traits or features, I knew there would be moments when I would be at the mercy of my memory and when my affection would be held to ransom.

But Rudy refused to listen, just as he never wanted to discuss the past. *We are the future, not the past*, he always said.

'Ah, Rudy, I'm sorry, but you know the answer.'

'I know I will never measure up!' he cried. 'But at least give me the chance to try.'

'Rudy . . . don't.'

'Damn it! Sometimes I think you want me to go away!'

I did not respond, for what he said was at the heart of the dilemma. Yes, I wanted him to go away because I loved him; I wanted him to stay because he loved me.

3

One day, in 1895, a young man is edging down the curling steps of Dublin's Nelson's Pillar when he comes face to face with a fetching girl making her way up. Tommy Raven of Leicestershire is a barracks orderly with the 4th Queen's Own Cavalry, stationed in Dublin at Marlborough Barracks. Annie Duffy is from Nan's Cottage in Sutton, the house her father – a gardener in the employment of Lord Barnmere – had purchased from his employer for fifty pounds. Tommy and Annie marry in 1896; my brother, Ultan, is born the following year; and in 1899 I follow.

The wedding took place in the Catholic Church in Baldoyle; I have the photograph. Annie, my mother, is wearing a dress I recognise: red with pleats, waist tucked, short sleeves; and she has on a funny little red headpiece with a feather. Not that there was red in the photograph, of course, but those were the colours I remembered. It is November, so, despite Annie's game smile, she must be perished. My father, Tommy, is in his British Army uniform, military cap. The bride and groom shine.

The priest, a canon, a man of ample jowls and girth, stands to one side, his smile triumphant. Papa was Presbyterian but Mother's religion had won the day. Although her grandfather was Church of England Anglican, from Dorset, he had turned Catholic to marry. Belief did not much bother my father – he always said he would have gone into a synagogue for Mother – yet he always identified with his own church in Howth, and with his pastor, the Reverend Gilmore. In 1920, when Papa died, it was Mr Gilmore's church he was buried from, and it is in the section of Saint Fintan's reserved for Mr Gilmore's congregation that he is laid down. Moreover, a year later when my mother followed, it was Mr Gilmore who badgered Father Shipsey, pointing out that Tommy Raven's grave lay on the corner of the path separating Mr Gilmore's former parishioners from those of Father Shipsey. Catholics reposed on one of Papa's flanks, Protestants on the other. The priest accepted the minister's interpretation of the cemetery's ground plan, which is how Tommy and Annie Raven lie together at rest.

4

Four years earlier, in the days when I could see, I first laid eyes on Rudy Saddler. I had gone to watch one of Ultan's cricket matches in the Demesne and was radiant with pride for my handsome, dashing brother, his fair mane bouncing as he sprang to bowl, his long legs in their whites, the taut bare sinews in his forearms agleam. His way of collecting his hair in both hands, smoothing down his blond mop as he strolled back from the crease to complete the over.

'Oh, bravo!' came a call from nearby when a wicket fell. 'Well bowled, sir!'

He wore glasses and the straw boater was too big for him. His moustache was scrappy above almost feminine lips.

'I am Mr Saddler, from Curzon Street,' he said to my glance. 'An acquaintance of your brother's. How do you do? My word! That is two wickets to his credit!'

He was Ultan's inverse: dark haired, small sized, bookish, and his spectacles reflected the sun offputtingly. Ultan may once have mentioned someone or other from Curzon Street, employed by the tram company as a ticket picker.

'I shall shortly be training as an accountant,' he said, as if I needed to be told. 'I shall be an articled clerk.'

The sun glare from his glasses had me shielding my eyes. 'Oh, really?'

'Indeed! It is the coming profession.'

I turned back to watch the cricket game unfolding below us.

'Oh, look! Look!' He was pointing animatedly to a thriving buddleia. 'A painted lady!'

'What is . . .?'

'Please allow me to show you!'

I feigned polite interest. The insect's wings shone like mottled tortoiseshell, orange and black.

'The French call her La Belle-dame, you know.'

'I did not.'

'They say she is from Africa.'

I laughed. 'That little thing?'

'I study them, you know. They're far more interesting than people, don't you think?'

The insect spun its wings and, as if theatrically, sparked its bright red underside.

'Would you care to learn more?' he asked as we re-joined the spectators. 'I would be more than happy.'

Ultan was exchanging ends. The new bowler's hair was on fire. All at once he turned and looked up at me, as if the cricket no longer mattered, as if time were at his command.

'Miss Raven?'

I turned.

'I said, it would be my pleasure.'

'What?'

'To teach you about lepidoptera, entirely at your convenience.'

I thought, vermillion. He is beautiful. As he walks backwards, still looking at me, polishing the ball off the leg of his whites.

'By Jove! What a smashing match!' said Rudy Saddler.

5

The Ancient Greeks thought of death as the absence of light; I was no Greek. I had lived nearly four years in darkness, but I was alive, even if I struggled sometimes to grasp what that meant. It was easier for me, in my position, to hold communion with the dead. We pooled our thoughts and jokes, and clutched each other's hands in rushing water. We assured one other that life is no great thing to lose, nor is the great divide something to fear. In the meantime, I learnt to employ my other senses in place of vision – Martha as she waxed the parlour, the Howth tram by our sea wall, the postman on the gravel, the milk dray drawn by the horse shod in heavy iron. In the back garden, up in the corner, my cabbages, beans and strawberries beckoned me with their singular foliage. My rhubarb, parsley and lavender spoke in their distinctive scents. The vividness of lavender in summer was strangely visible to me, as if the other colours of the world had been erased and lavender alone remained.

Other colours emerged under my touch, or at least I catalogued them according to how they felt. Rough was black, yellow smooth, red in between. I learnt to judge the size of a room that was new to me by clicking my tongue, or calling out and then listening for the reverberations.

6

I begged my parents in heaven to find Ultan a wife. Whenever Martha cawed, 'And why wouldn't he? Look at how handsome he is!' I shrank. I had made it clear to him that I would never be his obstacle. Our aunt, my mother's sister, lived in Donabate where she rented out a room. I could go to the aunt, I told him. Nan's Cottage was his, should he so wish.

Over the last year he had begun to come home late from his job in the *Irish Independent*. I lay awake, waiting for his latchkey, knowing that when the birds began to sing he would not be coming in. It was not unreasonable of me to fear for his safety in a city still recovering from war.

'You cannot do this to me,' I said. 'I will die of worry.'

'I am all right, Sis. Some nights, if it gets late, I stay with a friend.'

Three weeks earlier, he'd come in rank with beer. He'd been to the funeral of a colleague, he told me as he bumped around the kitchen. He'd been to the funeral of Harry Deegan – a prominent reporter – who had died that week in police custody, he said as he burned toast. I knew of Mr Deegan, since Ultan had often read out his articles. A prominent critic of the economic policies of our Free State government, Harry Deegan had given his whole working life to the cause of Ireland's liberty, but now that it was here they had murdered him, Ultan said, and went to bed.

Throughout that night, despite our sturdy walls, I could hear my brother weep. A week later, coming home on the Howth tram, he fell from the conductor's platform and had to be taken to the hospital in Baldoyle. Three days later he was discharged, a lurid bandage pressing moss to his head wound, I was told.

7

By the time we disembarked at Sutton Cross, and walked along the swerving bay where it lies on the isthmus, smooth as a child's throat, the east wind cut into us with venom. Rudy tucked his coat around me as his leather soles beat a tattoo – quick, short and sharp, even through the puddles.

Nan's Cottage, so named for an old Barnmere retainer, was a labourer's plain dwelling with the adornment of a new kitchen at the back, put up years before by Tommy. By then he was a porter in a Dublin businessmen's club off Saint Stephen's Green and taking home a decent wage. It was Tommy who had planted our birch. Trees, he used to say with innocent pride, were the mark of a gentleman's residence. My first memories of him: stripped to the waist, his tin-can figure that Annie ever despaired of fattening, pruning his roses, or forking seaweed on to the roots of hydrangeas. He had once served in Burma, where hydrangea plunged wild down steep ravines, he said. Our plot had been cut out of the adjoining Barnmere estate, Irrawaddy. As a child, I had walked up to Irrawaddy, sometimes every day, carrying my school satchel through the dense, variegated woods that marked our boundary. Lately, Ultan told me, Irrawaddy's lawns were in meadow, its chimneys throttled by ivy.

8

Needles of sleet danced noisily as we crossed the sea road and turned for home. Rudy put himself between me and the gusts. That afternoon, a parade of soldiers in their new uniforms due to take place in the Phoenix Park had been cancelled because of the weather, he said.

In the last century, his grandfather Rodolfo, a winemaker with a tenor voice from heaven, had shipped his wife and little daughter, Lucia, from Naples to the Cape of Good Hope to escape Italian wars. In 1899, Lucia, by then aged seventeen, small, dark and dynamic, danced with Sam Saddler, a corporal with the Royal Dublin Fusiliers on his way to the Transvaal. They fell in love and Lucia promised that if he returned she would marry him. A year later, as Sergeant Saddler, he was invalided home with a bullet in the neck. They were married in Saint Kevin's Church in Harrington Street in 1901. Sergeant Saddler became employed as a motorman with the Dublin United Tram Company, and the following year a son was born: Joseph Rodolfo. Rudy.

The Sergeant's right leg ended below the knee; each day he strapped on a wooden prosthesis. While inspecting the undercarriage of a tram car in the shunting shed he had been run over. Sergeant Saddler was now unemployed, and in constant pain. The damp of Dublin was killing him, Rudy said. He hallucinated about South Africa, a warm land where his pain would disappear, where every new morning saw the re-birth of the world. Lucia would hear none of it. She favoured the cool of Dublin and complained that the Cape reminded her of Naples, which she despised. Now they seldom if ever showed each other affection. The Sergeant spent his days in his canal allotment, or down beside the Camac River in Kilmainham where he helped Mr Potterton, the owner of a workshop, to service and repair engines. One day, when Rudy was sixteen, his father had taken him out in Mr Potterton's Dodge Brothers Touring Car and had taught him how to drive.

He was Lucia's project. She had put him in for the job as articled clerk with a firm of accountants and had scrubbed floors to pay for his night classes in bookkeeping. She baked soda bread, which she sold from her front window. Once a week, Rudy attended Signor Ricci in Dolphin's Barn for singing lessons. His grandfather, Rodolfo, could easily have sung in the Teatro di San Carlo, Lucia claimed, according to Rudy.

She did not approve of me. She saw her son make his love hostage to a burden – not to Rudy alone, but surely to her as well. He would one day be a partner in his firm, married to a normal wife, and with a family living in Ballsbridge, not attached to a blind woman out in Sutton.

9

For twenty-four months we had been drenched most days by vaulted black canopies from the Shannon that thundered down upon us. The rain swelled our tide and flooded our roads and pathways. Storms so fierce that crabs were being found in Marino, Rudy said as we came in the gate. Although the rain had stopped, our birch trees still dripped with persistence.

'Rose, you have visitors!' Martha spoke loudly, to let it be known I had arrived home, and drew me into the kitchen where she had been baking. 'Very strange. Asked for Ultan and when I told them he wasn't here insisted I draw the curtains in the parlour.'

I could hear Freddy snuffling at the back door. Whenever I left the house, Martha locked him out.

'I'll leave you be,' Rudy said.

'So no need to take off your coat, Mr Saddler.'

'Martha!'

'It's all right,' Rudy said, 'really, I need to be getting along.'

'You will stay here with me,' I said and thrust myself in Martha's direction. 'I'll talk to you later, Martha.'

'Is that you, Miss Raven?'

I could already smell the dampness off their clothes.

'Is that yourself? Goodness, what a lady you've become!'

I took Rudy's hand. The sing-song Cork accent made me catch my breath.

'It's Mr Barry, miss. Mr Barry from Clery's.'

'Yes, Mr Barry, I know . . .'

'And this is Mrs Barry. Here.'

His hands were small and warm, bird-like hands, meant to pin and tuck and cut. Hers were bony and I was able to tell she was as tall as me, a knack of mine.

'Ah, God bless you,' he said. 'I haven't seen you since . . . What I mean is . . .'

'I know.'

'Your father was a fine man, Miss Raven, don't ever let anyone tell you otherwise.'

'Thank you . . .'

'He was much maligned.'

'What a thing to say,' said his wife.

'I'm sorry, all I meant was that talk is cheap,' her husband said, 'the work of guttersnipes. You have our deepest sympathies.'

We sat without speaking, the weight of memory like a cloud. Tommy's porter's uniforms had come from Clery's, where Mr Barry worked as a tailor, and I had sometimes been brought along for Papa's fittings. Would have made a good jockey, Barry, Tommy always said. A tidy build, clever and intense.

'And who's this lucky chappy?' the tailor chirped up.

'Mr Saddler. How do you do, sir?' said Rudy. 'Ma'am.'

'We do well enough, thank you,' the tailor said.

'Mr Barry looked after Papa in Clery's . . .'

'Yes, yes, I know . . .'

I could hear the stiff crinkle of the woman's dress.

18

'Shocking bit of weather,' Rudy said.

'Hah!' Mrs Barry had a low voice. 'Crops flooded, wool and hides lost, animals drowned.'

Her husband blew air. 'A gentleman I fit from Ballina told me he saw pigs in a river cutting their own throats with their trotters as they tried to escape. Their screams could be heard downstream long after they had sunk.'

'Cyril, please!'

'I'm sorry, sorry, ladies.'

Martha brought in a tray, distributed delft, poured the tea.

'And you're back in your old premises at last, Mr Barry,' I said.

'We are indeed, miss, and proud of it. It'll take more than British gunboats to move us this time.'

'Will I not light a lamp?' Martha asked.

'Leave it as it is, please,' said Mrs Barry sharply.

'You were out walking,' the tailor stated.

'Mr Saddler and I have come from Howth,' I said. 'We share an interest in butterflies.'

'I see, I see,' said the tailor. 'That's a strange one, for certain.'

'And moths.'

'By golly. Moths as well?'

'They have flitters made of my woollens, bad cess to them,' Martha said, lingering, the way she tended to with visitors.

'I agree with you there, miss,' said Mr Barry. 'Delicious scones, by the way, congratulations.'

'Missus,' Martha said sharply. 'Mrs Merry.'

'Oh, Mrs Merry, pardon me.'

'My husband was killed at Gallipoli.'

'Ah, dear Lord, I'm very sorry to hear that, Mrs Merry, a

gallant cause to go out and fight those heathens and preserve our civilisation, God rest his soul.'

'And the souls of all the faithful departed,' Mrs Barry said.

Within the respectful silence Martha returned to the kitchen.

'So tell us, Mr Saddler,' said the tailor, clearing his throat, 'how do you study these insects at all? Through a telescope, is it?'

'I collect them,' Rudy said. 'In the summer, of course.'

'Golly – how is that done?'

'By net. The insect is always killed immediately upon capture – a pinch to the thorax – to avoid any damage they might subsequently inflict on themselves. Following which, each one is catalogued and packed in individual paper triangles, their wings folded back, and placed in a shoe box laden with mothballs. Against vermin.'

'Even the moths?' asked Mr Barry. 'They don't mind the mothballs?'

'They're dead,' Rudy said. 'They couldn't care less.'

I could hear Mr Barry's false teeth clacking as he chuckled, a detail I remembered.

'What do you do, Mr Saddler?' asked the wife in a cooler tone.

'I am training to be a chartered accountant,' Rudy said. 'I work in a small firm off Baggot Street.'

'Rudy works for Mr Fleming in Herbert Place,' I said. 'He has great prospects there, don't you, Rudy?'

'Fleming,' Mrs Barry said in a way that suggested Mr Fleming had yet to pass a test.

'It is a small practice, but Mr Fleming trained in Craig Gardiner,' Rudy said.

'Ah-hah!' cried Mr Barry. 'Only the best cloth in Craig Gardiner, let me tell you! Winceys and flannel from Huddersfield. No expense spared there, no sir! I was cutting cloth for a Craig Gardiner gentleman the day they bombed the post office!'

'Mr Fleming nearly lost his life during the Rising, didn't he, Rudy?'

'Well, there was a small incident . . .'

'More than an incident!'

'During the week of the Rising, when there was fighting down at Mount Street Bridge, Mr Fleming was crossing over from the office to go to Mooney's for a pot of coffee when a bullet whipped his hat off,' Rudy said.

'Gracious me!' the tailor cried.

'He still has the hat at home with a hole to prove it, although to this day he has no idea which side the shot came from.'

'Ah, stop!' laughed Mr Barry. 'That's the best I ever heard!'

Ultan said that the tailor had been against the Treaty, like many men from Cork.

'So what does this Mr Fleming think of Mr Blythe at all?' asked the tailor sternly.

'He says fair play to him, for it takes a man with guts to turn the screws at a time like this,' Rudy said. 'He says governments have to make decisions that are not always popular. What's the point of being free if we are bankrupt, he says.'

'But what about the cost to the common man?' asked Mrs Barry with sudden vehemence. 'The small man across the Shannon with a few wet acres? Is he free?'

'He most certainly is not,' said the tailor.

21

'Some help to him this *Irish* government!' Her voice trembled. 'What have they ever done for the decent people?'

I could hear Rudy's sharp inhalation.

'Mr Fleming says that we are all Irishmen and that is the important thing, ma'am. Unless the country comes first, no one can be free,' he said defiantly.

I could feel vibrations as Mrs Barry shuddered. 'It makes me sick,' she said. 'Sick to my core.'

One chilly morning, as Rudy and Mr Fleming crossed back over Baggot Street Bridge from Mooney's, a curious group was gathered on the pavement outside Cartwright's Merchant Bank, an imposing house on the corner of Lower Baggot Street and Herbert Place. A constable from the Dublin Metropolitan Police, wearing his new badge, stood on duty. Just as Mr Fleming and Rudy approached, the door opened and the president of the Irish Free State, Mr Cosgrave, emerged, his black bowler making him appear taller than he was. As he walked to his waiting car Mr Fleming called out,

'God save Ireland!'

'Good morning to you, gentlemen,' the President said and doffed his bowler.

10

Martha returned, fluttering with excessive purpose. She went home at four and saw no reason why visitors should loiter after her.

'How is your brother, Miss Raven?' enquired the tailor.

'Quite well, thank you. He will be sorry to have missed you – on these Saturdays he can earn a little extra by taking in the sports results.'

'Ah, the written word is sacred,' said Mr Barry, 'we'd all be savages without the written word. I'd have it up there on a par with religion.'

'I doubt Father Shipsey would agree with you there, sir,' Martha said.

I knew she wanted to tell me what my supper was – it was ray that she'd already said she'd bought it from a boat that morning – and that the gas was on, the milk bottles were out, and the time of the high tide.

'Martha, you mustn't be late.'

The bunch of keys tethered to her handbag jangled. 'I have to iron Father Shipsey's surplice for tomorrow's Mass. I'll call for you at ten, Rose.'

She also cleaned the priest's house one morning a week, dealt with his laundry and darned his socks since Father

Shipsey's housekeeper had grown too old and feeble for these tasks.

'Good day to you, Mrs Merry,' said Mr Barry, on his feet.

The hall door needed two tugs to open, one to close.

Mr Barry cleared his throat, several times. The chair creaked as he sat again. 'I was wondering, Miss Raven, if we might have a private word? By which I mean . . .'

'I've fed Freddy,' said Martha, coming back.

I could hear Mr Barry springing up.

'He'll need to go out in twenty minutes.'

'Thank you, Martha,' I said.

'Please mind the milk bottles, Mr Saddler,' she said, 'when you're leaving.'

Her keys sang and the door closed with a dogged scrape. Mr Barry's chair creaked.

'I'd best be going too,' said Rudy.

'I'm sure Mr and Mrs Barry have no objection if you stay.'

'This may not be for everyone's ears,' said Mrs Barry pointedly.

'Rudy is my dear friend,' I said, 'I cannot think of a matter in which I would not ask his advice.'

'What Mrs Barry means is that some matters are best kept private,' added her husband, 'especially in these difficult times.'

'But I would prefer if he stayed,' I insisted, 'if you don't mind.'

'But we do mind!' cried Mrs Barry as if suddenly unhinged. 'That is the point, girl! We do mind!'

'Look,' said Rudy, 'I must leave anyway . . .'

At such times I wished most that I could see, for if I could see their faces, I imagined, I would know what was in their minds.

24

'No offence intended, sir,' said Mr Barry.

'None taken,' Rudy said. 'I'll come out after Mass tomorrow,' he said to me.

'Make sure Freddy doesn't follow you.'

Nothing was said until the door tugged shut. I could tell it was still daylight even though we were forced to sit inside without it.

'I am fascinated, Mr Barry.'

'Tell her,' said his wife.

'Miss, we have come out here to deliver some highly important documents to your brother, but in his absence we will have to entrust them to you until he comes home,' the tailor said.

A sudden gust shook the cottage and rattled the parlour window.

'What kind of documents?'

The tailor liked to clear his throat each time before he spoke.

'As you know, Miss Raven, we are in the midst of a national economic emergency. Young Mr Saddler touched upon it earlier – a very estimable young man, I have to say, his erudition was a pleasure . . .'

'Spit it out!' cried Mrs Barry. 'Fifty thousand unemployed in commerce, the same number in agriculture, money leaving the country by the hour . . .'

'It is bleak, miss,' said the tailor, 'very bleak.'

'It's a disaster,' said his wife. 'Our so-called independence is a sham.'

The tailor said, 'The government fears that if our true state of affairs becomes known abroad, if a sensation were to be made of our impecunious position, then our ability to borrow money, at the moment so very difficult . . .'

'The government are cowards!' Each time she spoke I flinched. 'Every man jack of them! And as for our Minister for Home Affairs...'

'...were we to crawl back to London with our begging bowl, a hideous vista...'

'Few dare to mention the true position,' said Mrs Barry with passion, 'and those who do pay the price. Just as poor Harry did.'

I stared at them. 'Harry?'

'Harry Deegan was my brother,' she said.

'Oh... I am so sorry...'

'My younger brother,' she said. 'I reared him.'

Now I began to understand why we were sitting in my parlour with the curtain drawn when it was still light outside.

'They beat him,' she said, 'I saw his face in the coffin. His poor heart gave out.'

'We are Mass-going people, as was Harry,' the tailor said. 'This is repugnant behaviour.'

'One man in particular...' Mrs Barry said, on the brink of tears.

'A Castle man, Detective Sergeant Melody,' the tailor said. 'A fanatical type. Drummed out of Oriel House with blood on his hands and now he is trying to make amends by showing zeal to certain factions within the government.'

'A monster,' said Mrs Barry, 'he'll stop at nothing to get his way.'

'We disembarked the tram twice on our way out here today and waited to make sure we were not being followed,' the tailor said.

'Melody,' I said.

I could almost not speak. I was suddenly standing beside

Annie and Detective Sergeant Melody was looking me straight in the eye.

'Harry felt he had a Christian duty...' the tailor was saying.

'To reveal the true position to those outside the country,' Mrs Barry said. 'To broadcast the plight of the people in the west...'

My head spun. 'I'm sorry, what people?'

I was aware that Mr Barry had got up, parted the curtains an inch and was peering out.

'You see, Harry travelled west three or four times this past twelve months,' he said. 'Couldn't believe his eyes. The newspapers that have already reported the situation are not exaggerating, even though there are those in government who claim such reports are groundless. Ordinary people do not know which to believe, and when that is the case, they prefer not to believe the worst. But the truth is that widespread deprivation exists beyond the Shannon, even as we speak. Harry assembled these documents to prove it and was proposing to bring the scandal to a wider audience in the belief that only in that way would help be given. He had planned to hand over his report to a colleague who works for a newspaper in Boston.'

'But Melody got wind of Harry's plan,' Mrs Barry said.

'Probably tipped off from someone inside Harry's newspaper,' said the tailor.

'What is the west to Melody?' I asked. 'He is a Dublin peeler.'

'A peeler who is trying to prove his worth,' Mr Barry said. 'Who is terrified of losing his position and will resort to anything to impress his superiors.'

27

Mrs Barry sighed. 'He had it in for Harry for years ... on a personal level.'

Her voice was flat and fatal. I could hear the rustle of papers.

'Harry gave these to me the night before he was arrested,' she said.

'I'm sorry,' I said, 'I am unable to read.'

'Let me describe them for you, miss,' Mr Barry said. 'These are the sworn depositions of priests and doctors detailing the names of eleven men and women and six children who have starved to death in the west of Ireland in the last nine months, along with their addresses and the particulars of where they are buried. These photographs here show their bodies, and these ones are of live children, but in the grip of starvation, who by now may also be dead. Harry couldn't believe it. He was flabbergasted.'

'It is mortifying,' said his wife, 'for our country to find itself like this, after all we have been through.'

My heart knocked loudly as, within my darkness, the outline of something dread began to form. 'Did ... does Ultan know about this?'

They exchanged glances, but thought I could not tell.

'He does know most surely,' said the tailor carefully, 'which is why we are here. You see, my brother-in-law was a close mentor to Mr Raven, if you will, a caring older man. A Socrates, no less.'

I felt a fear I thought I had forgotten. 'But why do you say that Detective Sergeant Melody had it in for the late Mr Deegan on a personal level?'

I did not need to see the expression on their faces. Mrs Barry sighed again deeply.

The tailor spoke: 'Men like Melody are driven by self-righteous wrath, miss, which is often another word for hate. They see the best path to their spiritual salvation as marked by the blood of those they despise.'

I knew my breath was short, but I didn't care. I had to ask the question. 'Why would Melody have despised Mr Deegan?'

Mrs Barry was now sobbing audibly.

'Harry had great gifts to impart, miss, and was most generous to those whom he held in affection,' said the tailor eventually.

'Including my brother Ultan?'

'Yes! Yes!' Mrs Barry cried. 'They were friends!'

11

It was a name going back in my grandmother's line for generations, or so she used to say. It means a man from Ulster, but since Nana had no relatives up there and had been born and raised in Sutton, the connection remained elusive. When it came to Annie, it was never clear if she knew the meaning of the name she had given her son.

As a child you are chained to your family circumstances as a galley slave to his thwart. My mother cast me as her blight, for as hard as I tried to please her I was always at fault. With age, I came to realise that when she saw me she was envious, and so I think she saw me as a rival. Towards the end we had some sweet interludes, and I accepted that my mother's jealousy did not make her wicked.

Papa was seldom there to mitigate the results of her irritation, so I turned to Ultan. He sensed the injustice wherein he would always be excused where I was condemned, and this upset him. He could not risk losing the great bounty of his mother's affection by open revolt; instead he showed his support and affection in quiet ways, and read me stories at night, and shared his treats, and when I was ill with a rash, brought in soft cotton and dabbed me gently with calamine lotion.

I believe our upbringing forced Ultan to seek out fairness in the world. As we grew up he used to speak out with passion for causes that divided opinion in our household, such as Ireland's right to be free, or the destinies of other societies oppressed by empire. That he was now on the side of starving people in the west did not at all surprise me.

12

In step every Sunday, in every kind of weather, we walked arm in arm from Sutton Cross to the Tin Church. We were often assumed to be mother and daughter, and sometimes it seemed to me that Martha thought so too, and that this gave her the right to be present in every aspect of my life.

From the hum of voices and the renewed sea breeze we were approaching the church. Papa had once taken me by the hand and led me to a bed of sweet alyssum here. That magical, immortal scent.

'I didn't like one bit of that Mrs Barry,' Martha said.

Since we had left Nan's Cottage she had me pestered.

'She was a right horse,' Martha said, 'a big face on her, big feet. What did they want?'

'Martha, please ...'

'Why did they get me to draw the curtains?'

'They are afraid. Her brother died in police custody.'

'My husband is dead but I don't sit in a dark room,' Martha sniffed.

I had hidden the envelope beneath the linoleum in my bedroom. The thought that Ultan was involved in something that might draw the attention of the authorities terrified me.

I wondered who would have known had I burnt the Barrys' envelope in my kitchen range.

'I didn't like him either,' Martha said. 'A little ferret of a man.'

'At least he liked your scones,' I said.

I still went to Sunday Mass because there I was guaranteed to meet people, and hear voices other than those in my head, and catch the gossip of a world I could no longer see. I had long abandoned my respect for religion or the hope of a merciful God. Moreover, I disliked Father Shipsey's platitudes, his tutored reasoning bled of all feeling and how he took it for granted that men's souls fell within his purlieu. Soon we were back out in the air, buttoned up against the squalls tumbling down from Howth. Mr Murphy, the jarvey at Sutton Cross, always smelled of his horses, even though he now used a motorcar.

'They say they are going to reduce the pension again,' his wife was saying, 'can you believe it? What have we got ourselves into?'

'They should be ashamed of themselves,' Martha said.

'Two pensions in your house going down, Mrs Merry, so twice the grievance, no doubt at all about that,' said the jarvey.

'My late husband's pension comes from the Crown, Mr Murphy,' Martha retorted. 'It is going nowhere.'

'And now they're saying ten thousand pounds will be given to Croke Park!' cried the jarvey. 'So that people can run and lep and ride in motor-cycle races! Ten thousand pounds! Is that a sin or is it not, father?'

A heavy tread. Father Shipsey's clever eyes sat in nests of flesh. I wished we could be on equal terms, by which I meant, that he could not see me.

'I could build a church with bricks and mortar for a lot

33

less than ten thousand,' he said. 'Are you well, Miss Raven? Mrs Merry?'

He must have thought that because I was blind I was unaware of his gaze. The oil he used to plaster down his hair smelled oversweet.

'This weather has us all on our knees, father,' Martha said.

'Ah, I know, the people in the west especially,' the priest said. 'A dreadful time of it they're having, or so I hear.'

'Rivers bursting, I've heard that too,' the jarvey said, 'rumours of people starving again, if you can believe that in nineteen-twenty-four.'

'We should pray for them,' the priest said.

'And then maybe the Lord will provide,' I said.

'Thank you for that consolation, Miss Raven,' Father Shipsey said in a winnowing tone. 'Remember when we do build our new church that you will always be most welcome.'

As we walked home I could feel a clew of brightness in the southern sky.

'Did Ultan come home last night?' Martha asked.

'Very late. After three. Talked to Freddy for half an hour.'

'Is he in some sort of trouble, Rose?'

'What a strange question.'

'His behaviour has changed, that's all I meant. He's lucky he didn't come to more harm when he fell off that tram.'

'He's just a young man, finding his way, Martha.'

'I prayed for him this morning,' she said. 'That he would find a good woman.'

I put my face to the sea in the hope that her words would be plucked away.

'I can't understand it,' Martha harped on, 'a more hand- some man I have never seen.'

34

13

Despite the damp, Rudy was outside Nan's Cottage when we arrived, and smoking a pipe whose smell I had picked up at the seawall.

'Your daffodils are peeping,' he said.

'Did you not go home at all, Mr Saddler?' Martha asked, taking off her coat.

'I did and I got Mass this morning in Haddington Road, Mrs Merry, in case you're wondering,' he said jauntily.

'I have more to do, Mr Saddler, than to be wondering about you,' she said.

On Sundays, Martha made our lunch before returning to Baldoyle to cook for her mother. Rudy took my hand and sat me down beside him on the wooden bench where he had spread his coat.

'Did you say one for me?' he asked.

'Several.'

He leant in.

'Rudy! We're nearly out on the public road!'

He shaved every Sunday morning and then splashed himself with cologne. His family still went to Sunday Mass together, as ours had once done, after which his father went down to his allotment. Even on Sundays, he could not bear to be at home, Rudy said, but preferred his own company, sustained by memories of a place he would never see again.

I could hear Freddy inside the door, snorting to get out.

'What was the tailor on about that my ears weren't fit to hear?' Rudy asked.

'He just wanted to talk.'

'But only to you.'

'He's a sentimental man – he remembers my father. And of course . . . that day outside Clery's . . .'

'Of course . . .'

'I think he just wanted to express his condolences,' I said, and marvelled at how easily deception came to me. 'He's an old-fashioned man.'

'He seemed fishy to me,' Rudy said. 'And as for her . . . That kind of anti-government talk attracts attention, you know.'

'Do we have to spend our Sunday morning talking about the tailor?'

'I just didn't like the way they wanted to be alone with you, that's all,' Rudy said. 'He sounded as if he had come out for a purpose.'

'I told you his purpose,' I said stiffly. 'To offer his condolences.'

I hated lying to Rudy, but the less he knew about why the Barrys had come to see me, the safer he would be.

'Come here.' I took his hand. 'You obviously made an impression. He said he could tell you were a young man of great erudition.'

'I don't believe you.'

'I'd say if you ever want a good rate for a suit in Clery's he'll look after you.'

Two tugs on the front door and I could tell by the shuffle

of his feet that he was wearing carpet slippers, which meant he was still in his dressing gown.

'What a beautiful morning! Sis.' He kissed my cheek. 'Young Saddler.'

'Lord Ultan,' Rudy said. 'I just told Rose, your daffodils are coming out.'

'Ah, a host of golden daffodils!' Ultan exclaimed, his voice thick.

'Oh, please, spare us the poetry!' Rudy cried. 'It's too early, old man!'

'Beware of these little men who balance pennies on their noses, Sis.' He sat down heavily on the bench beside us and a little eddy of stale drink rode the air. 'Atta boy,' he said as Freddy jumped into his lap.

'Don't catch a chill,' I said.

He cracked a match and the sulphur swam lusciously.

'Sis? They're called Lucky Strike. From America.'

He put the cigarette in my lips; I held his hands and drew in deeply. For a molecule of time we were down on the sea wall, following our parents at a distance, and I could see Howth bending through the glamorous blue plume of my smoke.

'How goes the great news machine?' asked Rudy. 'The presses that never sleep! The drug of the unwashed masses! You editor yet, old man?'

'Not lackey enough, my boy,' Ultan replied, 'only bum-lickers need apply.'

'Ultan!'

'Horrible but true, Sis,' he said. 'Apologies. Sometimes my ire overtakes my manners. Oh, by the way, some bad news over the wires, I'm afraid.'

'What?'

37

'Your friend, Lucy Barnmere,' he said, suddenly gentle.

'What of her?'

He had to cough at length before he could proceed. 'Ah . . . dammit!'

'Ultan? What about her?'

'Fell from Tower Bridge in London, which is what we are reporting, out of respect for the family. I mean, that it was an accident.'

'Oh . . .'

'Found two miles downstream, I'm afraid. A post-mortem was carried out, but it's all hush-hush. The funeral is in London.'

In my private world a little girl listened attentively as I read to her and fluttered her pretty fingers. Later she and I sat side by side in the great bay window of her bedroom and looked out on the waves in Dublin Bay.

'Wordsworth lost a sister – did you know that?' Ultan was saying.

'Wordsworth again,' Rudy groaned. 'Please, my lord . . . '

'Tommy used to mention it. His mother coming from Lancashire, he thought of Wordsworth as one of the family, and for a long time I thought the same. I was devastated when Tommy told me he was dead.'

Rudy laughed. 'At least that's funny!'

'As a young boy Tommy was brought walking in the Lake District,' Ultan said. 'Never forgot it. The softness of it, he used to say. To be able to stand alone in such a tranquil wilderness. No factories, no smoke, no noise. An absence of the dire circumstances of big cities. The happiness of wild daffodils.'

The front door tugged open.

'Ultan, will you come in and have your breakfast,' Martha said. 'And get dressed, for goodness sake!'

'Good morning to you too, Mrs Merry. Is my dressing gown not a statement of that imminent intention?'

'There's tea inside by the fire,' she said. 'You'll get your death.'

Ultan coughed jaggedly before he said: 'He promised me many times that he would bring me there. We'd take a train from Lancaster to Penrith – the plan was clear in his mind, just the two of us. But we never did.'

He blew air as if the effort of so much talking had exhausted him.

'Breakfast,' I said and got up. 'Come along, gentlemen.'

But he began to cough again, a deep, phlegmy hacking from the chest that went on far too long.

'I'll get a bowl,' cried Martha and hurried in.

'You have a grippe,' I said. 'Get it out.'

'My grippe ... is not in ... my chest ...' he gasped and steadied himself. 'You see, as Wordsworth observed, so many enchanted places await us if only we take the trouble to look.'

He spat up at length as Martha held a bowl; and then he slumped beside me.

'Thank you. I refer to countries for whom our current problems are unworthy of notice. Economies that have been thriving for many centuries. Lands of plenty, with sunshine, abundant crops, settled, healthy people. Governments that do not need spies to keep them in power. Did you know that Eddie Kidney now works as a clerk in a government department?'

I was swept by the same dismay that always lurked there, ready to seize its moment.

39

'How is that possible?' I asked eventually.

'I thought he was in gaol,' Rudy said.

'He was, of course,' Ultan said, 'and had I my way he would rot in one. But now he's out under a partial amnesty, with some others of his kind, and helping to run the country.' He began to cough again, but gathered himself. 'I didn't want to tell you, Sis.'

'I am stronger than you think.'

'Eddie Kidney,' Rudy said, still in disbelief.

'We should go away from here, the three of us,' Ultan said. 'You're looking at me as if I've lost my mind, but I tell you with all my heart that I have never been more serious.'

14

He had declined Martha's breakfast and gone to get dressed as Rudy and I sat in the kitchen. Martha occasionally acquired tomatoes from stalls on the pier in Howth, and then beat them into duck eggs which came from a farm outside Malahide.

'There's something wrong with that man,' she whispered. 'He's not himself.'

'It's what happens if you stay out drinking till cock-crow,' I said.

'It's more than drink,' Martha said with unwelcome foreknowledge.

The Ultan I remembered, the Ultan who bowled so gracefully and who could run the mile in a decent time was now thin and pale, she said. He shuffled rather than walked. I remembered a time not too long ago when he used to eat his dinner faster than Freddy.

'Talk to him, Rose,' she said.

He was in the parlour, at the fire, sitting in the chair our father used to occupy, looking out. The cigarette he had just put a match to was the only fresh, vital thing about him, Rudy told me afterwards.

'Ultan, old man, do drink some tea,' Rudy said. 'You look as if you've swallowed a frog.'

I'd seen my father drunk, once a year, when he came home following his regimental reunion; next morning he looked like this, or as I imagined Ultan to now look, the energy hammered out of him.

'Here, I've brought you in a cup—' Rudy began.

'Ahhhh . . .'

'Ultan?' I said.

'Ultan!' Rudy shouted. 'His mouth is open but he cannot breathe!'

'Ahhh . . . ahhh . . .'

'What's wrong?' I asked. 'Rudy? What's wrong?'

'Ultan! Sit up, old man!' Rudy shouted. 'Good Lord, are you all right?'

'What's happening to him?' I cried.

'It's all right, he's just taken a turn,' Rudy said. 'Try to breathe normally, Ultan, come on!'

'Mother of God!' Martha had come in. 'What have you done to yourself, child?'

I could hear Rudy slapping him on the back, and then Ultan gulping air.

'I am perfectly well, thank you all,' he gasped. 'A temporary indisposition.'

'I don't know what they did to you in that hospital,' Martha muttered. 'Get out Freddy!'

'It could be the fire smoke,' Rudy said.

'There's no smoke from my fires, Mr Saddler!' Martha snapped. 'Ultan, please drink your tea.'

My brother took deep breaths.

'Thank you,' he said weakly, 'I am better now.'

'You should go back to bed,' Martha said.

'It . . . passes,' he said. 'It has passed.'

'What has?' I asked. 'What has passed?'

He was sounding most uneven.

'Look, now that we are all here . . .'

'You should save your strength and not speak,' Martha said.

'Be quiet, Martha! Go on, Ultan.'

'Well, I . . . I have been meaning to tell you something . . .'

I felt sudden dread that my deepest secret was about to be let out. 'Please! You don't have to—'

'I do, Sis. I do.' He cleared his throat and I covered my face with my hands. 'I . . . ah . . . I'm seeing a doctor.'

My ears resounded.

'*What?*'

'In Fitzwilliam Square. He's a member of Tommy's club.'

That's what we always called it, a joke at first, but that's what it was, after all. His club.

'Oh, well done, sir,' Rudy said.

Which, along with huge relief, was also my first thought: a doctor who treated those afflicted by a lack of temperance.

'It was recommended during my stay in Baldoyle,' Ultan said. 'He is hopeful.'

'Bravo!' Rudy said.

'Hopeful? Which doctor, Ultan?' I asked. 'Hopeful for what?'

'Mr Bradshaw. He remembers Tommy well, still talks about him. A surgeon. He is highly regarded but doesn't charge me for his advice because of the connection.'

'His advice?' I asked.

I did not need to see him frozen for words.

'What's wrong, old man? Tell us,' Rudy said.

43

I wished Martha would stop fidgeting so that I could hear.

'He wants to operate. To get it out, but . . . ' Blisters clung to his words. 'It may be . . .'

No one wanted to ask a question then.

'But he says . . . he says . . . '

I did not think I could bear it if he began to weep.

'There is a risk to my vocal cords. To my voice.'

'Oh, dear Jesus, have mercy on us . . .' said Martha.

'Martha—'

'There is also radiation, but he does not believe in it,' Ultan said. 'Not at this stage. I trust Mr Bradshaw.'

My mind was racing: scraps of old conversations, in this room, beside this fire, when my father used to come home from work. Papa's laughing voice. The phrase, 'a Tommy Special'.

'Mr Bradshaw will operate,' Ultan said. 'In Dr Steevens' Hospital.'

'Oh.'

'I'll be told when shortly.'

Down on the sea wall the Dublin tram went by. It was raining. High tide would be at three o'clock.

'We shall come in with you,' I said, trying to make the grotesque normal. 'I will be there with you.'

I was sure he would refuse, but instead he said, 'Thank you, Sis, I'd like that.'

Why I should at that moment have felt so grateful to a God I did not believe in that my parents were dead I could not explain. Or what about my first feeling, which had been one of huge relief? Too unspeakable to even contemplate. I knew this was a moment I would remember forever.

'You just let us know when, old man,' said Rudy shakily.

'The sooner the better,' said Martha, as if she suddenly knew what needed to be done. 'I'll ask Father Shipsey to say a Mass.'

'Just the thing,' Ultan said.

We were a queer little group, sitting there on a Sunday morning, facing a new enemy.

'Well, I'll let you know,' he said, 'and when this is all over, we can talk about what we discussed earlier, outside.'

'Of course we can,' I said. 'By all means, we will.'

'I have your word?'

'Yes, of course.'

'Rudy?'

'You have my word too,' Rudy said.

'About what?' Martha asked suspiciously. 'Have you been talking about me?'

15

Agnes Daly, whose father was the blacksmith in Fairview, was as tall as me, and her eyes were greenly lustrous and beautiful. We had sat in the same desk at school with the nuns in Raheny, and shared our secrets, and vowed we would be each other's bridesmaids. But now Agnes was working again as a chambermaid, in a hotel on the North Strand, changing beds and scrubbing baths. When Agnes wrote to me, Martha read out her letters.

'"*We are lucky we live in an age where the doctors know more than has ever been known. Consider Ultan fortunate to have been diagnosed in time.*" Did you tell her about Ultan?' Martha asked.

'She is my friend.'

'When did you last see her,' Martha asked. 'When has she ever come here to see you? To help you?'

'Martha ...'

'You pick your friends, Rose.'

The forge had closed; Agnes's mother had died; the blacksmith had fallen prey to the vapours. Now he sat all day in a chair, mute, faced towards the sea, and was fed with a spoon. Each night when she went home, Agnes had to lift her father into bed, she told me in her letters.

'"My news is that I have met someone kind and gentle. He drives the horse dray that delivers the Guinness to the hotel twice a week – would you believe it, his name is Arthur! Arthur from Guinness!" Jesus, did you ever hear the like?'

'Just read it, please, Martha, without adding to it.'

'"Modesty forbids me to describe our last encounter." Mother of the Divine! "Perhaps when Ultan is better I can come over and meet you, lovely Rose. It's been far, far too long."'

I heard her words but all I could think of was Ultan's impending operation; it filled my mind entirely; and all the while the Barrys' envelope lay hidden in my bedroom.

16

At times I wished Rudy would stay away. That was extremely self-regarding, for Rudy was nothing but loyal and supportive, and yet, with Ultan now mostly at home, I did not want Rudy there too. It would be like the old days, the pair of us in Nan's Cottage in the world we had made from which our parents had been excluded. We had often played at making house together and having children. Our charade took place in the tool shed up the back garden, where we had a kitchen and bedroom, cooked meals, sang lullabies at night, and kissed chastely the way our parents did when they knew we were watching.

Some mornings he was so weak he could scarcely get up, Martha said, adding that she had found blood on his pillow. Even milky tea hurt him to swallow. Mr Bradshaw had written a letter to the editor of the *Irish Independent*, advising of his patient's indisposition and stating that Ultan would be back at work by early April at latest. The newspaper, not known for its generosity of attitude, had written to Ultan saying that when he was fully recovered he could reapply for his position.

Mr Bradshaw's name was forever linked in my mind with a

Tommy Special. Papa said it was really a Curragh Whiskey, named for the officers down there who had invented it, and that he had simply brought the recipe with him, first to the officers' mess in Marlborough Barracks, and onwards to his club in Dublin, where in his honour it was renamed a Tommy Special.

'The most important job is to make sure the pips are out of the lemon.'

His voice, bell clear. White of egg, two fingers of whiskey, syrup and the pip-free lemon juice. Into a cocktail shaker with ice. Agitate. Serve through a Hawthorne strainer.

'A Tommy Special!'

His humble pleasure from such vicarious fame. And the club's main champion of this drink? Surgeon Bradshaw.

Ultan and I spent those days together, and the one time he went in to Dublin, where he had an appointment with the doctor's nurse, I waited like a child for his return. The opportunity to hand over the tailor's envelope never arose; I could not bring myself to bother him at such a time with the concerns of other people.

As rain wriggled in noisy worms down the window we smoked cigarettes and talked about our parents. The depth of his feelings surprised me, for I had always seen him as the favoured one, assured and happy with his place; instead I now learnt that as a boy he had yearned for his father's affection. Hard as Ultan had tried, Papa had never let him in, he told me. It was how his own father had treated him, reluctant to show emotion since it made boys soft. The Leicestershire Ravens, a military family, had believed in an approach to life that inured them against inevitable sadness. I could suddenly see my mother's strategy at work, as if her full attention had

49

been needed to correct this imbalance, and in the process of this overwhelming need she had overlooked me. It was a small consolation, but consolation, no matter how small, is always welcome.

17

'I never saw this coming.'

We sat as if awaiting a train we hoped would never come. Martha had been trying to build him up with soda bread and tripe, liver and coddle, but with only two days left, he was eating nothing and his belly was gone. He had just come back from Baldoyle and he had been drinking.

'Mr Bradshaw's nurse asked me the other day . . .' he was weeping all at once, '. . .she asked me . . .'

'It's all right, really.'

'Sis . . .'

'Tell me.'

'. . .if I would like to be anointed, and I said yes . . .'

'Of course.'

'She said everyone is,' he gulped, 'and she meant to put me at my ease, but why will they anoint me unless they fear the worst?'

The sudden image of my brother's body leapt at me: white, embalmed with olive oil.

'It is practised in all the hospitals,' I said with a wild, unfounded assurance, 'no matter who you are or what your condition. I have been in enough hospitals to know. They anointed Papa, for goodness sake, even though he was dead when they did it and he was a Protestant.'

In a small space of happy time we looked at each other and began to laugh.

'Oh, goodness, Sis, you're a tonic.'

'We're going to get through this, I know it.'

'You know – I wouldn't be surprised if you're right.' He poured tea and went to the rain-lashed window. 'There is something I have to tell you. It's just in case ... you know ... what I mean is, there is something I want you to do if I don't come back.'

'Of course you're coming back!'

'Please, Rose ... please ...'

He sat beside me.

'You see,' he said, 'I know that Barry, the tailor from Clery's, was out here the other week ... and his wife ...'

He might have struck me. 'How—?'

'Martha told me, and I know you haven't mentioned it because of my news.'

'I was going to tell you but ...'

'What Martha doesn't know is that he gave you documents for me. Sworn depositions, photographs.'

'How do you know?'

'I know, Sis, I just know.' He sighed. 'Listen, there are some people within the new government who think these documents should not be seen overseas. Particularly not in America at a time when our ability to borrow is so weak. We are ashamed, because part of our folklore is to hold the British responsible for the Great Famine ...'

He had to cough at length before he could continue and I could feel how ill he truly was.

'... but now our new government finds itself presiding over

a possible famine in the very first years of our freedom. The government has given what money it can to the west, but the situation is sliding beyond control. This was what Harry Deegan was going to write about, before Melody got to him. He had cabled a contact in Boston, someone who works in a newspaper there. They say they will publish the story but first have to ascertain the facts for themselves.'

I wanted to ask him about Melody's crusade against Harry Deegan, but I could not bear to have him suffer more.

'A reporter will come in early April and will let me know when he arrives.' Ultan caught my hands. 'I don't know who he will be, but when he gets here he will tell the authorities that he has come here to trace his ancestors. Ancestors – that's the key word Harry agreed with them.'

'How will he find you?

'He'll come to the *Independent* and find me, but if I'm not back at work by then there's someone I trust in there who will let me know when he arrives.'

'And what will you do?'

'I'll meet him and we'll travel west to meet the witnesses listed in Harry's report and verify the situation.'

I was crying with fear, but I didn't care.

'Sssh, Sis.'

'Let's go away, Ultan, like you said we would, the three of us. Let's leave all this behind.'

He sighed so deeply I could hear his heart. 'We will,' he said, 'when I've done right by Harry, we will.'

We sat for what seemed like an age, and I wished it would never end.

'You can't tell Rudy about this,' he said at last. 'It's too dangerous for him.'

'I know.'

'Promise me you won't. If you tell him, you'll be putting him in harm's way.'

'I've already lied to him.'

'Good. We are so alike, you and I.'

He could lift my heart by just being there, my dear brother, by us just breathing the same air.

'I've never even been to the west of Ireland,' Ultan said.

18

My parents went over there for their honeymoon and although I don't recall Annie ever mentioning Connaught, or the west, Tommy sometimes did. They took the train to Sligo and then cycled down the coast in glorious weather. Papa never forgot the emptiness of the landscape, or the uneven ridges on which the cornerstones of many past dwellings were still upright. He described to me the south-facing hillsides whose unworked potato drills broke through like the rib cages of buried giants. Although these hinterlands were elegies for the tragedy that had played out there, their beauty made it impossible for him to think of them as tragic or malign, Tommy always said.

In the settled places, where landlord clearances had not succeeded, cottages burned turf and asses grazed. Tommy said he could well understand the magic that had caused people to endure hardship in order to live there. Every morning a man only had to stand at his half door to reaffirm that he lived in a cathedral. Only death or starvation could drive people out of such a paradise, Tommy used to say.

19

Perversely I began to wish that Ultan would not recover sufficiently quickly from his operation to take the course of action he had proposed. I didn't want him going to the west of Ireland – I wanted him with me in Sutton, sitting on a deck chair in the garden, a rug over his knees. When he asked me to help him conceal the documents – the evidence, he called it – until he came out of hospital, all my sympathy was for my brother and not for people I had never met.

'I know you're asking yourself what will be achieved,' he said one afternoon when the sun broke through, an event as rare as it was wonderful. 'And the answer is: in itself, probably very little.'

Martha had left early and we were sitting outside the back door, alongside Freddy who lay on the warm slate flags.

'Harry used to talk about the accumulation of small facts in the evolution of a story. He used to say how historical events stand out as if they happened suddenly, whereas in fact they are just the climax of an almost infinite number of little steps. Delivering this evidence to an American newspaper is one such small step towards owning up to our plight on the international stage. People here will eventually realise that it is not shameful to ask for help.'

I could hear the strain in his voice and how he had to pause for breath.

'He was your friend,' I said.

For a long moment my brother was silent. 'He was my shining example,' he said at last.

'Why was he targeted?'

'Melody had it in for Harry. Always did.'

'He must have had a reason. I can understand that Harry was disliked in some quarters for his criticisms of the government, but this seems to have gone beyond that. Mrs Barry said it was personal.'

My brother was not normally short of words. 'Harry... Harry had a wonderful love of life. The way he partied! The way he dressed! He was different. There were... incidents involving illegal late-night drinking, years ago, when Melody was a peeler on the beat in Dublin. He would have come across Harry in certain company...'

I think I had always known, but I needed him to say it.

'Word is Melody's standing in the Castle is clouded by his past deeds. He needs to prove himself to keep his job, and so he made it his mission to stop Harry's story. He wants to be able to rush into the Department of Home Affairs, wagging his tale, showing what a great policeman he really is.'

Water echoed as Ultan filled his glass. 'But when he searched Harry's home and found nothing ...'

'His sister told me.'

'Harry had a weak heart. Some evenings he was so ill he could not write his copy – I used type it up as he dictated from his bed.'

'On those nights when you did not come home.'

A tiny hesitation. 'Yes.'

'You never told me that was where you were.'

'When you asked, I said, with a friend.'

'What did you talk about? Other than newspaper business?'

'Why do you ask?'

'I am interested in all your friends.'

'He used to tell me what it was like for him growing up in Drimnagh, how he felt . . . apart. Destined for better things, he used to joke. How he was often lonely. His first important assignment was the visit to Dublin of Queen Victoria. I've read his report. His description is so full of life and jollity!' He suddenly began to weep. 'That passion became his trademark in everything he did.'

'I am so sorry,' I said quietly. 'You must be grieving greatly.'

His ragged sigh. 'It has broken my heart.' After a moment, he caught my hand. 'You remember that last summer? How could you forget! The sun always seemed to shine . . .'

'Yes, of course I do.'

'And that party in Howth,' he said as my heart shrank. 'You remember that?'

'Of course.'

'You were the most beautiful woman there, the most beautiful that would ever be there. You shone like a star.'

'Don't, please.'

'And later, in the house—'

'Ultan, there is no need.'

'I saw you coming in, you know,' he said. 'I've always known you saw me.'

20

The morning arrived, wet and forlorn, a monochrome that sealed my darkness. We boarded the first tram to town, and huddled down in the damp among the other passengers. Martha had given Ultan holy water in a glass vial.

'Be sure he sprinkles it on the bed,' she whispered to me.

The bay lay grey as a shroud and people were walking about with their heads bent, Ultan said. From the sound of the sanding gear on the tracks I could tell we were passing Dollymount. The voices around the Pillar, where we changed trams, seemed muted. At half-past seven we arrived into Dr Steeven's Hospital near Kingsbridge.

'Goodness ... and how do you spell that?' enquired the admissions nurse when Ultan gave his name. She continued in a voice that reminded me of the nuns, 'Ah, here you are. Fasting, I hope, Mr Raven?'

I had foregone my own breakfast that morning so as to ease his fast, though he ate so little anyway.

'Next of kin?' she asked.

'I am,' I said.

'Name?'

'Miss Rose Raven, with the same address as my brother.'

The nurse wrote industriously. 'I love the north of the

county although I don't get out there as much as I would like to. Now, Miss Raven, you will be going home, of course, and coming back tomorrow. So, Mr Raven, I see you have a suitcase, very good, if you would like to follow me?'

'I am staying here.'

'Oh, I'm afraid that is not permitted,' said the nurse firmly, 'we have no such facilities. This is a small hospital. If all the next of kin waited we could not function for want of space.'

'In which case I shall wait outside.'

'Sis, it's not necessary, go home,' Ultan said. 'Rudy is dropping down later.'

'Under no circumstances am I going home,' I said. 'The hospital porter can bring me to the railway station. I shall wait there.'

'I'm afraid I'll have to ask you to leave now,' said the nurse unsparingly. 'We don't have the time for further discussion.'

'Mr Raven!'

I turned to the voice.

'And who have we here?'

'Mr Bradshaw, I was just explaining the hospital's regulations—' began the nurse.

'I am Miss Raven, doctor.'

'Well, well,' said Mr Bradshaw happily, 'Miss Raven, of course I remember you! Indeed you might ask, how could I forget? I never forget a pretty face. But you were no more than a young girl when you and your mother would come into the club to wait for the end of Tommy's shift. I take a liberty in calling him Tommy, but all the members did, and many of us, myself to the fore, considered him a dear, dear friend.'

The doctor smelled of strong antiseptic.

'Yes, we used to wait for Papa in the kitchens.'

'But then came out through the front hall!' the doctor cried. 'I can see you, perched on the club fender, pretty as a picture. And, my, just look at you now!'

I was later told that Mr Bradshaw was small and rotund, swathed in a green rubber apron, though his shooting white linen shirt cuffs with golden links in the form of golf clubs remained in place; and that two small corners of blood-clotted newsprint clung to his chin where he had cut himself that morning with his razor.

'Miss Raven, we were all so desperately, desperately sorry, of course ...' Mr Bradshaw started to say.

'Thank you, doctor, it's quite all right, there is no need,' I said.

'And your own suffering ...'

'Please ...'

'We started a fund in the club, of course.'

'For which I am most grateful. It went towards my operations,' I said.

'Ah, well.' He clapped his hands together as if to kill off any doubts he might have. 'Tommy is looking down on us today. He's probably making me a Tommy Special, as we speak!'

He laughed with excessive joviality and I suddenly wanted Ultan to come home. Mr Bradshaw was too giddy for that early hour.

The nurse said, 'I have your list here, Mr Bradshaw.'

'And put Mr Raven at the head of it!' the doctor called. 'To work!'

'Mr Bradshaw, may I please stay here until the operation is over?' I asked.

'Stay here?'

61

'I have explained to Miss Raven—' the nurse began.

'But by all means! Where else would you go, child?' Mr Bradshaw said. 'Nurse will escort you to the first floor landing and I will see you later. Come along now, Mr Raven, and we'll have you right as rain in a jiffy.'

21

At a bench, beside a throbbing, heat-filled radiator, I tried to distract myself by concentrating on the strict demeanour of the admissions nurse. Her respect for the hospital's rules. Her evident love of discipline. I saw her as one of the nuns in my old school, in her early middle-age, her grey hair, as I imagined it, protruding from a white headdress, her face sharp in authority but at the same time unable to conceal its natural kindness. The reason she had become a nurse. She had encountered Mr Bradshaw on many, many mornings such as this. All was well with the surgeon, for if not she would never permit him to operate on my brother. I must have dozed off on this thought, but for how long I could not say. I dreamt of people in a race, shouting to one another, calling out. Faster! Faster! The race was being run through a green building of many doors, and each door, as I ran through it, slammed behind me. Faster! I awoke to the thudding of my heart, and with my shoulder on fire where it had pressed the radiator.

'This was on the floor, miss.'

I struggled to wake up, my compass bearings adrift.

'Your hat. It was on the floor here beside you.'

I reached. 'Thank you.'

'At least you've made yourself cosy, I can see.'

I suddenly wished, without yet knowing why, that Annie was with me. Did he realise I could not see him? Sometimes men on the tram struck up conversations, but this was different.

'Visiting?' His voice was sly and it slid towards me like a snake.

'Waiting.'

'Ah, waiting. Waiting is always the hardest. Someone close to you, I daresay?'

How did I know he already knew the answer? I fought mightily to construct a face from the voice, for within his sibilant words was an echo from the past I was sure I recognised.

'A relative.'

'Your brother, they tell me.'

My mouth went all at once to chalk. 'Who—? How do you—?'

'Listen to me very carefully, Rose. Did Ultan confide in you? I expect he did. Before he came in here? We all need to get these things off our chests before we face our maker.'

Within the gaps of what he said I could hear the ticking of his pocket watch. I leapt to my feet.

'I know you!'

His hand fell heavily on my shoulder and I was forced to sit back down. 'Behave yourself, or I will have you sent away.'

'What do you—?'

'Now, listen very carefully to what I am about to say. I daresay you know the whereabouts of certain documents, false depositions. Purported photographs. All lies, but dangerous lies. Lies lead to sedition. Ultan was sadly misled. We understand how young men can be gullible, but we cannot allow fabricated news to get into the wrong hands and threaten the stability of our country – can we?'

I don't know! I wanted to scream, but could not speak.

'I think you know. I think Ultan told you, as his insurance policy – maybe even gave you what we are looking for. It would be natural. You will tell me.'

I gulped. 'Why don't you ask Ultan yourself?'

'Ah, would that I could.'

'What do you mean?' I got to my feet up once more and although he tried again to prevent me, I shook him off. 'I want to speak to a nurse. Nurse!'

'Be a good girl, now. Don't vex me.'

Fear must have suddenly injected me with sight, for I was sure I could suddenly see the dim outline of a gaunt face, yellow with hate.

'Give me what I need to know and I will go,' he whispered. 'Give it to me or you will regret it, Rose!'

'Nurse! Nurse!' I screamed.

Distant footsteps all at once, the tattoo of blessed leather soles.

'Rudy?'

'Rose?'

I shook violently. 'Oh, Rudy.'

'Rose—'

He was holding me. 'Sssh. When did they tell you?'

'A man ... someone ... he ...'

'It's all right, I'm here now.'

'Did you see a man? He was—'

'Oh, Rose, I'm so sorry.' Something fractured in his voice. 'What?' *What?*'

'Rose, it's not good.'

'Where is Mr Bradshaw?' I screamed.

22

Mid-March 1924

Those days were marked by rain so heavy and unrelenting that it had washed people from the streets, Martha said. On some days she had to make the journey from Baldoyle in Murphy's hackney. The wind was hurling the sea half a mile inland and suddenly every man in Dublin wore galoshes. Even the rats became more daring and tried to run Freddy's gauntlet, but they were no match for him. When he killed them he laid them out on the front step.

She made no effort now to hide her irritation whenever Rudy appeared, as if it were her house he was visiting and without an invitation. She saw me as her ward and more than once asked if she and her mother should not move into Nan's Cottage, as a short-term measure. Rain rattled the window as Rudy and I sat and talked. He brought me cigarettes that Mr Fleming had acquired wholesale when he was doing the books of a grocer.

'Smoking is by far the best way to keep the germs away,' said Rudy.

Sometimes at night, between the squalls, we went for walks along the sea and he described how the new gaslights over in Dún Laoghaire, as it was now being called, had become part of the water. He tiptoed around my grief and this, for some reason, irritated me. At times I wished he would treat me as a normal woman, which meant confiding in me when he was troubled, which I knew he often was, weeping on my breast, and crawling back into the womb that all men hanker for.

It pained me greatly that I was obliged to behave so badly. I tried to understand why I preferred my promise to Ultan over my genuine fondness for Rudy – why I was clinging on to a secret whose revelation would, as even my late brother had admitted, amount to little. I was terrified all the time. I had not imagined what had unfolded in the hospital: the weight of the peeler's hand on my shoulder, his ticking watch. I knew who he was. If I confided in Rudy, I would, as Ultan had warned, be exposing him to danger. So I said nothing. As a result, I was withdrawn and taciturn, and often discourteous. It was as if the weight of my fear drove everything before it, including my affection. I listened as he went through the *Independent*, at my request, reading out anything to do with the worsening conditions west of the Shannon.

'Why the big interest all of a sudden?'

'It was a subject that used to interest Ultan.'

'I never heard him mention the west of Ireland,' Rudy said.

'Believe me, he did.'

'Well, I never heard him.'

'I couldn't give a fiddlestick what you did or did not hear!' I cried.

The smell of chloroform would never leave me. It was Rudy who helped them hold me down as a nurse pressed the pad over my nose and mouth even as I shouted like a mad woman. In that instant before I sank, before I disappeared from view, I was sure I saw all their faces clearly, and the window of the

67

hospital, and the daylight. I wanted to tell them – this is a miracle! You have restored my eyesight!

I was devastated that I had not been able to see him in the funeral parlour. He was beautiful to me and would always be. His were surely the same sun-burnished limbs I had once known when he had played cricket, his hair the same endearing mop. I sat by his open coffin and stroked his forehead. At least he would no longer have to bear the burden of being who he truly was.

A few items of post arrived, addressed to me: a standard set of words from the *Irish Independent* and a Mass-card from Ultan's colleagues at work. Martha read them to me.

'And a letter from Miss Agnes Daly,' she said in a tone of disapproval.

'Please . . .'

Agnes wrote that she had only heard the news following Ultan's burial, otherwise she would have come to his funeral. We had laid him to rest in Saint Fintan's, alongside Tommy and Annie. Whenever I wanted to meet her, she was ready, Agnes said. Martha snorted.

'That one has some cheek!'

23

On the second Sunday in March, a rare day of airborne scent and ozone, Martha and I came home from Mass together, and I sat outside the front door in a sudden pool of sunshine as she went in ahead to put the kettle on. The heat of the elusive sun soaked my body. Grief for a moment relaxed its grip. This is good, I thought, even as I wondered what it was that was missing at that moment. Rudy and I will survive this, I thought. But then Martha began to yell.

We had never worried much about trouble out here on the sea where everyone was known to one another and strangers stood out like barnacles at low tide. No one I knew had ever suffered at the hands of thieves or villains.

Nan's Cottage was ruined. They had taken a crowbar to the floorboards and left us looking down at damp earth, I would later be told, although I could sense the destruction without needing to see it. In the front room, the seats were cut from chairs, cushions sliced and their innards disgorged, the backs of the armchairs slashed, the glass-doored cabinet – my father's wedding present to my mother – upended, and its crockery in a thousand pieces. Even the wooden mantelpiece had been jimmied from the wall and left to dangle. In the bedrooms, the drawers were on the floor, their contents pitched out, the clothes from wardrobes in a heap. The kitchen press had been torn from the wall and our food thrown everywhere. In Ultan's bedroom they had taken a knife to the mattress, I was told, down to the springs, all the wadding pulled. They had taken up the floor rugs and sliced them into pieces. No picture remained on the walls. But at first Martha saw none of this destruction. All she could see was Freddy, laid out on a pile of ruptured timber, his tongue hanging raggedly, the way it sometimes did when he slept.

'We'll have to get another ratter now,' Martha said.

24

Martha and her mother's house formed the end of a narrow terrace by the estuary in Baldoyle. Although I had been there years before, it felt much smaller than I remembered. I also now recalled the smell of the house from my childhood: over the years, gas must have leaked from the kitchen, for a gassy vapour was detectable in every room.

My teeth chattered so loudly that Martha put me into her own bed, along with a hot stone jar and a mug of steaming whiskey, which I hated. She answered my insistent questions as if dealing with a child in the grip of fever. The vandals had not gone near the back garden, she kept replying to my question.

'Why do you go on asking that, Rose? Did they not do enough damage to the house?'

Later that day, when Rudy turned up, distraught, she sent him packing without my knowledge. He had come out to Nan's Cottage, been shocked at what he had found and been directed on to Baldoyle by Murphy, the jarvey. It was Mr Murphy who had informed the Civic Guards, but I could have told him he was wasting his time.

Rudy came out again the following evening, and we all sat in the tiny kitchen as rain beat against the window. Rudy asked: who would pillage a simple cottage? For what purpose? I knew he was looking at me as he asked these questions, for I could tell by his tone that he was by now convinced I was hiding something.

'Poor Freddy,' Martha said. 'He never did harm to anyone.'

'He should be buried in the front garden,' I said.

'I will see to it,' Rudy said.

'At least then you'll have a proper job to do, Mr Saddler,' said Martha peremptorily, and soon afterwards showed him the door.

I should have stopped her there and then – I should have called him back and made it clear I cared, but I let him go, heard the door bang. Although I knew he would go home smarting from my failure to countermand Martha, as I would normally have done, my fear had not allowed me to do so. Moreover, I sensed an unlikely reserve in Martha, a culling of her words, as if she were holding something back, as if there were matters about which I was best not informed, all of which fed my anxieties. When she did revert to her garrulous tongue she told me that local people, led by the Protestant minister, Mr. Gilmore, had mobilised to put my cottage back in order, although I could tell she had misgivings about accepting help from such a quarter. Nonetheless, in the days that followed, she reported great activity at Nan's Cottage, even if she could not bring herself to praise Mr. Gilmore's part.

'It's well for him that has the time to do it,' she remarked, suggesting that Father Shipsey would also have sprung into action on my behalf were it not for his greater commitments.

My tiny bedroom in Martha's – really a box room at the head of the stairs – looked out towards Lambay. At home we lived within earshot of the sea, but here I was almost on top of it. Such a powerful, unending sound, the regular wash of pebbles being carried up, dragged back, carried up again. I lay in thrall to the ocean and imagined I was back again in Portmarnock. The water slipped above my head and I was part of it, floating with the current. I wished I was not alone. My thoughts were shameful, but I was past all shame. I knew I was betraying Rudy, but I didn't care. I wished my love was lying with me, in his flesh ... and that I could turn to him and kiss his mouth. Feel his body with my hands. Hear his gasps. Desire rose in me like a silver fish.

'*Baedeker's our man! All we have to do is pick up a Baedeker and go!*'

25

From what he told me later I could picture how Rudy must have felt. He was dismayed by what he saw as my changed attitude and had no idea what lay at the root of it. It seemed to him that whatever way he turned, he was met by opposition. He had tried to discuss the circumstances of Ultan's death with his mother, but she had refused to engage, as if she knew that any interest shown by her in Ultan's tragedy might be interpreted as a softening in her position towards me. The following evening he had come out to Nan's Cottage, taken a spade from the garden shed and dug a grave in the front garden, as I had requested. As he lowered the little dog into the earth he wondered if the good times would ever come again.

The next day's weather seemed to reflect the dark crevice into which our attachment had fallen, he told me. The sky was low and the wind cold as he finished up his work in the premises of a baker in Camden Street. He'd often described this assignment, where the invoices, cheque-book stubs, delivery notes, bank statements and petty cash receipts were all presented in flour-dusted cardboard boxes. In the years since independence the bakery had struggled to thrive. Flour had become more expensive with the poor weather, the quality of bread had declined. All the sugar came in from England and was often scarce. Customers still bought bread, but fancy cakes and chocolate éclairs had become a luxury. Besides, Rudy had the feeling that the baker – a stout woman – disapproved of him since she knew his mother sold loaves from her front room in Curzon Street. When the baker told him she was thinking of selling up, he sensed she held him partly to blame.

He left the shop with a bag of cupcakes to walk the short distance home. The sun had long declined and night was tightening around the city. When he turned into Curzon Street he saw yellow light welling out from the sitting room of his house. This room was used only for receiving visitors. He opened the front door with his latchkey.

'Rodolfo?' Lucia called.

He removed his coat, hat and scarf.

'We are here,' his mother called.

Rudy went in.

'This is Detective Sergeant Melody from the Dublin Metropolitan Police,' Sergeant Saddler said. 'Our son, Rodolfo.'

26

A tall man in a long woollen overcoat was standing before the unlit fireplace. Rudy looked at him intently. He had seen this jutting, spade-shaped beard before, but for the moment could not say where or when.

'Rodolfo, very pleased to meet you.'

A peeler's eyes, lazy, yet at the same time shrewdly knowing. That, and the uninvited use of the first name.

'I am Rudy.'

'Very well then. Have a seat, Rudy.'

Rudy turned to his parents. His father's gaze was to the floor, but Lucia's dark expression flashed a warning.

'Is there something wrong, sir?'

'Nothing that cannot be righted.' The policeman spoke in the kind of Dublin drawl that people like Mr Fleming sometimes poked fun at.

'Detective Sergeant Melody just wants to ask you a few questions, that's all,' the sergeant said.

'You answer him the truth,' Lucia snapped.

Sergeant Saddler's head shied from his wife's voice. She had woven her black hair into a long plait, now gathered over her shoulder and tied with a pretty red ribbon.

'Your parents tell me you're doing well, Rudy.' The bowl

of an unlighted pipe rested in Melody's right hand. 'Passed all your examinations with flying colours, so far. Very well regarded by your employer. Congratulations.'

Rudy saw his mother shake her lowered head.

'Good prospects,' said Melody, 'which is the way we all want to keep them.'

'Please be to God,' Lucia murmured.

An unsettling momentum was attached to this policeman, who now strolled to an armchair, and, when he had arranged himself in it, withdrew a box of Vestas from the pocket of his overcoat.

'Tell me, son, what you knew of the late Mr Ultan Raven,' he asked from within wreaths of pipe smoke.

Lucia emitted a disparaging rumble.

'Ultan?' Rudy said.

'A friend of yours?'

'Of course, we played cricket together, or at least, he played . . . Look, what is this all about? Ultan died recently in tragic circumstances.'

'Tragic, no doubt,' said Melody, 'especially for his surviving family.'

'Ah!' cried Lucia, as if hit.

'Rudy sees Miss Raven, we told you that,' said Sergeant Saddler.

'If we could please confine this discussion to myself and Rudy, Sergeant?'

The sergeant sank into his chair.

'How would you describe the late Mr Ultan Raven, Rudy?'

Rudy reminded himself that he was a professional man and that it was important to behave as such. He also needed to keep in mind that he was an exemplary citizen, he later said.

'Ultan was a first-class fellow, a good friend, excellent at his job, I would say destined to be successful. What happened to him was truly awful. He is sadly missed.'

'Missed by whom, may I ask? Apart from Miss Raven and yourself, of course.'

'By everyone who knew him – his colleagues, his friends . . .'

'These friends . . . How would you describe them?'

'I don't really know his friends. It was a general remark. But I'm sure anyone who knew Ultan loved him,' Rudy said.

'Hmmm . . . No names?'

'I know some people he played cricket with.'

'You met a man with him called Harry Deegan.'

'Who?'

Melody removed his pipe and smiled. 'Now, Rudy, please.'

'Harry Deegan?' Rudy said. 'Did he not work for a newspaper?'

'Indeed he did – the same newspaper your friend Ultan worked for. Which is why I assume you met him with Ultan.'

'I never met him,' Rudy said. 'Were they friends?'

'You might say that.' Melody placed his pipe in the ample glass ashtray which the tram company had presented to Sergeant Saddler on his forced retirement. 'What about Ultan's contacts in the course of his trade – people in government, for example – their names?'

'I don't know what you're talking about,' Rudy said as he tried to remain aloof. 'I met none of his friends or contacts, I cannot help you.'

'So it would shock you, would it, to learn that the late Mr Raven was consorting with sworn enemies of this Free State?'

'*What?*'

'Come now, Rudy, don't pretend! I think you know exactly to whom I'm referring.'

'If Rudy says—' began his father.

'Let him speak he-seff!' Lucia cried.

Rudy took a deep breath and tried to imagine how Mr Fleming would deal with this brazen intrusion.

'Listen here … Sergeant Melody, over the last few years, my connection has been with Miss Raven and not with her brother. I have little or no idea what he does, I mean, did, apart from working for a newspaper, where, as I understand it, he was well regarded. My interest is in his sister.'

'*Dio mio*,' Lucia said.

'And furthermore,' Rudy continued, 'her home has been vandalised in recent days, a crime which one would have thought the police would be best placed to address rather than pursue questions about her dead brother.'

'Ah, her cottage, yes,' Melody hummed.

'What is going on?' Rudy asked, even as the image of my plundered cottage, and my evasiveness, began to crowd in on top of him. 'I have done nothing to deserve this interrogation.'

'I understand, Rudy, that when a friend confides in you, especially a friend now sadly deceased, that you feel a strong loyalty to his memory. I refer to the information he shared with you before he died. Entrusted you with. Gave you to keep safe until he emerged well and healed from the hospital.'

Rudy saw his parents staring at him.

'Look,' he said with a little more dander, 'I'm quite happy to answer any question I can, but so far all I've heard from you is rot, sir.'

'Rodolfo!'

'It's all right, Mrs Saddler, it's all right. Rudy will answer in the end.'

Rudy steadied himself. 'Answer what?'

The policeman leaned forward. 'I can ruin your career,' he said softly. 'Just one word from me to Mr Fleming that his young employee is up to his neck in troublemaking and you're out on your ear. And who will employ you after that, eh?'

'Troublemaking?' Rudy cried. 'What do you mean?'

'Ever heard of the Public Safety Acts, son? No? In that case, allow me to fill you in. These Acts were deemed necessary to protect the integrity of this Free State from its enemies – from people involved in sedition, from the likes of Harry Deegan and Ultan Raven. A person found guilty on indictment of any of the offences listed in these Acts can be sentenced to death. Get the picture? Beginning to understand the kind of trouble your friend Mr Raven got himself into, are you?'

'Ultan never—' Rudy began.

'No, Rudy!' Lucia cried. 'Tell him what he ask! Now!'

Rudy wondered for a moment if this man was mistaking him for someone else which, under the circumstances, was impossible; or if he was awake.

'Perhaps you should acquaint me with these allegations,' Rudy said.

'By all means,' said Melody with stern amiability. 'The late Ultan Raven was in possession of documents and photographs which are proscribed by law. That makes him a criminal. Anyone assisting him in retaining possession of these documents is an accessory to his crime and faces a lengthy jail sentence, or worse.'

'What documents?' Rudy cried.

'Facsimiles concocted by his friend, the late Harry Deegan, that purport to tell the truth about the living circumstances prevailing in certain regions of our country, but are, in fact, vicious lies put about by a man whose lack of morality and repugnant unnatural behaviour with young men is too shocking to be recounted in front of decent people.'

Rudy was unable to speak.

'So I will put it to you again and I advise you to consider your reply carefully,' Melody said. 'Did Raven give you these bogus documents to conceal, or tell you about them? Do you know where they are? The truth, Rudy.'

Rudy felt the sudden terror of being at the mercy of a force over which he had no control and to which professional bearing had no answer.

'No,' he said, 'he did not. And this is the first I've heard of it.'

No one said anything. Rudy's parents were looking at the policeman. Melody was looking at Rudy.

'I believe you,' he said.

'Oh, thank God!' cried Lucia. 'Oh, thank the Lord!'

27

Rudy thought the interrogation was over. Detective Sergeant Melody was smiling.

'I apologise for this intrusion, but I have to do my job.'

'Of course you do,' said Lucia, 'without men like you this country she is sunk.'

Melody acknowledged the compliment. 'I wish you well in your chosen profession, Rudy,' he said, 'and in your life.'

'Thank you, sir,' said Rudy and rose to his feet.

'Over recent months, you have made numerous visits to Miss Raven in Sutton.'

'Yes.'

'As any young man might be expected to,' said the policeman cordially. 'And during these visits met Mr Raven. Sit down, please, Rudy.'

'Sometimes, but not always, yes.' Rudy resumed his seat, feeling that somehow he had been outmanoeuvred. 'He worked very hard and was often not there.'

'The demands of the press,' said Melody and shook his head in what might have been taken for admiration. 'Who else did you meet out there? You've already said his friends never came to the house – but who else did?'

'No one I can remember,' Rudy said. 'Mrs Merry comes in every morning.'

'Ah, yes, Mrs Merry. Who else?'

'The postman?'

Detective Sergeant Melody chuckled. 'Very good. And?'

'The local priest ... following the death ...'

'Father Shipsey, yes. I'm just trying to paint a picture, that's all, Rudy, a picture of the comings and goings in the Raven household. You and I are on the same side – I am trying to establish who Raven may have been involved with in this conspiracy.'

'Or not involved with.'

Lucia shot Rudy a dark look.

'So other than the Ravens themselves, brother and sister, you have never in recent months met anyone else but Mrs Merry, the priest or the postman in Miss Raven's house? Is that correct?'

'Yes,' answered Rudy even as, with blood pounding so hard he was certain it could be heard, he knew he had just lied. 'That is correct.'

'No visitors?'

'None.'

'What about friends of Miss Raven,' Melody asked. 'Do they come and visit?'

'Miss Raven leads a very private life,' Rudy said.

'She blind,' said Lucia.

'Yes, so I understand. So that means, no one else you can think of, Rudy?'

'No, I have met no one else in Miss Raven's,' Rudy said, his tongue fat with guilt.

'Well, well,' said the policeman.

Rudy thought the man could see right into his brain, but it was Melody who was on his feet.

'Mr Saddler, I want to thank you for being so open with me. You understand that in these exceptional times we have to do everything we can to uphold the rule of law. The future of our country depends on it, as I daresay you know. But in the event that your knowledge of what I'm searching for changes, I would appreciate it if you would contact me without delay. Here is my address and the number of my telephone.'

Rudy took the card. 'Thank you, sir.'

'I'll be watching your progress closely,' the policeman said and his eyes dwelt longer on Rudy's than was respectful. He turned. 'Sergeant, it has been my pleasure to meet you again. Mrs Saddler.'

Rudy remained in the parlour as his parents went out to the door with Detective Sergeant Melody.

'They say snow is forecast,' the policeman could be heard saying. 'What on earth can we expect next?'

28

Martha returned from Sutton saying that Nan's Cottage was restored to its old self. Every piece of damaged furniture and mutilated bedding, every broken cup and saucer, had been replaced. Two carpenters, one from Baldoyle, the other Portmarnock, had laid, nailed and sanded new timber on the bare joists, she said. Beds that had been stored for years in people's attics had arrived in Nan's Cottage. Despite the weather, they had even managed to paint the outside a warm yellow, like spring flowers, Martha said, and added, 'I didn't see Mr Saddler giving up his free time to help.'

I could feel her looking at me.

'Are you not excited, child?'

'I am looking forward to going home, yes.'

'What's the matter with you?' she asked. 'You're going around as if you're carrying the world on your back.'

'Please leave it be, Martha.'

'You can't mourn forever – I know that,' she said.

'Please.'

'Are you ill, then? Tell me and I'll call the doctor.'

'If I want the doctor I shall let you know.'

'If you're worrying about those thugs who killed Freddy, stop worrying! The police say they have a good idea who did it.'

I looked at her. 'Have the police spoken to you?'

'I didn't want them to upset you,' Martha said, 'so I talked to them, yes.'

'It's my house!' I shouted. 'I may be blind but I'm not an imbecile! Stop treating me like one!'

At four that afternoon, Rudy appeared. It was mid-week and he should have been at work. Martha had gone down to the dairy in the village for butter.

'We must speak.'

The estuary wall lay partly in darkness. Out on the water, as a southerly wind brought spits of fresh rain, I could hear the soft chat of fishermen on the ebb tide. Rudy linked me and we came to the shelter of a boat shed. As he began to describe the visit to Curzon Street of Detective Sergeant Melody, my blood plunged.

'He seemed to know so much about Ultan,' Rudy said. 'About you too – about us. About that reporter who died, Harry Deegan. The things he said . . .'

I could not bring myself to speak. At that moment, I knew that unless I acted quickly I could no longer protect him.

'What is the matter?' he asked.

'I am sorry, I'm just tired.'

'What is going on, Rose? And please don't say again that you don't know. What was Ultan up to?'

'What on earth can you mean?'

'Something is going on, isn't there? Something I'm not being told. Something Ultan did. Melody spoke of documents and photographs. He used the word sedition. It's why the tailor didn't want me in the room that day, isn't it?'

'I have no idea what you're talking about.'

'You're not being straight with me!' Rudy cried. 'Melody is looking for documents, damn it! And I think you know where they are! It's why your house was upended – and I think you know that too! I've had enough of your dodging. You have to tell me what I want to know.'

'My brother is dead, my house has been ransacked and my dog killed,' I said with as much passion as I could muster. 'Do you not think that for the moment I've suffered enough?'

'And I have been there for you whenever I could,' he appealed. 'I helped you arrange Ultan's funeral. I dug a grave for Freddy, in your front garden, and buried him. And now I've lied to Melody about the tailor. But you have to tell me what is going on – and you have to tell me now.'

'Are you threatening me?'

'I lied to a policeman, Rose!' he said. 'I never mentioned the tailor because somehow I knew what Melody was after.'

Dread had seized me. I turned away.

'Listen, Rose. You either accept me for who I am, and trust me completely, or you don't. But I won't be shut out any longer. I have been prepared to tolerate your evasion, up to this – but no longer. So tell me now what is going on, or I walk away.'

I wanted to cry then, for I knew I could not keep my promise to Ultan much longer.

'Off you go, so,' I said, my flippancy a wonder.

'Rose . . .'

'Off you go, Rudy. I have nothing to tell you and you have no further business here.'

He gasped. 'After all we have been through?'

'In fact, it may be for the best if we go our separate ways for a spell. After all, you may need some time to come to terms with these evasions of mine you are so intent on having me confirm.'

'I think you are overwrought and tired.'

'I am perfectly well, thank you, and I don't need your sympathy or patronage.'

'Rose ...'

'I think we have said everything.'

He sighed. 'I'll walk you home.'

'There is no need.' I looked towards Portmarnock. 'As you pass Martha's, kindly knock on her door and ask her to be so good as to fetch my cane.'

'You are being stubborn,' he said. 'Please.'

'Since when has it been your right to direct me?'

'Rose, this is not you.'

'Go, please, and do as I ask.'

'I may not come back,' he said with feeling.

'Then don't,' I replied. 'It is not as if your toing and froing are matters that concern me.'

'Sometimes I wish I had never met you,' he said and walked away, his quick leather soles the last I heard of him.

29

On Wednesday morning, the day I was due to return to my refurbished home, Martha came in from the sea wall to say the wind had dropped and a thick fog had settled over Dublin. She prattled on in her enervating way, suggesting that since I would be unable to see the new arrangements in Nan's Cottage, she and her mother should spend the first night, or two, along with me, and help me to settle in. I thanked her for her concern, but told her very firmly that since I would be living there on my own I had better get used to it.

I yearned for Rudy, for his gentle voice and his caring nature. As I was drinking my breakfast tea in Baldoyle, Rudy, I would later learn, was setting out along the fog-bound canal for work, pushing his bicycle, a loaf of his mother's bread wrapped in paper for his employer, Mr Fleming, in the pocket of his greatcoat. The night before, fog had thickened in his dreams and crept around brick corners. Rudy had found himself in streets he did not recognise, where every door lacked a number. He kept thinking someone was in step behind him. Now, walking to work along the canal, it was as if he had never woken up.

He was convinced that the break between us was temporary; yet he was still smarting from my rebukes and needed time to recover. His mother, Lucia, had sensed the crisis in him. He had told her of the damage done to my cottage, but my misfortunes were of little interest to Lucia.

'It is better that you come home here after work for a week or so,' she had said and smiled. When happy, Lucia was beautiful. 'Much better for you here and not out there, in the country.'

She had meant with me, and he knew what she had meant; but to reveal our row to her would be fatal, as she would pounce on the information and weave from it a cage from which he would never escape. He had often told me of her Italian sayings, and how he had admired her for them. '*A mali estremi, estremi rimedi,*' she used to say in the aftermath of the Rising. It meant, desperate times call for desperate measures. '*Al piu potente ceda il piu prudente,*' meant, at times it is better to bow than to resist.

That morning, he was the first into Fleming & Son. I had never seen Mr Matthew Fleming, of course, much less met him, but even so I felt from all of Rudy's descriptions that I would recognise him. He was aged fifty, tall, inclined to stoop, his fair hair was thin and his nose was a formidable beak. He lived in an old house on that part of the Strand Road that runs down to the Merrion Gates. Twenty years before, Mr and Mrs Fleming had made a pilgrimage to Jerusalem in pursuit of the fertility which had up to then eluded them. They sailed first to Cairo, and then set out on the gruelling journey overland. Three months later, exhausted, but convinced they would have offspring, they returned to Dublin. Their call was not answered. Nonetheless, when he commenced in practice, Mr Fleming described his firm Fleming & Son Chartered Accountants; any other name would have been an

90

unthinkable rebuke to the spirit of a young man who was, to his parents, alive in almost every way. Shortly thereafter, Mrs Fleming had fallen down dead one afternoon, pruning roses in her garden. Now, each Christmas, Rudy was invited out to Merrion Gates for dinner, an overwrought and lonely affair. The house lacked warmth and the touch of a woman.

Fleming & Son occupied two interconnecting rooms, used in a different era for dining and entertaining: Mr Fleming's desk and Rudy's stood in the front room; the inner room was reserved for meetings with clients. Behind Mr Fleming's desk hovered a large wooden crucifix, acquired in the Holy Land, our Saviour's agonized body carved from ivory. Down on the half-landing, where sat Miss Doreen Longley, the secretary – a lady in her early thirties – a painting of the golden city as seen from the Temple Mount could be admired. Miss Longley typed letters and sets of accounts, and directed clients up to Mr Fleming. She also made the tea, set mousetraps in the winter and in the summer months tacked up fly-papers. Her silver-rimmed spectacles were attached to her person by a silver chain and when she looked at Rudy her gaze was always soft. Ever since Rudy had told her about us, Miss Longley had given him little cards for me containing pressed flowers and with messages of support.

30

Rudy spent that morning dealing with the accounts of a solicitor who, according to Mr Fleming, presented his affairs in such immaculate order that something had to be awry. At noon, as the Angelus rang out over Dublin, the boss excused himself and said that he might be late back that afternoon. On Wednesdays, Mr Fleming always took lunch at home and then, weather permitting, proceeded to Milltown Golf Club. There will be no golf today, Rudy thought, as out of the window he saw the boss turn up his collar against the chill wind and huddle southwards along the canal bank.

He made a pipe and sat back at his desk. During winter, the sweet tobacco smoke acted as a corrective to the prevalent smell of mice. Rudy tried to regiment his thoughts. He had wanted to describe his interrogation by Melody to Mr Fleming, but had been too nervous to do so. He valued the boss's judgement and experience, not to mention his business contacts, but how could he explain to his employer that he had lied to the policeman? He had no way of knowing how Mr Fleming, a daily Massgoer, might react. On the other hand, the boss was used to keeping secrets in the course of his profession, and Rudy looked on him as a friend, just as, he dared to hope, Mr Fleming saw him as a son.

Pipe in hand, he strolled to the boss's desk, a handsome escritoire panelled in oak and finished in tooled yellow leather with brass fittings on its twin sets of drawers. An inkwell, diary and a trim square of blotting paper sat centrally on the desktop, a testament to Mr Fleming's sense of order. Rudy sat in the deep chair. He imagined himself some day looking out from here at his articled clerk, signing off the accounts of solicitors and shopkeepers. Leaving early to play golf in Milltown.

A brown file lay to one side, beneath a closed diary. Rudy lifted off the diary and opened the file. A letter to the new government requesting a telephone awaited Mr Fleming's signature. Beneath this unsigned correspondence lay embossed stock certificates, in different colours and shapes, all in the name of Mr Matthew Fleming: the Imperial Burma Rubber Company, Tate & Lyle, Taylor Woodrow and United Steel. Rudy was familiar with these investments, for the boss had often spoken of them and had urged Rudy, in time, to start his own portfolio.

'Ah, you're well suited to that desk, Mr Saddler!'

A cigarette jutted from the corner of Miss Longley's mouth as she carried in two cups of tea and the newspaper tucked into her oxter. On the days Mr Fleming left early, or was working from the premises of a client, a more familiar regime prevailed.

'He'll have to find a desk as good for you when he makes you his partner,' Miss Longley said, and settled into a chair.

Rudy felt a fresh stab of dread as the threats of Detective Sergeant Melody and his own lies assailed him.

'I had a chat with the boss yesterday,' she said quietly.

Rudy looked up.

'I handed in my notice.'

Rudy stared. 'What? You're leaving?'

'Not until May, but yes. I'm going to live with my sister in London.'

'Oh, I'm sorry to hear that,' Rudy said. 'I mean, sorry that you won't be here.'

'She is a war widow with a large residence in Battersea. I am going to help her run it as a boarding house.'

'You'll be badly missed, Miss Longley,' Rudy said. 'This place won't function without you.'

'Oh, he'll find someone else,' she said, looking around her with an air of passing disdain that Rudy had often noticed when she spoke of Mr Fleming.

'Why?' asked Rudy. 'Why leave?'

'There is nothing for me here,' Miss Longley said. 'Dublin is a wasteland. Look outside! There's no fun here anymore.'

'And there is in London?'

Miss Longley's pleasantly round face grew animated. 'I was last there at the time of the Great War, staying with my sister, and even during that upheaval there was ten times more excitement to be had than in Dublin. London is parties and the cinema and ice cream! You should visit it, Mr Saddler. Believe me, when you first set foot in the gaiety of Piccadilly Circus you'll never want to come back here again!'

Rudy felt a surge of longing for a place he had never been.

'Here there's nothing but darkness,' Miss Longley complained. 'I read the other day that we still have nearly ten thousand men in military custody. Incarcerated for their political views and branded as criminals. I'm leaving all that behind. And the weather in London is better too, believe me.'

94

'We can't be all that bad,' Rudy said, feeling that he should defend Ireland.

'Hah!' Miss Longley said. 'Every day you pick up the paper . . .' She folded out the *Irish Times*. 'I sometimes can't bring myself to read it.' She shook herself, as if to banish thoughts of bad news. 'So, tell me now, Mr Saddler, how is my friend in Sutton?'

Rudy winced. 'She is . . . in fact she is most distressed. Her home was burglarised,'

'Oh, I'm so sorry to hear that. The blackguards took advantage of her indisposition,' Miss Longley said.

'She was not there, but they as good as ruined her dwelling. She has had to lodge with Mrs Merry, her housekeeper, who lives in Baldoyle.'

'This is what I mean,' said Miss Longley grimly. 'Bring her to London, Mr Saddler. My sister will take you in until you get started. I will see to it. But get out of here.' She collected his cup. 'Please convey my sympathies to Miss Raven.'

31

He was in near panic as he hurried across Baggot Street Bridge. Passing by Mooney's, he checked behind in case Miss Longley had also decided to emerge and cross the bridge for coffee, something that had never happened, but still. He continued at speed down Pembroke Street, his head on fire, all ideas of professional aloofness abandoned. At the kiosk on the junction, he made the crossing into Lansdowne Road and onward down towards the railway station, one foot bidding to outpace the other. Mr Fleming would know what to do, or if not, he would know someone who did.

The day before in Booterstown, he had just read in Miss Longley's copy of the *Irish Times*, a woman had leaped to her death from the first floor window of a house rather than be interrogated by detectives from the G-division of the Dublin Metropolitan Police. The woman's husband had been arrested and taken into custody, despite his wife's body lying dead on the road. No reason was given for the deceased woman's behaviour. Her brother, the report went on, had been a well-known journalist, also recently deceased, Mr Harry Deegan. The police declined to explain why they had been at the house. Mr Cyril Barry was helping them with their enquiries.

Rudy ran down the tunnel under the railway line and

climbed the steps to the southbound platform. He could see the tailor clearly, in the darkened parlour of Nan's Cottage, getting up to peep out nervously between the drawn curtains; and his wife, sitting upright, her face drawn, her big hands clenched in her lap. It was as Rudy was reading the report for the second time, his eyes so enlarged that they hurt him, that he suddenly recalled where he had seen Detective Sergeant Melody before. It had been in Doctor Steevens' Hospital on the morning of Ultan's death. Rudy, who had come to the hospital to see Ultan, but had been greeted by an ashen-faced nurse with the dreadful news, was hurrying distractedly to the upper landing, trying to work out how he would relay what he knew, when a bearded man had passed him, walking quickly downstairs.

Rudy had come of age through wars and a revolution. One night he'd gone to bed in one country and awoken in another. He'd known of men who had chosen poorly and had been shot. Now it was only a matter of time before the tailor talked.

The Dublin & South Eastern pulled in at twenty minutes past the hour and Rudy boarded it. He was familiar with this journey; he had delivered files when Mr Fleming was confined to bed with influenza; and for the last two years he had come out here for those awkward Christmas dinners. He pressed his forehead against the train's chill window glass. He knew the boss's ordered mind, the way he insisted on the control account being balanced to a farthing. When a problem arose that needed the boss's attention, Rudy always marshalled his facts in advance in order to present the picture with the utmost clarity.

At Sydney Parade he disembarked and made his way out

on to Strand Road. It began to sleet, penetrating squalls of easterly ice-laden rain that soaked him in an instant. He ducked right, down a muddy track that wound itself between the backs of the houses and the railway, and although his feet too would now be wet, at least in here there was some shelter from the weather.

Despite trying to make himself as calm as double-entry, Rudy realised his account might still seem fanciful to a man used to probity and moral order. He almost baulked. What if the boss terminated his employment on the spot? Or what would happen if Mr Fleming was already aware of what Detective Sergeant Melody had described as Harry Deegan's repugnant behaviour? Rudy had not even dared to consider if this remark had included Ultan.

A green wooden door led into Mr Fleming's back garden. The house, two stories over a garden-level cellar, loomed. Rudy took a deep breath. He had no option but to proceed professionally – a favourite word of the boss's, which summed up everything he stood for. Above the garden-level door rainwater spouted from a ruptured gutter. Rudy knocked and went in. The kitchen was directly upstairs, but the boss's meals were always served in the dining room, which overlooked Sandymount Strand. Midway up the back stairs, Rudy was about to call out, announcing his presence, when he drew up sharply. He had heard voices. He listened carefully. There it was again, coming from the direction of the kitchen. The voice of a man who was simultaneously struggling to breathe. In a rush of fear, as he sprinted upwards, Rudy wondered if something dreadful had befallen Mr Fleming, as it had his wife. He reached the head of the stairs. The sound was definitely coming from the kitchen; the door lay partially ajar. All at once, a woman's voice, gasping as she spoke. Rudy halted at the partly open door. Something inside of him contracted with pain. Mr Fleming, unclothed, was braced at the kitchen sink behind a woman. She was equally bare, her elbows on the draining board, and bowed before him. Rudy had never seen his mother naked before.

32

At half-past five, as the heavy sky bore down with great force on the sea, as the wind spat globs of water and the deep growl of thunder shook our ears, Martha and I boarded Murphy's jarvey car for Sutton. Rain hammered the car's tin roof. Eventually, we pulled up. Mr Murphy carried in my suitcase and hurried off abruptly, refusing payment, telling Martha he would be back for her in an hour.

'Wonders will never cease,' Martha said as she fretted about, lighting the kitchen range and unpacking my clothes.

My house smelled fresh and new: wood smells and paint smells. I ran my hand over strange fabrics and tried to guess their colours.

'You are now the proprietor of a Singer Sewing machine, if you don't mind, Miss Raven!' Martha cooed.

I lay on an unfamiliar bed in my room, listening to the steady, warming tick of the kitchen range. The downpour was relentless. I felt as if I were on a little boat in a cold sea, drifting beyond reach of land. When Martha cooked me an omelette, I ate it quickly in the hope that when Mr Murphy arrived she would not linger.

'I can still stay the night,' she said, 'my mother can cope.'

'Martha, please ...'

The jarvey came back, as he had promised, with news that the Shannon had burst its banks in three places and that a whole family had been swept away. I no longer cared. I closed the front door behind them and sat by the range, waiting for the rain to stop. The door scraped open.

'You are not to try to use that sewing machine on your own, Rose,' Martha said.

'Oh, I won't, don't worry.'

'I've put out the milk bottle,' she said.

33

By this time, Rudy had left Mr Fleming's house and, like a man already drunk, had stumbled down the lane. At half-past three he got back as far as Mooney's, where he sat drinking until five, the hour at which Miss Longley went home. Ten minutes later, he lurched in to the big front office, which up to that morning had contained his life's ambition. He couldn't bear it. He tore down the crucifix from above the boss's desk.

Lurching crazily around the room he ripped up all the stock certificates and pitched the silver inkstand from the beautifully tooled leather desktop. The keys to the desk drawers shone at him sullenly. Rudy was possessed by the need to destroy, to expunge all traces of Matthew Fleming, to obliterate the boss's achievements and his revolting shadow from the world. He unlocked the top drawers and flung their contents around the room. A gagging odour of mice assailed him. He dragged out the deep bottom drawer. Abruptly, in a moment of lasting horror, a grey swarm sprang out at him. He screamed and toppled backwards. A frenzy of squealing mice swarmed over his chest, his face, and into his hair. He tried to roll away and thrash them off. The rodents were now dispersing in their dozens, around the big office, into the wainscoting and out the door. Rudy got to his feet, terrified, tearing off his jacket and waistcoat, and then kicking off his shoes and his trousers for fear that mice had burrowed into his clothes. As he shook out his trousers and then dressed himself again, he stared. In the deep drawer, a pile of bread loaves glowed with mildew. Rudy gaped. In some cases, small squares of paper poked from the mottled dough. Rudy picked up one. It said, *mercoledì*.

Wielding a poker from the fireplace in Miss Longley's office, his mind teetering into madness, he pounded the boss's desk to kindling. Exhausted, he rushed down to the toilet and was sick. His mother. His poor father. Rudy felt demeaned, for he was sure that Mr Fleming's decision to employ him, and the regard in which the boss had said he held him, arose not from Rudy's ability but from the fact that his mother was his employer's whore. Exhausted by what he had seen, paralysed by fear for what he had just done, with no job now and a home he could not bring himself to return to, he slumped down at his desk and slept.

34

The boat oar knocked softly in its rowlock. The joyful softness of the sea. I reached out to quiet the oar but jumped as my flesh met hot metal. How long had I slept? It was still raining. The oar still knocked. I jumped up as I suddenly realised that someone was rapping at the kitchen window.

'Miss Raven . . . Rose . . .'

My first thought was, *Rudy?*

'Miss Raven? Don't be alarmed.'

Crawling with fear, I went to the back door as the busy new kitchen clock marked six.

'I'm a friend of Ultan's, from the Indo,' said a man's voice. 'I have a message.'

With the chain still clipped, I opened the back door an inch.

'Who are you?'

'A friend.'

'How do I know?'

'Please.' His voice was full of alarm. 'Just listen.'

I didn't know what to do, or think. I felt so alone. 'Go on.'

'Mr Christopher O'Hare from Boston arrived today and

is staying at the Empire Hotel in Great Denmark Street,' he said.

My head spun. 'And why should that be of any interest to me?'

'He is here to trace his ancestors,' the voice said.

35

I pulled on rubber boots and a hooded gabardine, put a bread knife in my pocket, spent five minutes feeling my way around the parlour till I found matches, then went up into the back garden. It must have been dark, but to me that was of no consequence. The incontinent rain put me inside a drum. I had last been in this tool shed with Ultan, a month before. The handle of the digging fork, when I found it, was still encrusted with specks of clay, left there by his hands. Grief leapt at me, tried to rob me of my resolve, to make my purpose secondary to its needs, to sink me to my knees in the shed.

'Where do you suggest, Sis? Beside the cabbages?'

'Not far in enough. Go to the rhubarb stools.'

'Poor rhubarb.'

'Dig out one of them and plant it back again.'

The new urgency took me over calmly. I waded in among the vegetables till I could kneel in the muck and feel the knobbly stools, lone survivors of the winter – immediately identifiable – the reason I had chosen rhubarb. I was already sodden – my hands and face, my clothes – as was the ground, the raised bed. The first three plants I tugged upon held firm. The fourth gave up easily; I didn't need the fork. Scraping with my hands, down through soaking clay to the depth of my elbows, my fingers touched the biscuit box. Ultan had taped the lid in place. I lifted it out and ran the knife along the edge, but as I did it slipped and I knew I'd cut my index finger. I tried to suck at it as I peeled off the tape. The lid gave.

The envelope was thick to my touch as I tore it open and shook out a wad of papers. The tin box would make a good stove; but the documents were now being pounded by rain. I could feel the glossy consistency of the photographs. Some of the matches spilled as I fumbled one out; cracked it; but it doused. I cracked another and it broke and burnt me. Taking three together, I brought them alight in my cupped hands and put them to a corner of a photograph. Flame leapt. I dropped it into the tin with the other papers. I'm sorry, Ultan, I said.

A door banged.

'Who's there?' I called, adrift with fear. I gripped the knife. 'Who's there? Don't think I can't see you!'

'Rose? Rose! What are you doing?' Rudy cried.

36

When wind from the bay swept through Tommy's birch, it teased each bole and branch, tugged out song from calluses of bark and gave a voice to high bundles of mistletoe. Whenever I heard this winter chorus I could see our trees again. As a child, I had tried to count their branches, and then the twigs on each branch, and marvelled that no matter how hard I tried I could never succeed.

He had brought me in from the deluge. He stank of cheap whiskey.

'I know what these are!' he gasped and I could hear him going through the documents I had tried to burn. 'Oh, dear Lord – these are what Melody is after! Oh, Christ! Look at these poor children!'

I had never heard Rudy blaspheme before.

'Why would you burn them, Rose?'

'To keep you safe.'

We were both crying.

'Ultan made me promise.'

'It won't work,' he said, as, to my dismay, he recounted how the tailor's wife had met her end and her husband was in custody.

'He'll talk. He will say he brought these out here. He will

tell Melody he met me here and Melody will know I lied.'

We made toast by the fire and he drank strong tea. I thought he had nothing left to say, but then, in a halting voice, he described going out to Mr Fleming's house. The range crackled with old floorboards the carpenters had left behind.

'Did they see you?'

'No. Nor do I want to see either of them again.'

He was in a dark cave, which made us more alike than we had ever been. We sat in silence, disturbed only by the rain and the clock's tinny pendulum. I stroked his head, his hair. He told me about finding the loaves of his mother's bread in the boss's desk. He felt so sorry for his father.

'I am finished up here. I am going to London. Miss Longley has a sister there who will give me lodging.' He took a deep breath. 'Will you come with me?'

'Rudy?'

'Be my wife, Rose. We can start again.'

I felt a soaring leap of hope.

'Leave all this behind, yes,' he said. 'Go where no one knows us.'

I was giddy, for I knew that I had loved him all along.

'What is there to hold us here?' he asked. 'Nothing. Ultan was right.'

I took his hands and faced him. 'Let us talk some more,' I said.

37

At first light, even though it had begun to snow lightly, Rudy sat on the garden deck of the Dublin tram. Seabirds made lonely calls from the salty marshes and flocked along the peeled cadaver of the bay. Rudy had a vivid image of me at his side in Piccadilly Circus, a place he had seen only on postcards, as he would later say. We were radiant with laughter. In Clontarf, a civic guard on the beat paused and looked up at him narrowly. Rudy shrank into his seat. He could feel the outline of the envelope at his ribs. Shameful facts, dreadful times. The tram lurched inland on groaning iron. His ears stung with cold. He preferred the bustle and noise of the city to our fields and lonely seascapes. He felt emboldened among people, less conspicuous. In London the gay throngs were beyond imagining, Miss Longley had said.

He peered down at the snow-garnished railings of the Custom House. Soot-streaked buildings with broken windows reeked of hardship. In Sackville Street, drays and ass-carts were standing idle, and hansom cabs waited in a line. Seagulls strutted on the plinth of the ruined post office as Rudy disembarked at the Pillar, and then, eyes to the fore, walked briskly into Rutland Square, up Gardiner Row and into Great Denmark Street.

It was five minutes to nine and the life of the city had yet to gather pace, although wheel marks glared blackly from the centre of Great Denmark Street. The red brick of the Jesuit College enlivened the searing black and white as Rudy approached the hotel. He had worked out his approach. A shilling to the hotel boots, although extravagant, would smooth his way to the right bedroom. He was about to cross over, but halted. A blue Model T Ford with red-spoked wheels stood outside the hotel's entrance. He recognised the car as a former Castle car, now assigned to the new Dublin police force. These four years past the vehicle had been in and out of Potterton's for repairs.

Rudy stayed on his own side and tried to hide behind a lamppost. He was blinded by sudden bright sunlight and could not make out if there was someone sitting in the car. He was summoning his dwindling courage when unexpected movement caught his eye. On the same side as he was standing, no more than fifty yards away, opposite the hotel, pipe smoke hung on the thin air. If Rudy moved ever so slightly towards the roadway he could see the source of this smoke: the brim of a hat, and beneath it, a spade-like beard.

Alarm pounding, breath caught in his chest, Rudy turned and walked back down the street, trying not hurry or to look around.

38

Later that morning, snow squalls surged over the Bailey. I felt the gradient of the hill press me as the tram climbed. Martha had needed to be reminded firmly that there were days when I preferred to go out on my own. Even so, I could not be sure that she was not following me. Earlier, when she had again pressed me to consider her moving in to Nan's Cottage with her mother, I had seen red.

'If you bring that up once more, I will sell this cottage, give the proceeds to the nuns in Raheny and move in with them!' I had shouted.

It was not yet eleven. I could tell the sun had all at once unwrapped the hillside; whenever I felt sun on my face I could see the world again. The tram levelled out. I hoped she would turn up, for even though I could never tell her I was saying goodbye, I had to meet her one last time. I disembarked at the Sutton end and, when the tram had left, as I tried to find my bearings, I smelled her perfume.

'I remember coming up here the day of my First Holy Communion,' Agnes said. 'Your Papa gave me sixpence. It was the most money I had ever had.'

The little teashop was set dramatically above the sea. On a good day the Wicklow Hills could be seen.

'And Papa wasn't even a Catholic,' I said.

In school I used to invent stories just to see Agnes's eyes enlarge into their beautiful, fathomless irises.

'Can you still manage at home?' I asked.

'It's horrible. It's not just that he can't speak anymore, or that I have to clean him – but he's so heavy! Some evenings after lifting him into the bed I think my back is broken.'

I would have loved to be able to see her one last time, but Martha had told me that Agnes had gone to weight now, and had not minded her appearance. For me she was the same Agnes, unchanged and beautiful; and of course with Martha it was hard to untangle venom from the truth. We talked of our days at school and laughed when we remembered some of the nuns.

'They meant well,' I said.

'That Mother Mary Superior had the hands bet off me,' Agnes said. 'Old bitch.'

'She actually wasn't too bad when you got to know her,' I said.

'Oh, I'd forgotten,' Agnes said. 'Excuse me.'

'All I'm saying is, she wasn't too bad.'

I could imagine Agnes's expression of doleful resentment.

'Listen – I heard something . . .' She caught her breath. 'I don't know if I should say this.'

'Say what?'

'I better not.'

'Go on, please.'

'I did not for a second believe it, Rose . . .'

'Of course not.'

'I heard that Ultan was caught up in something, you know, with anti-Treaty types, spreading rumours . . . saying dangerous things. That if he hadn't died he would have been arrested.'

'At least he was spared that,' I said with some relief. 'What is the source of this rubbish, may I ask?'

'I'm just a friend telling you what I heard, Rose,' Agnes said with a spike of indignation. 'There is no need to attack me!'

It was ever so, for as long as I could remember, as if Agnes had a wound that would never heal. I suddenly wished I could level with her, and tell her the way out of this darkness.

'I often wonder which of us is the unluckiest,' she said haltingly. 'I often wonder, you know, if we had just been allowed to go on the way we were . . .'

She began to cry, little gulps of sadness, eerie in their reminders of our childhood. I reached out to her.

'What about your Arthur?' I said. 'Arthur from Guinness?'

Her crying deepened.

'Agnes, be kind to yourself.'

'He's gone!' she wept. 'I thought he loved me . . . I would have done anything for him . . .'

'Oh, Agnes . . .'

'Told me lies . . . made use of me . . .'

'Sssh . . . .'

'Talked about us going down to Limerick together, that he had a new job set up there, but all along he was living in the Coombe with a wife and children.'

All the years merged in the only place I could still see, all the images of what might have been, the fond glances, the voices of those I still loved and the smells of that summer.

'I am so sorry,' I said. 'I really am.'

She drew back.

114

'He was all I had, Rose. You knew that! But I didn't hear you saying you were sorry then!'

'Agnes, don't . . .'

'How do you think I felt to lose all I ever wanted to a blind woman? I could almost hear you laughing! All you had to do was crook your finger and he came running!'

'That's not true, I never did.'

'Like your little dog! Here Rudy, Rudy. Sit! Good boy!'

'It wasn't like that.'

'It was the same in school – Saint Rose! All you had to do was look at the nuns and they melted. One smile from Saint Rose! Oh, yes, you suffered, we all know what happened, but you're like a cat who always lands on her paws. Lady Rose Raven! What do you know about how good it feels to have a drunken man lie on top of you and hope when you wake up he'll still be there? To pray to God that he'll come back and take you away with him? Because you hope that his hell is better than yours? That's all I have left to hope for, Rose, you made sure of that. So don't tell me you're sorry. You think of no one but Rose Raven and one day Rudy Saddler will find that out too.'

39

Rudy later described for me what happened next. Every so often, as he stood in thickening snow across the canal from Herbert Place, a spasm overtook him. He felt a thief, even though he had stolen nothing. The snow fell beautifully, and twice so, it seemed, since its fall was reflected in the water. In the previous two hours, he had observed tradesmen removing the giblets of the boss's desk; and, fifteen minutes after that, a new desk and chair being delivered. A further thirty minutes went by before the blue Model T with the red-spoked wheels glided up from Mount Street Bridge and halted outside Number 8. In terror Rudy watched through the dizzy dance of snowflakes as Detective Sergeant Melody, wearing a belted topcoat, stepped from the car and walked up the steps to the office. Five minutes later, Melody re-emerged and the car was driven away.

The sight of Melody for the second time that morning struck Rudy with petrifying impact. He doubted Mr Fleming had called in the police: when the boss had walked into the destruction of his office that morning, and when Rudy had subsequently failed to appear, Fleming would have understood. He was probably in there now saying his rosary, Rudy thought grimly. No, Melody was there, not on account of any action Mr Fleming had taken. Melody was looking for Rudy.

Just after one, Miss Longley appeared at the top of the steps, peered into the snowstorm, opened her umbrella and made her way towards Baggot Street Bridge. The sight of her neat figure made Rudy yearn for the normal life he had just forsaken, their chummy cups of tea, her gifts of pressed flowers, her way of making Rudy feel he was important. He kept level with her, on his side of the canal, until she turned right; at which point he ran up the tow-path and crossed the bridge. Although he understood she lived in Lower Baggot Street, he did not know where. When she left the office each day, Miss Longley disappeared into a world of which Rudy knew nothing.

People kept appearing from the snow, sometimes hugely, and then as quickly, vanishing back into it. He stayed fifty yards behind the small, somehow resolute figure, her head bowed into the snowfall as she bowled along. He realised that he would have to tell her everything if she was to remain his ally, although he dreaded doing so. Neither would he put her in danger by giving her the documents still concealed in his undershirt; rather, he would ask her to simply go down to the Empire Hotel and pass on a message.

The car across the street seemed to be keeping pace with him; its windows were partly obscured by snow; Rudy scarcely dared to look; but suddenly the vehicle increased speed and was lost to the whiteness. Miss Longley turned right into Herbert Street, a surprise, since he had assumed she lived on Baggot Street. Halfway along the narrower street, as snow swirled into a vortex, she walked up steps to a door and folded her umbrella. Rudy sprinted forward just as she reached with her key to the latch.

117

'Miss Longley!'

She turned and looked down at him, as if nothing had ever happened, as if they were alone in the office together, about to have tea.

'Miss Longley, I am sorry for this intrusion,' he began.

'Ah, Mr Saddler, I was wondering when you would turn up,' she said.

40

Part of me still believed that what I was living through – my sightless day-to-day existence – was a temporary phenomenon and that I was merely marking time until my former life resumed. This delusion may have arisen through living in darkness, where I could with ease revisit the scenes of years before and, in the process, re-live them. In that way, I sat again through all the cricket matches in Trinity that Tommy and I had attended. The steward in the pavilion had seen service too, so we were able to sit out on the terrace – like royalty, Papa unfailingly remarked. He drank a half of bitter and smoked his pipe. He used to say that being there reminded him of the cricket he had watched in England as a boy. I never took much interest in the matches, but I loved the pageantry – the men in their bright whites, the picnic groups in their merry hats spread over the little grass rises around the pitch. The whack of the cricket ball on willow and the cries when the players appealed to the umpire were as sharply audible to me as when, as a child, I had first heard them.

That day, as I came back from meeting Agnes in Howth, it struck me that I would never walk into Trinity again. The absolute nature of what we were about to do made me afraid. Would I forever look back longingly across the Irish Sea?

How could I engage with a world and with people I had never seen? With a shock I realised this was a dilemma I had faced once before. At Sutton Cross, a neighbour took my arm and brought me home, the snow crunching beneath our feet.

'I've never seen weather like this in March,' she said.

I thanked her and went in. Agnes had offered to come back to Nan's Cottage with me, but I had declined. I did not want her to come in and see the packed suitcase on my bed.

41

At four o'clock, in a thickening blizzard, Rudy cycled towards the canal. A tram laboured by, its upper deck empty, its lower level crammed with passengers. Lights glowed from the frosted windows of many houses. He knew his father would be in the allotment.

He had been amazed to learn the extent of Miss Longley's dislike of Mr Fleming. She had long suspected his affair with Lucia, she told Rudy – one of the reasons she was leaving. She had not wanted to alert Rudy to her suspicions for she did not want to upset his prospects with the firm. When Rudy told her about the conditions in the west, and shown her the photographs, she had immediately agreed to go to the Empire Hotel. After less than an hour, she returned to the flat, where he had sat waiting.

'He's almost as young as you are, Mr Saddler,' she said, and confirmed that she had delivered his message.

Rudy kissed Miss Longley's cherry red cheek.

'Not goodbye!' she said sternly. 'The French say *au revoir!* Which means, until we meet again.'

He had to push the bicycle the final one hundred yards. The allotment lay as if beneath a shroud. A little tail of smoke rose from a shed. Not until now, through all his years at home, had Rudy fully grasped why his father preferred this tiny cabin to his own hearth.

'It's Rudy!'

The sergeant was well wrapped, warming his hands over warm coals in a makeshift grate. He filled the blackened kettle from a bottle and placed it on the primus. He heaped tea from the caddy to the pot. Rudy had loved this ritual since his childhood, the sense somehow that this damp shed was central to the universe.

'You are troubled,' the sergeant said, after some time had passed.

Rudy held the tin mug for warmth and wondered how he should begin. Snow clung to his moustache and clogged his nostrils.

'I know it in you,' the sergeant said. 'Always have. I know it too when you lie. Like when you lied to that peeler.'

Rudy's tears rushed into his eyes.

'It may be none of my business,' said the sergeant, 'but if you want to talk to me I'll listen.'

'Mama cannot be told,' he began. 'I mean . . . it would upset her.'

An ember of hearth light crossed his father's deep-set, pale blue eyes and in that small moment something beyond wisdom was evident in the sergeant.

'I'm sorry—' Rudy tried to say. He began to cry. 'You're a good man.'

He felt his father's hand in his hair. He held it there, and then kissed it.

'It's all right, really,' the sergeant said. 'I will survive.' He made himself a pipe, attending to the bowl with grave deliberation. 'I often dream of the day I taught you to drive.

We're in the Dodge, just the two of us, the engine is purring, the wind is warm and we're driving into the park. I always wake up thinking how lucky I am to have you as a son.'

The warmth of the shed made a mockery of the engulfing bone-cold landscape.

'What else brought you here?' the sergeant asked. 'You know you can tell me anything now.'

At first haltingly, but ever growing into his father's open decency and affection, Rudy described what he was bound up in, beginning with the day he had met the tailor.

'They have him up in the Castle yard,' Sergeant Saddler said grimly, 'I heard about it yesterday from a peeler who came down to Potterton's with a motorcycle.' He shuddered. 'You wouldn't do it to a dog.'

Rudy showed his father the photographs and the sergeant's head sank.

'And all we fought for,' he said.

They sat in silence. From a bag in the corner the sergeant produced a whiskey naggin and topped up the tea mugs.

'I knew it as soon as Melody showed up,' he said. 'He's a horrible sort. Changed sides after 1920 when he saw which way the wind was blowing and has been trying to prove himself ever since. After the Treaty he was part of a gang down in Oriel House that went out and murdered Irregulars. When they were disbanded, most of them scarpered, to places like New York, where their talents were appreciated, but Melody stayed on in the DMP. They say he's terrified now that the families of the Irregulars he put down are going to come after him, so he spends his time trying to impress the hard core men in Home Affairs, hoping they'll think he's too valuable to ever be thrown to the wolves.'

'Why didn't he get out when he could?' Rudy asked. 'Go to New York?'

The sergeant shrugged. 'He has a wife and children in Phibsboro. He owns his house there. He made a decision.'

The crypt-like silence was broken by the muffled sound of snow toppling from the shed's eaves.

Rudy explained to his father what he proposed to do.

'Until things settle down,' he said.

'I understand,' the sergeant said.

'Rose is coming with me,' Rudy said, defiantly, for he expected his father to argue against it.

'Of course, she has to,' the sergeant said. 'Of course. They as good as killed a man's wife – imagine what they'll do to a blind girl.' They drank the laced tea and the sergeant bared his teeth as the whiskey found its mark. 'Where did you tell the American to go?'

42

When he came to my back door at midnight and told me the landscape was white and devoid of human life, that the bay shone like a sapphire, and that the full moon was hanging like a lantern in the sky, I pictured us two, in this vast, dead landscape, sealed in forever.

'Some of the stars are red,' he said. 'I heard an old man on a corner saying the world is coming to an end.'

He was certain he had not been followed, but he would leave before dawn, he said, since he was sure that Melody would come looking. His father had said that if we sailed from Waterford as passengers on a cattle boat, we would evade Melody. Sergeant Saddler had offered to drive down with us into the southeast the next day, and bring home the car.

He set a fire in the grate of my parents' bedroom, and then stripped the bedding from the wrought-iron bedstead and laid it out before the flames. He boiled water and filled the stoneware jars that had warmed my parents' nights for eight months of every year. We kissed deeply. He undressed me slowly, easing each button from its eyelet with great respect, and when my shift fell away he kissed the rounds of my shoulders. My hands found his chest and hips, as smooth as apples, and he came to me, his length on mine, and I could feel the cleft of his back as I lifted into him.

Later, he brought in cushions from the parlour and set them before the bedroom fire. He told me he was spreading out the papers and photographs across the hearth because, despite keeping them close, the paper was still damp. At noon the next day I would go by tram to Terenure where he and his father would meet me.

'After London, we'll sail far away,' he said. 'We'll look back and wonder why we stayed here so long.'

'Tell me.'

'To somewhere settled and at peace, with chestnut trees, where the sky is always bright and the earth is warm. We'll lie down together and let the heat of the ground rise into us.'

He held me close.

'There will be sea, as there is here, but it will be warm sea,' he said. 'I'll make a picnic. We'll fall asleep in the shade.'

'Sing to me,' I said.

'We could be heard . . .'

'So, sing to me softly.'

I smiled as I imagined the formal set of him as he prepared himself, how he joined his hands and raised his head.

'It was down by the Salley Gardens, my love and I did meet,

She crossed the Salley Gardens with little snow-white feet . . .'

I knew in that moment that my parents were near us, and that they approved; and that my love for Rudy was no betrayal of the past.

'She bid me take love easy, as the leaves grow on the tree,
But I was young and foolish, and with her did not agree.'

As much as I strove to hear the world beyond the cottage, I
could not. I wondered if that lack of sound was what the dead
heard as they lay in their graves, that universal numbness.

'I remember years ago,' he said, 'my father used to bring
me with him down to Potterton's and in good weather I'd go
out on the banks of the Camac with the local children. I was
seven or eight. It was magical. We'd strip off and play in the
water. I taught myself to swim. I'll never forget the power
of that – neither of my parents could swim but I could. I
remember floating on my back in mid-stream and looking up
at the turrets of Kilmainham Gaol. It all seemed so peaceful.'

We sat with a blanket over us.

'At the beginning, my father used to come out from the
workshop and check on me, but after a while he didn't need
to. One of the boys was called Micky Dugan. That wasn't
his real name, he was called after the famous comic strip.
Micky Dugan was simple and slow. He was partly bald and
his teeth were crooked. People said his parents were very old.
Everyone in the gang looked after Micky Dugan. The older
boys carried him on their backs; they taught him to smoke;
he shared in their sweets. He couldn't swim but he had a
lovely smile. You'd give him anything just to see him smile.'

I kissed Rudy's cheek.

'One day, it seemed we were all together, but the next, only
a few of us remained. Most of them went into the army. They
died on the Somme or in Passchendaele. A few of them were
out in 1916 and were shot by the British. They're buried in
Glasnevin. I knew Micky Dugan couldn't have joined up, but

during the school holidays I used to hang around to see if I might see him. I never did.'

'What do you think happened?'

'I really don't know. Funny, isn't it? Tomorrow you and I will be gone from here, maybe never coming back – and who is the one person I'm thinking most of leaving behind? Little Micky Dugan, a lad who's probably been dead for ten years and whose real name I never knew.'

43

My mind was filled with sunny dreams. Floating just above deep sleep, I could feel the sand of Portmarnock between my toes, and wet seashells, and hear the tide that threatened the hem of my dress. Freddy rushed to me from the corner of a dune, a low-flying, lazy gull fixed in his sights. So comical: the little, bustling dog, the languid gull. I saw an old oil drum where someone had set down a pair of polished, two-tone leather shoes. If only I could paint, I thought, that is what I would paint: that rusty drum, those two-tone shoes.

At first, I had no idea of the time. At some point in the night he had got up; I had heard the bones in his bare feet settling as he walked around the bed, but I had fallen back to sleep. I sat up, taxing the limits of my absent vision for a hint of light, at the same time knowing it was early since I had not heard the milkman, but snow may well have delayed his dray. No rain, or wind, or traffic on the sea road. Even the tide was silenced. The new clock in the parlour suddenly dealt out eight in shrill little beats, as if time were forever snapping at its heels. I imagined Rudy on his way to town, disembarking at the Pillar, changing for the Inchicore tram from which he would alight beneath Kilmainham. And, in my imagination, the American had slipped out of his hotel, unobserved, on his way to meet Rudy.

I lit the gas, put on the pot of steeping porridge and took out the bread. The house was tomb cold; Rudy had said the snow was up to the window ledges. While the pot on the kitchen range began to simmer, I went back to the bedroom, dressed myself quickly, and then gathered up the cushions from the hearth. They were still warm. My fingers came in contact with a smooth surface, then a charred edge. White, by the touch of it. I gasped. I was holding one of the photographs that Rudy had put out to dry there – the one I had attempted to burn.

'Rudy!'

I was dizzy in an instant.

'Rudy?'

As my heart thudded, I turned off the gas and hurried out to get my coat. With my suitcase to hand, and the photograph safely in it, I tugged shut the front door, put my key under the milk bottle, and walked down the snow-covered path of Nan's Cottage. Kittiwakes were calling from the estuary.

44

A woman at the tram stop remarked that snowdrifts sat along the seashore, an unheard of event.

'Will it ever stop?' she asked into the biting, snow-laden wind. 'They say we'll have no spring this year at all.'

Women from this hinterland often worked in Dublin, in shops and hotels, and took the early tram to town. The conductor knew me and helped me to board.

'Are you off on your holidays?' he asked.

I was not seeing Dublin Bay, or the Sugarloaf, as we trundled inwards; I was seeing London in the pictures of a book that Mother Mary Superior in Raheny had kept in her desk. I wondered what car would be used for our drive down to Waterford. I hoped it would be the Dodge, with its gleaming black body and huge headlights, the first motorcar I had ever sat in.

It had begun to snow in earnest, wet flakes of it, dappling everyone abroad, someone said. The break with his mother would be harder on him than he had bargained for; but in time, he would forgive her, especially if he was far away. The tram halted at the Pillar and I could hear hawkers calling. I alighted, the city's noise oddly softened in the blizzard.

'Do you need someone to guide you, miss?'

A stranger who had seen my cane.

'You're very kind. To a taxi-cab, if you could, please.'

He cupped my elbow and took my case. 'Frightful bit of weather,' he said as we crossed the road. 'A day to stay at home, if you ask me.'

I was encouraged by this uplifting spirit and knew that everything would be taken care of.

'Here we are,' he said and I heard the vehicle's door being opened.

'Thank you,' I said and got in. 'Please bring me to Rowserstown Lane in Old Kilmainham. I am in a great hurry.'

45

I could scarcely hear the engine as we spun through the blanketed streets. The taxi hummed with the rich aroma of its leather, which, when I removed my mittens and felt the tooled grooves, I imagined to be burgundy. As the driver hooted, I could almost see the barrow women in the roadway, selling their flowers, despite the weather, and children making a snowman. We stopped, but I knew we had not arrived because the journey had not been of sufficient duration. I heard the front passenger's door being opened; the cab's springs acknowledged that another person had come on board; we resumed.

'Good morning, sir,' the driver said.

I did not bid the newcomer good day; conversation with a stranger was the last thing I needed. As we slipped down towards the Camac, as the brakes squealed to govern our descent, as the cold seemed to penetrate more deeply the lower we went, I wondered why the driver had picked up another fare since I had told him I was in a hurry. Sometimes cabs took on extra fares to divide the cost for the passengers. Perhaps he had done so because of these dreadful conditions. *A mali estremi, estremi rimedi.*

'She's finding the hills very difficult in these conditions,' the driver said.

'I daresay she is,' said a new voice.

46

They say that our instinct to flee danger began in the jungle, that we are born with the heart and lungs of apes. These organs flood with primal energy when faced with danger as we momentarily vault over our fear in an electric rush of action. It has nothing to do with bravery or cleverness. We are in that short space seized by the need to save ourselves, or another even dearer than ourselves, an imperative that trumps all others. We revert in that tiny moment to the jungle.

So it was that even before I knew it I was out of the car and skidding down the hill. I screamed out Rudy's name. I screamed. All I had to guide me was the gradient, and my image of the hill, bridge, river and valley, seen years before, but crystallised in a place deeper than sight.

'*Rudy*! RUDY!'

Behind me I could hear a voice commanding me to stop or be shot. I was past all fear. I could hear the curious deadness into which my screams collided, as if I was calling out from behind a pillow. I screamed as my ears rang, as my soaked feet somehow carried me.

'You bitch—'

'RUDY!'

A weight hit me square across my back and I went face

down into slush and snow. He had me caught. I lunged and bit at his big hands with righteous hate.

'Bitch! I will have you flogged!'

Metal doors were being dragged open up ahead, scraping the ground, and releasing the noise of a car's engine. At that moment, I believed I could see. The inside of the garage, a black contrast to the snow that I was part of; Rudy's father standing to one side, proudly, the garage owner to the other; a stranger; Rudy.

I have heard that there comes one moment in every life when we are bestowed with the gift of omnipotence. A tiny second, often before the end, when we can see into every heart and mind, when puzzles fall away, tears are dried and love is confirmed in all its glory. It is, they say, as if we have lived all our lives for this twinkling of total understanding, and having achieved it, must then move on.

'HALT!'

Even as the order was called the shots rang out. A fusillade. Lead ripped through metal.

'Rudy—'

My wrists were held, but I still managed to kick.

'Please don't hurt her, sir,' Martha said.

'Martha?'

I could hear a man sobbing up in the garage. I was so glad that I could not see. Thank God I was blind and could not see.

PART TWO

Four Years Earlier

Sutton, County Dublin,
United Kingdom of Great Britain and Ireland
Summer 1920

1

On a Sunday of joyfully blue sky and warm sea we strolled
along the sun-drenched coast road where palm trees flour-
ished, where the bay was dotted far out with sails, where
seagulls paced the shore and hawks quivered mote-like far
above our heads. We had been to Mass in Sutton, following
which Tommy, my father, had met us at Sutton Cross, at
the gates to the Marine Hotel, and with a little bow to us,
his children, gathered my mother's arm and led the way for
home. Every two months or so Tommy attended his own
church in Howth, but even on those Sundays when he prayed
alone he was back at Sutton Cross before us.

Ultan and I trailed the old pair, allowing the gap to widen.
Tommy's slight but square frame, still regimental; Annie's
head as it bobbed from side to side with every step, a woman
always about her business. Ultan paused, removed a cigarette
from a little leather case, bent his head into cupped hands
and cracked a match.

'You have an admirer, Sis.'

Rakish smoke trailed from his arched nostrils; the pollu-
tion of the morning was exquisite.

'Really? I don't think so.'

'Since the cricket match two weeks ago he has spoken of no one else, believe me. Want a pull?'

'Not out here.'

'Come on, Rose! Who's going to see you?'

I nestled into him by the seawall as the ozone moiled our faces and he set the cigarette between my lips.

'He says you're the loveliest creature on earth,' he murmured.

'Mmmm ...'

I adored that first fat explosion as I drew down on the cigarette, and then let it back out in a blue veil to float between me and the distant Hill of Howth. Gorse glowed like bullion from the flanks of the Demesne. The thrill of memory possessed me and with it the feeling that something amazing, but which I had yet to understand, lay just within my grasp.

'He's quite a catch,' Ultan said and retrieved his cigarette.

I loved my brother's tall, graceful figure, his sauntering nonchalance, the daring dip of his straw boater.

'I thought all he caught was butterflies.'

'Butterflies?'

'Seemed very taken with them.'

'Oh – you mean Saddler!' Ultan threw back his head and laughed. 'Where did you meet him?'

'At your cricket match in the Demesne!'

'Good Lord! He's a trier, Saddler, I'll give him that. Worked on the trams since he was twelve as a ticket picker. Had to, mother's a virago.'

'He seemed kind ...'

'He's a grand bright lad,' Ultan said. 'But it's not Saddler, Sis, it's Mr Holly. Mr Chink Holly, no less.'

I felt something delicious kick inside me. I thought,

vermillion. I thought, *he is beautiful*. 'Oh, come on, Ultan.'

'A gentleman, I assure you. Knows how to behave. And he's got a business to walk into.'

'A bit too forward for his own good, I would say.'

'Do I detect a blushing rose? Hmm? A little quiver in her lovely stem, by Jove?'

'Stop it!'

'Can't fool me, you know. Besides which, he's right. You are ambrosial!'

Way ahead, Tommy and Annie slowly receded, two black figurines on the rim of the bay. We stepped in to let a tram pass and the conductor acknowledged us from his platform.

'Why do you call him Chink? Is his name not David?'

'In Belvedere apparently a teacher said his hair was Chinese red – whatever that means. It stuck.'

'Sounds dreadful.'

'He's not a bit like you might think,' Ultan said. 'I've been in his house—'

'When you were a child. When you went to school together.'

'They're normal people. He works in the family shop in Capel Street. He is my friend.'

'You may well think so, but you may not be his.'

'That's unfair, Rose!'

'His father is a member in Papa's club. Mr Holly is a wealthy businessman. These people mix within their own.'

'These people . . .?'

'You know exactly what I mean.'

'Look,' said my brother sternly, 'there's another cricket match in ten days' time, after which he's invited everyone back to his house. He's asked me to tell you he would love nothing more than if you came along.'

I stopped and looked at Ultan. 'And then I will fly to the moon.'

'He will have the house to himself! His parents will be in Birmingham for an exhibition that weekend.' Ultan put on an accent that was vaguely how Tommy spoke. 'The latest shovels from Sheffield, lass!'

'I'm not going up to Holly's, Ultan. Forget it.'

'Rose, please . . .'

'You go, if you like, but without me.'

'I shall, but it's you he wants there, not me!' Ultan flung his cigarette into the sea. 'You have him bowled over, Sis! I should not be surprised if you were the whole reason for this party!'

'You are being ridiculous,' I said and resumed my walk as the urgent lap of tide against the seawall marked the turn for home, as the morning soaked me with its splendour and the distant, troubled city lay quiet and far away.

'Rose!' Ultan was abreast again. 'Chink doesn't care for convention. His father started out thirty years ago on the shop floor, working for *his* father. Just as Chink is doing now.'

'Have you spent the last twenty-one years with your eyes closed? Do you really think I would ever be more than an adornment at a party up there? Grow up, Ultan!'

'These differences soon won't exist, mark my words!' he cried. 'Chink thinks the same way! Soon we will all be the same, flattened out, no bosses and workers anymore, no us and them. That is what being free will mean!'

'I think,' I said as I walked at speed, 'that you are getting so far ahead of yourself, there's a danger you'll meet yourself coming back.'

2

My brother and I were part of a new generation in which change not permanence would define our lives. Change was afoot, and swiftly, as Ultan told me when he came home at nights from the newspaper office in Middle Abbey Street where a few months earlier he had begun work as an office boy. Change was devouring people's minds, not just across Europe, but in Dublin too, he said. Ireland was now in a state of permanent insurrection, although few in authority admitted it. Nothing would ever again be the same.

'Try telling that to Tommy and Annie,' I said.

3

On the slight incline, a hundred yards from Nan's Cottage, a tall and gangling young man, dressed in the white jacket and bow tie of a hotel waiter suddenly appeared. His shoes looked too big for him and it seemed as if he might topple over. As we came face to face, he drew up.

'Hello, Rose. You look smashing this morning.'

'If you say so, Eddie.'

'Where's your Enfield, Kidney?' Ultan asked. 'Or has it been confiscated?'

Eddie Kidney's face was livid with pimples and he had a way of staring when he spoke.

'You hardly think I'm going to bring it to work, do you, Ultan the Sultan?' He laughed. 'Ultan the Sultan!'

'You smell like a tart, Kidney,' Ultan said. 'Come on, Rose.'

They had been in the same class at school when Eddie's father was killed in the Rising, although it was said that Ted Kidney had been shot as he looted a shop in Mary Street. Eddie now worked in the dining room of the Marine Hotel. It was unfair of Ultan to make fun of Eddie's beliefs since I knew Ultan too believed in a free Ireland.

'I've got balcony tickets for the Picture House, Rose,' Eddie said. 'One of them's for you.'

144

'Maybe another time, thanks.'

'One day you'll say yes,' Eddie said.

'Can the IRA not give you a better uniform, Kidney?' Ultan asked.

'You'd want to be careful with that mouth of yours, Sultan,' Eddie said.

'You better hurry up or you'll miss parade,' Ultan said, walking backwards. 'Hup! Two! Three! Four!'

'Fuck you, you son of a dirty Brit,' Eddie said and spat as he turned and walked off.

'Fuck you, you sad little rebel shite!' Ultan called after him.

We continued up towards home.

'There's no need to be so unkind,' I said. 'Especially since you both share the same point of view.'

'I don't care what his point of view is, I hate him,' Ultan said. 'It was Kidney and his mates who set fire to the hay in Barnmere's last winter. A hundred pounds worth of damage.'

'There's no proof.'

'What would have happened if there had been children in the barn? We used to play up there when we were kids.'

'How do you know it was Eddie?'

'Told everyone his hair nearly went on fire, more's the pity it didn't.'

'Stop it, please.'

'Steer well clear of him. He's a dangerous little bastard, mark my words,' Ultan said.

4

We came up from the sea, the sun on our backs, the blue sky so enormous and faith giving that it was hard to imagine the country was not contented. Nan's Cottage was my father's manor: a respectable garden to the front, quarter of an acre behind, with a bountiful vegetable garden, grazing for a cow – although we never had one – and a fox's covert. We seldom saw the fox since Tommy's Yorkshire terrier, Freddy, patrolled the garden like a little hussar. But sometimes, in the dead of night, I awoke to the airborne dread of a rabbit as the fox – a vixen – hit her mark. Only country people like us were aware that rabbits could scream.

Our parents knew their place. It was the way they had been formed and lived their lives. Upon their marriage, they moved into quarters in Marlborough Barracks, two rooms and a scullery, a rare privilege granted on the strength of the esteem in which Papa was held by his regiment. Diligent, hard-working and loyal, Tommy Raven had been a cavalry groom, but he became allergic to the dust in the stables which made it impossible for him to work with horses. Most men would have been invalided out, but Tommy was so liked that his officers made him a barracks orderly. Gave him a smart tunic and put him in the officers' mess. Tommy's station in life was to serve, and he excelled. His ready acceptance of life's immutable structures, his happy face and his refusal to complain made his superiors smile for Tommy Raven. Papa was a hardworking, humble man, whose only personal indulgence was a flutter on the horses, which he followed avidly, especially Chanticleer's Notes in the *Irish Times*.

Freddy rushed out at us, his tail a blur. I could hear Annie in the kitchen, talking to Martha, as she took off her coat.

'I couldn't hear a word of Father Shipsey's sermon, I think I'm going deaf.'

'He mumbles something dreadful for a priest,' Martha said, coming from the kitchen, licking her fingers and then wiping her mouth on her apron. 'It has nothing to do with your ears, ma'am.'

Father Shipsey's gaze on me exceeded well-mannered curiosity. I'll not confess my sins to Father Shipsey, I'd long resolved.

'We're lucky to have him as our parish priest,' Annie called. 'He's a fine man.'

'And very easy on the eye,' Martha said.

Papa had once remarked, out of Annie's earshot, that in a perfect world Martha would have married Father Shipsey.

Bull Island bathed in Sunday sun. I loved these Mass days on which Tommy did not have to work, when he started a pipe and sat with his Sunday newspaper in the parlour, facing Howth. Every few minutes he looked up and shook his head.

'This is not the same country I remember coming to,' he said with regularity.

In one of the more peculiar substrates of our social universe, my mother, who worked for Mrs Wilder on the Burrow Road, enjoyed the regular services, including on

Sundays, of Mrs Merry from Baldoyle. This relationship arose from a sense of obligation. After her husband's death in Gallipoli, Martha Merry and her aged mother were evicted from their cottage in Portmarnock. Even though a law had been introduced to prevent rents being raised, or war widows evicted, Martha's landlord trumped up an excuse to tumble her dwelling. She and her mother were left destitute. We, in Sutton, knew nothing of this till one night a woman, who introduced herself as Mrs Martha Merry, appeared at our door and spoke to Annie. She carried herself with dignity despite her indigent position. An end-of-terrace house in Baldoyle was up for rent, she said, but the agent would not entertain her. The house was the property of a Dublin gentleman who, she believed, was a member of the club in which Mr Raven was employed as porter.

Annie spoke to Tommy, and Tommy, choosing his moment in the club, made the approach. Within a week, Mrs Merry and her mother were installed in Baldoyle at a nominal rent.

Papa might as well have backed the winner of the Derby. 'It's not what you know, it's who you know,' he said happily when he heard the Merrys' news.

Martha took on an obligation to our family as one takes on a mortgage. She cleaned Nan's Cottage, even as my mother worked for Mrs Wilder; she set our fires and prepared our Sunday lunch when we went to Mass. As Annie pegged out bedsheets on the Burrow Road, at home our bedsheets, washed by Martha, billowed in the breeze. Because she refused flatly to be paid, once a year Papa went over to the grocer in Baldoyle and paid off the very modest balance on Martha's account. She called him 'sir'; he addressed her as Mrs Merry.

5

'Mrs Merry has a way with parsley sauce,' Tommy said.

Despite the lovely day, we sat in the kitchen around the small, deal table covered with an oilcloth acquired by Annie in a McBirney's sale. Martha had waited until we were so seated before she had left for Baldoyle, then Tommy had carved the bacon in thick, fleshy, fat-topped slices. When the front door was tugged to we all sat and looked at one another, trying not to smile, although Annie frowned furiously to warn us not to give offence. The hall door needed two tugs to open, one to close. Half a minute went by.

'Freddy is fed,' Martha said as she reappeared.

'Ah, thank you, Martha,' said my mother.

'Hey-ho to you, Mrs Merry,' Tommy said.

'Thank you, goodbye, sir.'

This time, when she pulled the door behind her, Ultan went into the parlour where I could see him peering out.

'She has cleared harbour,' he said when he came back.

I laughed aloud.

'Your manners, miss!' Annie's eyes were two little points of reprimand.

She could never bring herself to scold Ultan, but saved her ammunition for me. I kept my eyes on my plate as Annie spooned out the butter-glowing cabbage. I often wondered how Ultan and I could be the children of these two people. Ultan, tall and broad, with his lovely clean limbs, his hair like summer hay, and his bright blue eyes stood as a contrast to his father almost too extreme to be explained. Tommy looked so much older than fifty-two years. My mother, too, despite her energy, seemed newly stooped, as if bad news was ever expected. She had become slower in her movements, and her skin lacked the lustre I remembered. Ultan and I, blossoming with the sun, our lives ahead of us like waiting treasure, seemed a different species to Tommy and Annie. It was as if we had discovered the secret to something they had never known.

'A lot of trouble in town,' Annie said, 'or so I hear.'

Tommy shook his head, as if by doing so he could forestall a discussion whose conclusion was laden with uncertainty.

'Being caused mainly by factions of the British Army,' Ultan said, and when Annie looked at him severely, 'Ask anyone. If the country wasn't against them before, it is now.'

'The government is only responding,' she said. 'Responding to the ruffians who are trying to bring this city to its knees.'

'I'm not sure they're all ruffians ...' Tommy began.

'Ruffians,' my mother repeated. 'Mrs Wilder had a gentleman from the Castle to dinner last week who told her it will all be over by Christmas.'

'Mmm,' Ultan said, 'I wonder what he meant by over.'

My mother had a way of establishing her authority in an argument by sighing and closing her eyes.

'The disruptive element will be rounded up and deported to Van Diemen's Land,' she said, 'following which the King will visit Dublin and make a tour of the country. It's what the people want.'

'Tasmania,' Tommy said, 'is what it's called.'

'Does it matter what it's called?' asked my mother sharply.

Lunch proceeded in silence. Although Ultan believed in the cause of Ireland's self-government, and the men who were taking a stand against the British, he would never admit it in front of Annie. In fact, of the four of us, she was the only one fully committed to preserving Ireland's status in the Empire.

Our Sunday ritual had remained unchanged for years. We always used what was called the good cutlery, Sheffield plated knives and forks, a wedding present to my parents from Annie's family. Among my daydreams at such times were: sailing away forever, living in a house of my own, and finding a man I could love for the rest of my life, regardless of his station.

'Are you up or down with Mr Silverstein these days, Papa?' Ultan enquired cheekily.

I could never dare such a question, for it would be seized upon by Annie as another dart to launch at her husband; but from Ultan's mouth the dart, like all his words for her, was honey.

'Your papa brought me home a florin last week, didn't you?' she said warmly. 'He's very clever at cards.'

Tommy shone under her approval. Twice every month he played in a poker school that included Mr Silverstein, someone he had known in the barracks. Most of Tommy's friends were leftovers from his army days, men who in some cases had served, or, like Mr Silverstein, had provided services to the crown forces. In Mr Silverstein's case he still delivered beer to the officers' mess in Marlborough Barracks.

'I may soon need that florin back if Mr Chanticleer lets me down, mum,' Tommy said.

For a moment Annie's eyes became enlarged.

'Hey-ho! Only joking!' he said, and we all laughed to show our support.

'You should be working in the music hall,' Annie said.

6

Mother Mary Superior in Raheny said I was her prize student. She had once taken a secretarial course in London, and as a consequence, as well as history and English, she taught me basic bookkeeping and how to type. I was almost seventeen when I left school, which was considered old – most of my friends, including Agnes Daly, had left a year or two before me in order to find jobs. I didn't want to be a wage slave like Agnes, who worked ten hours a day in the hotel in Fairview. Soon after the end of my final term, Mother Mary Superior invited me back to work in the convent kitchen. I also began to supervise some of younger children in class. I think she saw me as a recruit to their ranks, which was flattering. For some months I continued to study under her guidance, as the prospect of a warm, safe life in a beautiful residence overlooking the sea beckoned. But as I came to know these women as colleagues rather than as lofty disciplinarians, and saw the sacrifices they had had to make for their privilege, I decided to end the arrangement.

Tommy was confident he could find a position for me in Dublin. Even with the grave uncertainty abroad, the club was full of men who were employers, he said. Annie sounded notes of warning. Dublin to my mother was a place that tainted its inhabitants, especially its young. She had grown up with stories of the tenements and brothels, of how young girls were taken advantage of – 'especially the good looking ones' she always said with an implied rebuke – and ended up with half a dozen children in a damp room and a drunkard for a husband. Moreover, she feared that should such a fate befall me in a job where my employer was a member of Tommy's club, that this could put Tommy's job in danger, since, as she reasoned – her fancy knowing no bounds – the gentleman would not like every day to be reminded of my plight whenever he saw my father.

Tommy, ever ready to please my mother and acquiesce to her views, came up with a somewhat different solution. His club uniforms were cut in Clery's, where he had struck up an acquaintance with one of the tailors, a Mr Barry, someone I had met years before when Tommy had brought me in with him for his fittings. During the days of the Rising, Clery's had been ravaged by fire, its windows had melted with the heat, but within a few weeks the store was operating from temporary premises in Lower Abbey Street. At the right moment, Tommy said, he would approach Mr Barry to see if a position could be secured for me in the department store, perhaps in the ladies' section.

'They're building a completely new emporium on the site of the old shop,' Papa said. 'Mr Barry says they will be taking on up to a hundred new staff.'

'It will never be as good as the old Clery's,' Annie said.

7

Regardless of weather, our parents always sat indoors, a habit evolved out of their sense of decorum. If Tommy had come up the back garden after Sunday lunch, lain himself out on a rug and unbuttoned his shirt, as Ultan had now done, Annie would have threatened the asylum. Some Sundays, when the weather was fine, my brother painted out here, simple watercolours of the trees; but today he lay back, one arm behind his head, a cigarette in his mouth, eyes closed as the sun picked out the appealing contours of his chest.

'I've been thinking,' he said.

I sat on the low cane chair used by Tommy when he was weeding his beds. The heat beat down from a spotless sky. Every weekend, from Portmarnock to Howth, people could be seen bathing in the sea.

'About young Saddler,' Ultan said drowsily.

'Oh, yes – and his butterflies.'

'Tommy cries blue murder when the whites eat his cabbages.' Ultan spread his arms wide so that the tips of his fingers arched into the grass. 'He showed me once that when you pinch a caterpillar no blood comes out, just green.'

'Stop!'

He smiled drowsily as bees worked a bed of lavender. He

was a man whose beauty lifted the moment and drove the mood.

'I have a crafty plan,' he said.

'Oh no, what now?'

'For you, Miss Top of Her Class. For Chink Holly's cricket party.'

'I've already told you, Ultan—'

'Agnes Daly *qui tollis pecata mundi,*' he said.

'Who?'

'Agnes Daly, Miss Faultless.'

'What about her?'

'Agnes,' Ultan said, 'would be ideal for Rudy Saddler. Absolutely perfect.'

'What are you talking about?'

'Young Saddler is ambitious, wants to get ahead. He'd jump at the chance to be invited up to Holly's after cricket.'

'Why should that be of interest to me?'

'Would it not be deeply kind of you to introduce Miss Daly to Mr Saddler? Let me finish! How many times do I hear, "Poor Agnes"? Poor Agnes. Poor, poor Agnes. Well, Little Miss Mother Superior, why not give poor Agnes a chance to meet someone who may improve her life?'

'This is nothing to do with Agnes! You know that were she to accept then I would have to too!'

'Never occurred to me.'

'You don't give up easily, do you?'

Ultan propped himself on one elbow and carefully buried his butt. 'I am trying to help you to break out of the strait-jacket we have been reared in, that is all.'

'Mr Saddler has never met Agnes, he may not be taken with her.'

Ultan's eyes sparkled. 'Of course he will! She's a dish, you know – or so I've heard it said.'

I looked at him. 'What do you mean by that?'

'Means she's attractive.'

'Yes, but why did you say you've heard it said? Do you not find her attractive?'

'I've just said so.'

'No, you didn't. You gave me the impression you weren't sure if she was attractive or not.'

'Of course she is,' Ultan said, 'that's what I said. Agnes is a dish.'

'But not to you,' I said, firmly, knowing that I sounded like our mother. 'You don't find her dishy.'

For the merest moment, I saw a pleading in my brother's face, as if I should not have needed to say what I just had, as if I had forced him into a place he did not want to be and made him say too much, but he just smiled and shook his head.

'Agnes is not my cup of tea, Sis, is all I mean, but that doesn't mean she can't be Rudy Saddler's.'

I could hear Annie's raised voice down in the cottage as something Tommy had said earned a rebuke. This little unit had become too small for all of us, I suddenly knew. I wanted to let the sun at my limbs, I wanted to break free.

'What are you suggesting?' I asked, all at once exhausted.

'Get Agnes to go with you to Chink Holly's party,' Ultan said, 'and I'll make sure young Saddler comes along.'

8

I hurried over the railway – the gatekeeper was closing his gates and said, 'Quick as you please, love!' – and down the Burrow Road. Crossing that train line was a ritual for me, a gate into another world. Beyond it, as if protected by the steel railway, people played golf, and swam, and lived within sight of Ireland's Eye without the worries of our agitated country – at least, that was how I imagined it. The scent of woodbine claimed the air as voices from the links floated out in soft snatches.

Ultan had a way of making me promise to do things I did not want to. Although I was sure that Agnes, no more than me, would never dream of going to a party in a house belonging to people like the Hollys, nonetheless the image I could not shift from my mind was of Chink Holly walking backwards from the crease during his cricket match, polishing the ball off the leg of his whites, his eyes locked on mine.

I recognised her parasol: I had given it to her for her birthday and had picked it out in Clery's for its vivid redness. All at once, the Great Northern thundered by, full of noise and fury.

'I don't know how they live here with that noise,' Agnes said.

'I'm sure they don't even hear it.'

'Not to mention the smell of soot,' she said.

The tide was rising but even so, out at sea, the tops of sandbars still prodded up like the humps of whales. A strip of grass ran above the high tide line, and ended some yards from an old stone wall that had partly crumbled. In the distance, looking back towards the golf links, the white hems of bedsheets jigged in a little breeze.

'Oh, ham sandwiches,' Agnes said with a shiver of disapproval when I unpacked my basket. 'I just brought Bovril.'

She valued her figure, which was slim and shapely, and made do on scraps for fear of gaining weight. For as long as we had been friends I had seen my role as her protector. I was never sure why this was so, but it was, and I felt powerless to change it. I spread out a rug. We unbuckled our shoes and peeled off our stockings. Agnes's raven hair was wound up tightly beneath a hat into whose wide rim an elaborate confection of paper flowers had been stitched. Her pale skin did not take the sun well; she kept her face in shadow. It was a shame to hide her eyes – large luminous eyes, green as jade.

'I should wait till after I bathe to eat,' I said. 'But I'm too hungry. If I get a cramp I'll expect you to jump in and save me.'

It was an old joke, for she had never learned to swim despite living as near the sea as I did. Some old wives' tale from her mother's side, about fishermen going straight to the bottom when their boat capsized, a mercy compared to trying to stay afloat.

'There's talk of them bringing back the curfew to ten next winter,' she said and from pages of newsprint unwrapped two china cups. 'If that happens, they say they want me to sleep in the hotel, but I've told them I can't.'

'Ultan hates the curfew, even though he has a pass,' I said.

'I hate this country,' she said.

I wanted everything for Agnes that I wanted for myself. Whatever it took for me to be happy, I would try to find a way for her to share it too.

'The Hollys above in Howth?' she said when I told her about the party. 'You must be joking! The only time anyone from my family was allowed in there was years ago when my father welded their gutters.'

'They're not like that, Ultan says. And he has a friend he wants you to meet. Someone he says you will like.'

'I wouldn't be seen dead in Holly's,' Agnes said, 'even if I was there to meet the Prince of Wales.'

As my image of Chink Holly on the cricket pitch lingered, as I wondered how soft his hair would be to touch, I felt myself rallying to the side of people I had never met or known. 'Why do you say that, Agnes? You don't know them.'

'What's more, there's talk about them in the hotel.'

'The Hollys?'

'Word is he's given money to the illegal government.'

'Who?'

'The father. He's in with the Shinners. From what I hear, if he doesn't watch himself he'll end up blindfolded against a wall in Kilmainham. Too good for him, I'd say.'

'Don't say that,' I said. 'His son is a friend of Ultan's.'

'The last time I saw your brother was on the tram and he didn't even bid me the time of day,' Agnes said. 'If you ask me, he's grown too big for his boots, Lord Ultan.'

'He thinks you are ravishing, Agnes,' I said with all the candour I could muster. 'He said, "Agnes is a dish".'

'Why doesn't he tell me so himself?'

'Maybe he will – at Holly's party.'

'I couldn't care less what he says,' Agnes said, 'I'm not going.'

I took a deep breath. 'Well, I am,' I said, and in one small moment leapt across the great chasm of all the prejudices I had been brought up with. 'I don't see why I shouldn't. The Hollys are no better than us.'

'They're different to us,' Agnes said, 'just you wait and see. It's chalk and cheese, and we're the chalk.'

Agnes's position seemed all at once so self-damaging that I was seized by the need to convert her.

'Times are changing! There's nothing wrong with going to a party in a house owned by people your father, or mine, might work for. The only difference between us is in your mind!'

Agnes sighed. 'You do as you please, Rose, as you always do. I'll stay in the world I've been brought up in, where we all know each other and we're safe.'

Above the nearby tide a man was walking a dog. He glanced up with a cheerful smile and raised his boater.

'Did you see that?' I said when he had gone on. 'He's probably a member of the links here, a man of property and substance. He looked up into the dunes and what did he see? Two pretty ladies with a picnic. Do you think he gives a fig where we come from? For that matter, who is he? A rebel? A spy? A soldier in disguise? Do we care? No one cares any more – that's the point!'

I finished my sandwich and Agnes screwed back the top on to her flask.

'What's his name?' she asked as if nothing was farther from her mind. 'The one Ultan wants me to meet?'

'Saddler,' I said, 'Mr Rudy Saddler.'

'Oh, God!' Agnes said and threw the dregs of her cup into the bushes. 'He sounds awful! Is he a Jew?'

9

A southerly had risen from nowhere and was blowing straight in our faces. Where minutes before the sea to Lambay had lain smooth as glass, now white-topped waves had appeared. We packed our things and started back towards the shelter of the dunes.

'Stop, girl!'

I froze.

'I know you!'

An elderly woman in a black straw hat, and widows' weeds to her ankles, was sheltering within an overgrown escallonia. A cat glared out from the crook of her elbow.

'I know you,' she said again.

'It's Rose, Mrs Wilder,' I said. 'Rose Raven, Annie's daughter.'

She looked at me intently. Her face was pale, thin, and dominated by spectacles.

'Rose Raven!' She lunged towards me. 'How lovely you look! How lovely you are, both of you!'

I had known her since Annie had come to work here, and had sat on her hammock the other side of this wall listening to her berating the sea for stealing her land. Robs me of ten perches every year, had been her lament.

'This is Miss Daly, my friend. This is Mrs Wilder. And that is Poody.'

The old woman dropped the cat and shooed it off, then grasped Agnes's hands in hers. 'Do you know that I was once as beautiful as you?'

'I can easily believe that,' Agnes said.

'Oh, she has your charm as well, Rose! You'll go far, young lady. I keep telling Rose that – don't I?'

'You are my inspiration, Mrs Wilder.'

'Listen to Rose, she is far wiser than her years,' said Mrs Wilder as a strengthening gust bowled us back several paces. 'I am alone now, of course, but I wasn't always.' Her eyes were suddenly tearful. 'Oh, he was a fine, big man, but that was no use to him. Stepped off the train in Howth and was dead before his feet met the platform. Thirty-five years of age. Dear Lord, if only he had made it home and I could have seen him one last time. How can someone live with that thought? But I do, every day, and every day when I weep to see him one more time I pray to God to take me.'

Agnes stood, wide-eyed.

'I try to tell myself it's a blessing he was spared this madness, the ambushes and assassinations. In my day your dinner party would not be deemed a success without the presence of an officer. Look at us now! My husband was so proud of Dublin. It would have broken his heart to see what they've done to it.'

She sighed deeply.

'But look at you two!' she cried, recovering as if in a single bound. 'The world at your feet! And as for you, child—'

Agnes shrank back.

'My goodness, you have the most wonderful eyes I've ever seen.' The gale rocked us backwards again. 'Now off you go, both of you, before we're blown to the Hebrides!'

10

We climbed a sand dune, the wind billowing our skirts, and then skittered down the other side, wicker baskets before us, to the safety of the empty fairway.

'Such a terrifying old witch!' Agnes gasped with laughter. 'Did you see her witch's cat?'

'Poody.'

'"Oh, Lord, my poor husband, if only I could have seen him one last time!"' Agnes rolled her eyes.

'Agnes . . .'

'"Thirty-five years of age . . ."'

'Stop, please! She still misses him.'

'They're all the same out here,' Agnes said.

'What do you mean?'

'In their big houses, with their army officers for dinner. "My husband was so proud of Dublin!"' She laughed without mirth. 'I wonder has she ever scrubbed a bath, or walked with her eyes to the ground for fear she'll miss a farthing.'

Sooner or later, a point was reached when my esteem for Agnes faltered.

'Agnes,' I said calmly, 'that terrifying old witch is not what she seems, believe me.'

'Oh, please, Rose! What do you take me for? Everyone

165

knows what these people are like. "It would break his heart to see what they've done to Dublin." Boo-hoo-hoo!'

I stopped short of the road. 'What if I told she's not from these parts at all? That she's not one of *these people*, as you call them?'

Agnes shrugged. 'Does it matter?'

'It seems to matter to you!' I shouted, despite myself. 'All you can do is disrespect the man she loved because you're caught up in your own stupid little world! What do you know of Mrs Wilder? You know nothing! You mock her because you are so fixed in your own narrow ways! I sometimes find it hard to know how you are my friend.'

She began to gasp, her breaths hard to find. She sat down abruptly on a tuft of pampas grass, hands atremble.

'Very good,' she whispered. 'Where is she from?'

'From Sheriff Street.'

'What?' Agnes shook her head.

'She's a tenement girl.'

'I don't believe you!'

'Mr Wilder was a photographer, one of the first. Spent his days in Dublin, taking snapshots of buildings and people. His photographs are still famous, even now, forty years after his death.'

Agnes was dabbing at her eyes with a white handkerchief.

'One night, after a day in the inner city, he was developing his plates, when the image of a beautiful girl swam up out of the chemical solution. He stared at her. Cast his mind back but, though he tried, he could not remember having seen her! And yet he must have – or his camera must have, for there she was, standing by the railings of a house in Sheriff Street.'

Agnes was looking at me dubiously.

'He went back into town, but he couldn't find her. It drove him to near distraction. He spent days trying to track down the exact spot where his camera must have captured her. After a week, when he was on the point of giving up – of accepting that some miracle had intruded into his lens from heaven – he walked up a lane near Sherriff Street and she walked out of the door of a tenement.'

Agnes fluttered her eyes. 'Is that true?'

'It is gospel,' I said. 'She has told my mother fifty times if she's told her once.'

We resumed our way towards the road.

'I'm sorry if I shouted at you,' I said.

'You always shout at me,' she said.

'Not always. Are we still friends?'

She leaned across and kissed me. 'You know something?'

'Tell me.'

'One day I would love to know how to swim,' Agnes said.

11

I sat on the upper deck, at the seawall side. As Howth shrank away and the chimney of the Clontarf Power Station loomed, I shivered with excitement. A letter from Agnes had arrived that morning saying that, on second thoughts, she would be prepared to be introduced to Mr Rudy Saddler. The tram's warning gong sounded twice, followed by the squeal of its braking notches. Although I had seen Chink Holly only once, I felt I knew him, and this made me giddy, for I had read how love needs only a glimpse to take root, and I had grown up hearing from Tommy how he had instantly fallen in love with Annie, even within the gloom of Nelson's Pillar.

We veered inland. Public lighting had been fixed to many of the tramway poles, but few people walked out after curfew any more for fear of being picked up by the law, or the army. The doors and ground floor windows of some buildings had been fortified by sandbag emplacements; military checkpoints, with soldiers sprawled in the sun, could be seen at many of the intersections. The tram emptied out at the Pillar, and for those first seconds the excitement of the beleaguered city gripped me: jingling tram bells, hawkers bawling, the screech of metal on metal, and the surging energy of hundreds of converging people. The crowds suddenly parted for a foot patrol, helmets strapped, arms to hand, moving through briskly. I boarded the Number 14 and we set out in the direction of O'Connell Street Bridge.

The truth was that, even with Ultan as my chaperone, I would not have had the nerve to go to Chink Holly's party had Agnes not changed her mind. Her attendance somehow legitimised mine, whereas turning up as a girl on her own to a house where I knew no one would have smacked of brazenness. All I had to do now was pray that Agnes would not change her mind again.

Nor could I dare tell my mother of Ultan's plan. Our parents disapproved of social mobility and saw themselves as part of a great, safe tradition in which good servants, as they were, were looked after by those above them in an equilibrium sustained by mutual respect. One kept to one's station and, for as long as anyone could remember, this meant that one's children were expected to do the same.

Half a dozen soldiers lounged on the wooden tram seats behind me, smoking, caps removed, rifles akimbo.

'Good morning, pretty missy!'

I could hear their quiet laughter. Agnes despised army men, especially English soldiers, and said no girl was safe with them when they had drink taken. And yet, over the years the soldiers I'd met with Papa had been cheerful, their banter mostly harmless. We passed derelict and gutted buildings, and, at the bottom of Dame Street, a street stall with plucked chickens hanging by their legs from a rail.

'Care to join us for a cuppa, my beauty?'

They were disembarking on Lord Edward Street, probably to take up duties in Dublin Castle.

'I bet she only drinks Mazawattee, aye?'

'But she's sweet enough without any sugar in it!'

Not all that long ago my father had been a soldier, living side by side with such men. I'll never marry a soldier, I thought as the tram resumed. Unless he's one like Tommy Raven.

12

The city quickly gave way to green countryside. I was on an errand to Dartry for my mother, delivering a basket with two pots of strawberry jam and a tray of scones to her friend, Miss Sinnott, once the governess in Irrawaddy. Miss Sinnott's terraced cottage had its back to a meadow that swept down elegantly to the Dodder River. Inside, her living quarters were cramped and suffocating with low ceilings and a smell of clinging peat smoke. Tommy said that for Yorkshire people a smoky cottage was home from home.

'You lift my heart,' she said. 'Be sure to thank your mum. Her jams are champion.'

Annie and Miss Sinnott had become friends when Annie had worked in Irrawaddy, something my mother said would never have happened had Miss Sinnott been Irish. Only an English governess would have had time for an assistant housekeeper, Annie said, inferring that an Irish governess would have been too intoxicated with her position to recognise her. Out of Miss Sinnott's back window I could see carpets of wildflowers tumbling through grass to the welcoming riverbank.

'Would you not sit out in the lovely afternoon, Miss Sinnott?'

'And get my death? Not likely, duck. How's your dad?' She scrutinised me. 'Will he go home?'

'You mean—'

'When we leave. We are all leaving, you know, it's been decided. Charles has told me. One half of the Castle now run by people you wouldn't want to be introduced to, the other already packed and waiting for a place on the mailboat.'

Miss Sinnott's father, twice a widower, had died in the Battle of Modder River. Charles Sinnott, his only other child – at that time a boy of fourteen – then came to live in Irrawaddy with his half-sister. Charles had remained in Ireland and, through Lord Barnmere's connections, was now employed as a clerk in Dublin Castle.

'My mother says the King will soon come over, and make a tour,' I said. 'To make things better.'

'Ah, Annie was always the chief royalist in Irrawaddy – even more so than Lord Barnmere!' Miss Sinnott chuckled. 'But I'm afraid she's wrong this time. No king will ever come here again. This place is lost to the likes of us. We're only marking time these last few years.'

I had never thought of it in that way.

'This is home for Papa,' I said, 'he will never leave. He loves it here.'

'I hope you're right, child, and maybe if I had met someone it would be different, but Charles and I will have to go. You see, he knows just how dangerous it has become. He receives information in his position.'

Miss Sinnott's brother always wore a bowler to work, and his trousers had a stripe in them. He could have been walking down Pall Mall instead of Dame Street, Tommy said. I had seen him once, on a visit here with Annie:

172

low-sized, in his undershirt, a tanned head, suspicious eyes.

'Charles says the rebels have lists,' Miss Sinnott said.

She did eventually allow me to bring our chairs outside the back door. I took in grateful gulps of sweet air, but Miss Sinnott had me wrap her in a woollen shawl. I made tea and heaped butter and strawberry jam on to the scones.

'Were you ever in love, Miss Sinnott?'

She looked at me sternly and I thought I had overstepped the boundaries of our friendship; but then she sank back in her chair.

'A year after I arrived here as governess, I was already old, you know, thirty-two, but still dainty.'

'I can well imagine.'

'Never beautiful like you, dear Lord, no. But I had good hips, I was educated, Daddy saw to that . . .'

She seemed to fade off into the afternoon.

'Oh, those days!' she cried all of a sudden. 'The parties. We had Earl Spencer out to Irrawaddy every other week. He loved cockles. Nanny Skipton, he used to call me – imagine! I was right chuffed! There was no trouble here at that time, we all had our jobs and knew our place. It was like a dream. I thought it would go on forever.'

She stared past me.

'He was head coachman, his name was George Byrne. He came from the Liberties. You should have seen him in livery! Gorgeous George he was known as in the kitchen. I used to walk with him in the Botanical Gardens, on his days off. It was there one day when . . . I couldn't read the description of a tree, it were too high up. I remember the moment . . . I asked him to read it for me . . .'

Miss Sinnott was crying.

173

'Daddy would never have allowed it, had he been alive ...
He put such store in education, I couldn't ... I couldn't ...'

Her swollen hands clenched.

'Could George not have learned?' I asked gently.

'He laughed when I suggested it. He was too proud, you
see, but so was I. I'm sure he joined the Irish Fusiliers to show
me how good he really was. When he died in Ladysmith they
gave him the Queen's Medal for bravery. I would have loved
to have seen it. They sent it to his parents, I was told. I didn't
deserve him, you see, and I've paid the price ever since.'

A warm wind scooted butterflies up from the Dodder.

'Where will you go when you leave?' I asked.

She turned her face to the sky.

'My mother left me a cottage near Skipton. Been in our
family since we fought Bonaparte. I think of it last thing
every night, and when I wake up I often imagine I am back
there.'

'Is it very different to here? Look around you! This is so
beautiful.'

'White rose, lass, that's the difference. Folk understand
each other, you never have to say something twice. Here, I
never know what's coming next. Charles was walking to the
tram two weeks ago, on his way home, when across the street
from him a young man went up behind a policeman and shot
him in the neck. The bobby was no older than the gunman.
He was an Irishman, on the beat. He bled out on the pavement, Charles said it was a dreadful sight. If they do that to
one other, what will they do to us?'

13

I took out my only good dress, a sleeveless, needle and thread cream affair with a low waist and a hemline to my calf. It had pretty white flowers embroidered through it, and it fell straight and loose from my shoulders. At least Agnes earned a wage, and had been doing so since she left school, and had money squirrelled away to spend on clothes. I had to rely on my mother's generosity.

At half past seven, as I disembarked at Somali Village, the sun had begun to slip over Dublin Bay. When I had told Annie I was going to Howth to meet Agnes it was not untrue, except that Ultan would be with us and we were going to Chink Holly's party. Three Saturday evenings a month Tommy was on duty in the club, and on those evenings Annie went to her quilting bee in Raheny.

Ultan and Agnes were sitting on a low bridge, the smoke from their cigarettes lying on the evening air. Ultan's smart navy blazer, one I had not seen before, sported a triangle of white handkerchief in the breast pocket. Gel glinted from his tight-brushed scalp. I knew at once, from the crooked grin hanging on his face, that he had been drinking.

'The ball cannot begin without the princess,' he drawled and produced a leather encased hip flask. 'One for the road?'

'May as well,' Agnes said and took a swig. 'Goodness! What *is* that, tell me?'

'Gin and lime,' Ultan said, pocketing the flask and tossing his fag butt into the stream. 'Shall we?'

Agnes rose, radiantly. I looked in amazement. Her hip-clinging, grey flapper ended at her knees in probing tongues. Silver beads sparkled from the fabric. A double string of imitation pearls came to below her waist and her white, elbow-length silk gloves showed off her bare arms like alabaster. Atop this ensemble she had put on a simple straw hat, banded with further pearls. Her lovely dark hair had been cut so that it now clung to her beautiful neck like pelt.

'I don't know about this . . .' she said to me.

'Goodness! You look beautiful!' I exclaimed. 'Doesn't she, Ultan?'

'Enchanting,' he said. 'Come on. The rumour is he's made a fruit punch – let's hope there's some left.'

We walked downhill until the bulk of Howth was lost behind us. The houses down here were substantial, with big gardens and cypress trees that looked back over the bay towards Dublin.

'There's good money in hardware,' Ultan said as he stopped, extracted his hip flask once more and this time kept it upturned on his head.

We had reached bright blue entrance gates. Dance music tumbled out to meet us. I had not known what to expect, since I had never been to a do like this before.

'Oh, I really don't know . . .' Agnes said.

I linked her closely. 'Come on,' I said and in we went. 'Hang on tight!'

Bright, dashing motorcars smelling of rich leather, with

running boards like furled wings swooping the length of them were parked on the gravel. A crowd was gathered before an immense, red brick, wisteria-drenched residence. Gramophone music yawed from an upstairs window. No one greeted us, or even looked at us, and for a terrifying moment I wondered if Ultan knew where he was going. A man called out, 'By Jove, you made it!' – but not to us. The intense noise of so many people talking and laughing made me feel dislocated. Out on a wide lawn, flower-decked young women sat or sprawled on cushions, hammocks, and rugs. Some men sported boaters and those who didn't shone of brilliantine. None of them looked as if they had recently been playing cricket. On a higher lawn, I saw teams at croquet. Agnes was staring, her mouth partly open. Just beyond the front door, on a garlanded pedestal, three nymph-like girls wearing only white bedsheets were feeding grapes to a strikingly handsome young man dressed in the tunic of a Spartan warrior.

'Ah-hah!' cried Ultan. 'Tally-ho!'

He pitched full tilt towards a silver tureen that was being attended by a white-gloved waiter. A moment later he was back, three glasses aloft. All at once he seemed to have mutated into a personality far lordlier than even his usual grandiloquence.

'They say he's spiced it with *poitín*!' he whispered gleefully.

I hated the taste of alcohol, but Agnes seemed to have no such issue.

'*Sláinte!*' she said and swallowed a good draught.

'I say—'

Mr Saddler must have seen us arriving, but I had not noticed him until that moment.

'Ultan—'

177

'Rodolfo the butterfly!' Ultan snared a lobster claw from a passing platter. 'What a spread, aye?'

'I decided you weren't coming,' said Mr Saddler and ran a finger across his struggling moustache.

'Better late than never!' Ultan cried. 'I believe you know my little sister? And this is her friend, Miss Daly. Miss Daly may I introduce the amazing, the extraordinary, the one and only Mr Rodolfo Saddler?'

Mr Saddler's young face glowed. 'It's Rudy, just Rudy,' he said, and fumbled off his boater.

'My pleasure, Mr Saddler.' Agnes cocked her head prettily.

'Now, young Saddler, you are quite surrounded by beauties!' Ultan gasped and pretended to be dizzy. 'How on earth can a chap manage?'

He reached over heads for a tall jug going by and refilled Agnes's glass, followed swiftly by his own. 'Mr Saddler has *prospects*!' he said and winked in Agnes's direction. 'Those innocent features are just a ruse. Rudy is a coming man! Can tot a column of figures quicker than I can bowl a leg-break!'

'Oh, come on, take no notice,' Rudy began.

'Are you not having a jar, Saddler?' Ultan demanded.

'Perhaps in a moment.'

I suddenly saw our host. He was to one side of the hall door, flaming head bowed, in deep conversation with a waiter, a tall young man whose deportment was lopsided. The waiter suddenly turned and looked directly at me.

'Miss Raven and I . . .' Rudy Saddler had begun to say.

'I'm sorry,' My breath had vanished. 'I have completely forgotten something.'

I hurried for the gate, my head on fire. I was trembling. The last person I had expected to see was Eddie Kidney. Up

178

to that day – that moment – I might have persuaded myself that everyone was entitled to their opinion, and that the likes of Eddie Kidney deserved a chance; but all I could think of was the last time we had met and the hate that had poured out of him for our family. I didn't dare look back. I turned out the gate and made up towards the high road at a furious lick. The others had not even noticed my retreat. I needed time to think and to be on my own.

'Miss Raven!'

I had never heard his voice before, but I was determined not to be diverted.

'Miss Raven—' He was agitated as he drew level with me. 'Is there something amiss?'

14

The sea flicked in bright pulses through the cypresses. I had followed him back reluctantly, to his blue gates. His expression was almost comically serious and he seemed unable to stand still.

'May I, with your permission, suggest a short cut?'

A stepped path led sharply downwards, so that soon all the music and party noise ceased. He hurried down every two steps, before rebounding, and offering me his arm, which I did not require, and frowning hugely in his attentiveness. I knew I would not be able to adequately explain the reason I had fled and for which I was already beginning to feel remorseful. On a lower terrace, in a kitchen garden, bamboo canes were smothered in runner beans. I was forced to admit that my panic of minutes before had abated and that every time I looked at him my heart warmed.

'I apologise for not being more alert to your arrival,' he was saying. 'I did keep watch earlier on, but then, when you did not appear ...'

'It was my fault, I was late, I kept the others waiting.'

'Nonetheless, it was inexcusable of me. But why did you leave when you had just arrived, if I may be so forward to ask?'

'It was just ... I was suddenly assailed by ... by indigestion.'

'Ah!' His hands shot into the air as if something incredible had been revealed. 'My mother always recommends baking soda! I shall see to it immediately!'

He led on, as if he had no brakes, but was simultaneously aware of this fact, and every so often had to restrain himself. We proceeded by beds with salads and peas, carrots and onions. Every couple of steps he looked back, as if to check I was still following, or perhaps to see if I had succumbed to a fresh bout of indigestion.

'You haven't been here before?'

He must have known the answer to his question.

'My grandfather built this house. He was no gardener, so this was all in rum shape until my father's time. Be careful . . .'

His intensely bright red hair was swept back from his forehead. He was dressed in white linen plus-fours, and mauve stockings that dived into cream and blue shoes. His dark blazer was beautifully cut and the blue spots of his dickybow matched his eyes.

'We are so lucky to be able to eat the year round from this garden,' he said and rushed forward to open a door set into a high wall. He stepped back, quite dramatically, and bowed me through. The surprise was wonderful. A small, tidy lawn, surrounded by hydrangeas, perched above Dublin Bay. A honeysuckle-drenched pergola framed a distant view of Sutton in the dying light.

'Oh, look, I can see our cottage,' I said, and instantly regretted it.

'Yes, I know. In the tumult of my existence since I first set eyes on you . . . please, Miss Raven, I mean every word I say . . . I have often searched for you down there with my telescope.'

'You . . . what?'

'Oh, don't worry!' He began dragging wicker chairs to a table. 'It's an old glass and the most I can see is a very small and fuzzy outline of your house.'

I had to laugh at his brazenness.

'Miss Raven,' he hurried on, 'if it's not too impertinent, may I suggest you sit here whilst I fetch the baking powder?'

'The baking powder?'

'For your indigestion.'

'Oh, yes, of course, that is kind.'

He tore off into the house. His energy had drained my breath. I looked around. Red monarchs were flocking on a glossy Hebe. I thought of our little back yard at home, where all one could see were Tommy's birch trees. I turned to a clatter of cutlery and glass.

'Now, this is how Ma does it . . .'

He set down a silver tray on which he had laid out a tumbler, a jug of water, a small tin of Royal Baking Powder on a saucer, and a teaspoon.

'She advises a level spoon of the powder directly, followed immediately by a glass of water.'

I could think of no way of reversing my position.

'Perhaps a half spoon, to begin with . . .'

'Very well.' He made a spoon of the white powder and tapped it down until it was less than flat. 'Open wide.'

The taste was odious; but he had the water ready. I swallowed it all and he filled the glass again. Now the pain in my chest did not need to be invented.

'Ohh!' he grimaced, crouching to examine me. 'How is that now?'

'Much better.'

'You see? I told you. It never fails. Ma swears by it.'

I fixed my eyes on the view in order to compose myself. He was now sitting, one polished foot resting on the knee of the other leg, tapping his fingers against his heel.

'May I tell you something, Miss Raven?'

'By all means.'

'I said prayers you would come here tonight.'

I turned to him. 'I beg your pardon?'

'To Saint Raphael, the patron saint of happy encounters. A full rosary, kneeling by my bedside. He is smiling on us as we speak.'

'Perhaps you should pray to my brother Ultan. It was he who persuaded me.'

'A fine chap,' he said. 'I like him.'

'He is talented and he works hard.'

'We've known one another since we were children.'

'I know.'

'He tells me that if he had half your brains he would be editor of his paper by now.'

'He loves to paint and write,' I said. 'He is much more artistic than me.'

'But you, Miss Raven, are yourself a work of art, by which I mean, that if any artist was able to capture even a fraction of your loveliness he would have made his name.'

I laughed. 'Mr Holly—'

'Chink.'

'Mr Holly, we have just met,' I said.

'But we also met at that cricket match in the Demesne,' he said and leapt to his feet.

'I'm not sure I remember an introduction . . .'

'There was not one, I accept, and of course there should

have been, and again if I am too forward . . .' He looked like someone about to perform a dance routine. 'I of course apologise.'

'Mr Holly—'

'Chink, please, I beg you. I am not yet twenty-one years old. And again, I am sorry if—'

I took a breath. 'Please don't keep apologising.'

'But you do remember – the cricket match?' he said. 'I know you do.'

'How can you possibly claim to know what I remember?'

'It's a feeling I had when we first saw each other! A connection. This moment is ours, I thought!'

'You presume a lot.'

'And ever since that shared moment I have imagined meeting you,' he said and sat down again. 'Every day, every evening. You have consumed my imagination.'

'You are going very fast,' I said, 'Chink.'

'I cannot stop myself! You are so beautiful—'

'You need to slow down.'

'That every time I think of you my knees become helpless. It's true!'

I tried to be stern. 'Please.'

'And can you imagine the dickens of a job it will be to wash grass stains from the knees of these breeches?'

I returned to the view.

'You must feel very privileged,' I said, 'to live here.'

'Privilege?' He shook his head. 'I don't believe in it.'

I laughed. 'Easy to say when you have it in abundance.'

He leaned forward until I thought he would fall. 'I've never been more serious. It's not important where you live, or where I live. Only we as human beings are important.'

'Do you always go on like this?"

'It's what I believe in.'

'We may all be equally important, but we are not born equal,' I said. 'Far from it. Yet we have to get on with our lives.'

'Exactly! But that does not mean that the benefits enjoyed by the few should not be enjoyed by the many.'

'Such as?'

'Human dignity, the right to decide one's own destiny, the ability of self-determination for a sovereign people.'

'You sound like a politician.'

'What I've just described is what this war is all about,' he said.

I sat back. 'What war?'

'The war. The war here that is currently being fought against the British. Our war.'

I looked at him closely to see if he was joking. 'You mean the outrages?'

'No, I mean, the war.'

I knew that I had blenched. 'It's not a war! People breaking the law is not a war!'

For a moment he looked distraught; but all at once he sprang to his feet and began to pace up and down. 'How else but war to describe a situation in which tens of thousands of British troops are dug in across the land? In which Irishmen are tried without representation by the military courts of an occupying army and shot by firing squad the next dawn? What is that if not a war?'

As I tried to establish if I was hearing him correctly, the image of Eddie Kidney kept coming back.

'This occupying army, as you call it,' I said carefully, 'is our army. Irishmen serve too, you know.'

'It is the British Army, Miss Raven.' He had vaulted on to a low wall and for a dreadful moment I though he was going to fall backwards. 'The King's army! Not ours!'

'I'm sorry,' I said, 'but are our courthouses not being burned by criminals? Has the government not had to introduce a curfew in order to stop these gangsters in their tracks? Have not three bishops spoken out against the outrages? Is it not preached from our pulpits that these men are going against the law of God?'

He was looking down closely at me. Suddenly he jumped from his perch and went on his knees before me. 'Change should not be feared, Miss Raven, but change is happening as we speak. The old order is being overturned. We have our own courts and government, albeit underground. We will soon be completely in charge of our own destiny and when that happens we will be free!'

I'm not going to parrot my parents, I thought. I'm not going to be Annie or Mrs Wilder.

'Is that what you and Eddie Kidney were talking about earlier?'

He frowned. 'Eddie? You know him?'

'He lives not far from us in Sutton.'

'Ah, Eddie is a good lad, deep down,' he said. 'Not blessed with many brains, granted, but he does his best.'

I had begun by being amused by what I had heard, but now I was muddled and not a little concerned.

'What will be the cost of this new beginning you speak of?' I asked. 'How many will have to die before we are free?'

He had stopped fidgeting. 'Every other means have been tried, but the Brits seem to understand force alone. We have to fight, that is the shame of it. We have to fight.'

All at once I remembered with a shock what Agnes had said about his father.

'My God,' I said, 'you can be shot for saying these things, you know.'

'Will you turn me in?'

'Should I? Are you in the IRA? Do you break the law?'

He smiled. 'I never try to impose my views. Please forgive me.'

'There is nothing to forgive. Please get up. I happen to believe in free speech.'

His eyes widened, and then he performed a backwards somersault and returned to his feet. 'For which, as you have observed, good men are sent to prison,' he said. 'And good women too.'

'But I'm afraid I shall not be joining them, Mr Holly,' I said, still blinking at his antics. 'You should be careful. These are dangerous times.'

'And will remain so,' he said, 'until the country is relieved of its discontentment.'

The sun was sinking like a prize apricot behind Dublin. 'I had better find my friend, Miss Daly. She may be looking for me.'

'Of course! This is meant to be a party!'

He jumped over to the door of the kitchen garden. 'After you, Miss Raven.'

'Thank you, Mr Holly.'

We climbed the steps, back up into the chatter and the music. I could smell a complex mixture of honeysuckle, cut grass and his pomade. It seemed we had arrived very quickly at a point to separate us.

'You see, I have been brought up to stay clear of politics,'

I said. 'Politics means trouble in Ireland, my mother always says.'

'And I'm sure she's right,' he said amiably, 'mothers usually are – as we have seen this evening.'

15

Insect hatches stiffened the warm night as bats began to dart between the trees. I made my way up the dusky garden, in search of Agnes, stepping over figures entwined on rugs, avoiding abandoned jugs and glasses. Two of the Greek maidens from the earlier tableau lay beneath a tree, asleep in each other's arms.

I prided myself on my ordered mind and my facility to relegate matters into their separate compartments. In that way, I was able to distinguish between Chink Holly's dangerous political views and the fact that I found myself drawn to him. Except obliquely, or from the mouths of the likes of Eddie Kidney, I had never before heard the case for the rebels stated as if the outcome were a foregone conclusion. And yet, as I stepped over abandoned croquet mallets, and plates, and rugs, it was Chink's passion for what he had said that I most remembered.

Agnes and Rudy Saddler stood as one, near shrubs at the far side of the high lawn, lost in contemplation by a Hebe.

'Sssh!' Agnes put her fingers to her lips. 'Don't alarm them.'

A quivering colony of sooty moths appeared to be imbedded in the bush.

'*Biston betularia*,' Rudy whispered. 'Observe the exquisite markings on the underside of the wings.'

As I watched, one tiny creature flipped over and changed colour, from riveting brown-black to sober grey.

'I don't think they are bothered by us,' Rudy said. 'They are for all intents and purposes intoxicated.'

Agnes giggled. 'Mr Saddler has been introducing me to his friends.'

An empty beaker and glasses lay beside the fragrant bush.

'Miss Daly has a natural affinity with lepidoptera,' Rudy said.

'Whatever that means,' Agnes hiccupped.

'I am thinking of going home,' I said.

'Shall I escort you to the tram, Miss Raven?' Rudy asked.

'Not at all, I'll find Ultan.' I looked at Agnes. Her straw hat was askew, but her face shone radiantly. 'You must stay and enjoy the evening.'

Rudy said, 'In that case I shall take the tram later with Miss Daly.'

'Don't forget there is a curfew,' I said.

'But not till midnight!' Agnes cried.

I picked my way back across the ever-darkening garden. Would there ever be a night without a curfew or a day when armed patrols were not a feature of our streets? Perhaps, but not when we were at war. There! I had used the word.

The hall door lay open. All at once I heard Chink Holly's voice from the garden; I went in. I didn't want to engage with him again, not until I had had time to consider what he had said. A staircase soared from a beautifully panelled hall to a gallery. I could hear the business of the kitchen underway as I tried to work out where Ultan might have got to. Part of him, the lordly part on view earlier, would imagine that a house like this was his natural lair.

The hall curved away, its rich panelling enlivened with photographs of family groups, many of them taken outside this house. Through a door to my left, an imposing room was presented, with a central, gleaming dining table, and a sideboard, almost as long as the table, set out with tiers of silver. At the far end of this room, glass doors reflected my own approaching image. What drew me in, I just then could not say. I caught a scent, sweet, like holy incense.

'Ultan?'

The glass doors led to a vaulted greenhouse whose silky dark fronds reached for the night. By way of tomatoes strung to the roof, and ferns, and smooth lilies that seemed to glare, I made my way in. I stepped around a stout watering can. Five paces away was a further door, beyond a curtain of verdure. I crept closer and heard a voice coming from what appeared to be a potting shed. This inner door had not been fully closed. My eyes swam into the tiny space. Lying on old cushions, his skin luminous in sudden moonlight, was my brother, his eyes closed, a smoke-weeping hookah at his lips. Alongside Ultan, also in his flesh, lay the Spartan warrior.

16

That summer rolled out in a succession of glorious, never-ending days. Even the sea grew warm enough for Tommy to remove his shoes and stockings and wade out in search of mussels while Freddy stayed up on dry land and howled.

A letter came from Chink Holly, signed 'Your admiring and obedient servant', with an invitation to walk on the pier in Howth; I declined. Each time I thought of him, and of his house, the image of my naked brother terrorised my mind. Chink's outspoken political views, shocking though they were, faded when put beside the dangers associated with Ultan's behaviour. I was seized with dismay, for I suspected that others, including Chink, were bound to know. Nor did I grasp exactly what it was I had seen, even though in truth it came as no surprise. On the other hand, I had heard what opium did to those who fell under its spell, and indeed I prayed against the odds that what I had seen was no more than such sorcery at work. The thought of our parents finding out convulsed me, for while I would always love Ultan dearly, and be ever happy for him, and not embarrassed, no matter how aberrant his choices, I knew that Tommy and Annie would die of shame.

I could not bring myself to confront him. Ultan was not

an easy man to engage. He often flirted with the curfew and was gone next morning before my parents appeared, but even when I had him to myself he had a way of deflecting questions to his benefit. For all these reasons, I also decided to avoid Chink Holly, for I was convinced that each time he saw me he would be reminded of my brother.

Meanwhile, Agnes, the reluctant party guest, about whose happiness I had so fretted, was spending all her free time with Rudy Saddler.

'He calls me his darling little bunting!' she whispered.

When I suggested we go to Dublin on her day off, and sit in Fullers, as we sometimes did, she did not quite laugh outright at my idea, but brushed it aside, as if I should have known that her precious free days were now reserved for Rudy Saddler.

I kept longing for another letter from Chink, even as I dreaded its arrival; yet, the days went by without one. It's probably for the best we don't meet again, I told myself. Annie and I bottled gooseberries. Behind us, in Irrawaddy, they were making hay. And then, one Monday evening, when swallows sailed high in the heavens, Tommy came home from work, looked at us as if he had just seen a ghost, sat down heavily in the kitchen and dropped his face into his hands.

'Papa?'

'Oh, girls,' he whispered, 'something dreadful has happened.'

17

Beneath an otherwise blameless sky, Annie and I hastened out to Dartry, where Miss Sinnott sat stunned and unable to speak. Her neighbours too were badly shaken. Charles Sinnott had been a thorough gentleman, they said, who had never once refused them help, no matter how poor the weather or difficult the task. Charles had been a thoroughly selfless soul who kept himself to himself, attended his local church and worked each Christmas Day in a soup kitchen in the inner city. Whoever has done this should swing, everyone said.

Charles had alighted from the number 29 tram in Dollymount at seven the evening before. As the tram pulled away, two men walked forward, both wearing masks, caps tugged low. At five paces, a single shot was fired. As Charles fell, both men aimed their pistols and shot repeatedly into his prone body. The attackers then turned and strolled away, leaving Charles Sinnott dead across the tram tracks. Over ten eye-witnesses had come forward to report the outrage.

At home, my parents sat in the kitchen, dumbfounded. They remembered Charles from his days in Irrawaddy, a kind, if solitary boy. His work as a clerk in Dublin Castle had been exemplary, by all accounts; but when Ultan came back from work he had a somewhat different story. It seemed Charles had worked in the G Division of the Dublin Metropolitan Police, a branch of the law so feared that even I had heard of it.

'I don't believe it,' Annie said. 'Not Charles.'

'They're saying he was a spymaster,' Ultan said, 'that he had a network of snitches all over Dublin.'

'May God forgive you,' Annie said and covered her face with her apron.

In the days that followed, the scene of the assassination was much discussed. Why, when he lived in Dartry, had Charles Sinnott been in Dollymount at five on the evening in question? Ultan was again full of the latest. Charles had been on his way to see a key informer, it was being said, although, as Ultan pointed out, the fact that less than two shillings had been found on his person put this theory into doubt.

'Two bob would hardly pay a squealer,' Ultan said.

'Ultan!' Annie shrieked.

Tommy had a different story. Apparently, Charles had been making regular visits to a house in Dollymount, the home of a lady who lived alone, whose husband, an army officer, had for many years elected for overseas postings. Charles's well-beaten track to this lady's door would have been well noted by those with an interest in Castle employees, Tommy said.

Annie was furious with Tommy, for she feared that Miss Sinnott, who believed her brother had come to Dollymount for a drink with old friends, would herself die if such ill-founded filth, as Annie described it, were heaped atop her grief.

Charles Sinnott's funeral was conducted by Mr Gilmore, in the Presbyterian church in Howth. Except for Tommy, we waited outside. At Mass in Sutton the previous Sunday, Father Shipsey had made it clear: if a Catholic, however well-intentioned, stepped inside the door of a Protestant church they faced excommunication.

18

And yet, those days were sweet as honeycombs. The skies were radiant from dawn and the sea breeze came to us laden with goodness. We climbed the stile into the adjoining meadow, Annie and I, then, arm in arm, made our way towards Irrawaddy's rippling trees. My mother looked pinched and grey of late, despite the sun, and could not take more than a dozen steps before stopping to recoup her breath.

'You should see a doctor,' I said.

'Half of Sutton has this chest.' She wheezed and tried to fill her lungs. She wore a hat and a lace shawl whenever she went out. 'It will pass.'

Bees thrummed and swallows swooped for the high midges. I was glad to be out with Annie on her own. Two letters, written on soft yellow vellum and in matching envelopes, had already come from Chink that week. He had asked permission to come to Sutton and present his compliments. It was unthinkable that I could allow such an appearance without Annie being forewarned.

'I met a friend of Ultan's recently,' I began, 'a gentleman.'

'Ah, the one who's been writing to you.' Annie paused again as we entered the wood. I was not aware she had seen the letters coming in.

'Yes, his name is ...'

'I know who he is, Ultan told me.'

'I see,' I said. 'I would have preferred you to have learnt his name from me rather than from Sir Ultan.'

'Ultan is very caring of you,' Annie said sternly, 'you're much too hard on him.'

I felt angry that Ultan could not contain my modest secret whilst I was left paralysed by fear that his would become known.

'David Holly,' Annie said.

'Yes, his name is David, although because of his hair he is known to everyone as Chink.'

'I think I have seen him,' said my mother, unexpectedly, 'on the strand in Sutton. Swimming. Groups of them come down from Howth.'

'How did you know?'

'His hair, you couldn't miss him,' Annie said and actually smiled.

She would have looked down on Sutton strand only on those occasions when she was hanging out Mrs Wilder's washing. What would Chink have seen, had he glanced up? A prematurely old woman in a maid's uniform, pegging out linen against the sea breeze?

The ferns in the cool wood had leapt mysteriously since our last walk in here.

'Just be careful,' my mother said and raised her hand to block off my reply. 'With times as dangerous as these, you must pick your friends with care ...'

'By which you mean ...'

She sighed. 'There is talk in Howth about those people.'

'The Hollys. Why don't you say their name?'

'I will say what I choose.'

'But . . .'

'I have heard it said that Mr Holly is not a gentleman.'

I wanted to shriek. 'What does that mean, Mother? And who said that anyway?'

Annie hated being challenged. 'I put great store in what Mrs Wilder says,' she said defiantly. 'She is in touch with the people who matter.'

I wanted to denounce everything that Mrs Wilder represented, but I forced myself to be calm.

'Mrs Wilder is an old lady stuck in the past, Mother. She still lives in the day her husband died, back in the last century. These people you refer to tell her only what she wants to hear.'

'Dublin is a tinder box and sparks from it are starting to fly,' Annie said trenchantly. 'Don't blame me for being concerned for your behaviour.'

It was true that in the weeks since Charles Sinnott's murder a new phase had begun in the escalating conflict. Public gatherings had been proscribed, barricades manned by sentries were now common and civilians were being halted and required to show their curfew permits. Armoured cars had even started appearing in Sutton and Howth. We reached a wall on the other side of the wood and Annie rested again, this time on the large step stone that had been set into the masonry.

'There are rumours, Rose, is all I'm saying, and I blank my ears to most of them, but I have heard that Mr Holly has given money to the IRA.'

I felt fear and excitement, side by side.

'Oh, Mother! They're decent people. Chink has a business

to walk into. They're not going to risk everything they've achieved by breaking the law! I know I haven't met his father, but Chink is most assuredly a gentleman!'

In that instant, as I defended him aloud to Annie, all my caution about Chink Holly evaporated. But Annie was unmoved.

'You never can tell,' she said. 'You should ask your father about Mr Silverstein.'

I laughed. 'Mother?'

'Listen, child! They burned his motor lorry and the poor man can no longer earn a livelihood! They wrote "Get Out" with tar on the walls of his home even though his family have lived here for centuries and his grandfather began delivering ale to the army in 1870. He's now destitute!'

'I ... I am sorry for Mr Silverstein,' I said, 'but what has this got to do with Chink Holly?'

'You are the daughter of a British soldier,' Annie said. 'For some people that is a sin for which you can never be forgiven.'

19

I wanted to go back to the cottage after that, and be on my own; I wanted to clear my head, but Annie insisted we keep going up to Irrawaddy and find someone in the kitchen to give us a cup of tea.

'It will cheer us up,' she said.

The north lawn of Irrawaddy was more than an acre of mowed and manicured turf, criss-crossed by beds of blazing roses, all of which required the full-time attention of four gardeners. I had come up here as a child for Lucy Barnmere's birthday parties and been amazed by the many books in Lucy's nursery, even though she could not yet read. Since I could read, even though I was younger by a year, Lady Barnmere seized on my ability in order to motivate her daughter. I became Lucy's little friend. Then, as the years passed, Lucy went away to school in England and the invitations to her birthday parties dried up. Once, at Easter a few years before, as I had walked up here, alone, Lucy suddenly appeared out on the lawn near the rose beds, chatting with people of our age. She had become elegant and beautiful. When she saw me she wobbled her fingers in a half-hearted greeting, then turned and said something to her companions which made them laugh, after which we never met again.

*

Since it was frowned upon for employees to walk directly across the lawn where they might be visible from the reception rooms, we followed, as we had always done, the path along the lawn's north edge that led to the kitchens. Normally, noise and chatter would push out to greet us, but that day we could hear nothing.

'I wonder where everyone is,' Annie said as we looked around the long, empty kitchen with its enormous coal range and hanging rows of copperware.

My mother had worked here since she was fourteen and was familiar with every inch of the huge house. Beckoning me to follow, she bustled down the long service corridor that linked the kitchen with the dining room. The smell of polish was what I best remembered in the dining room, rising from the gleaming floorboards, tables, sideboards and cabinets. Generations of Barnmeres, side by side with turbaned and bejewelled Burmese princes, watched from their portraits. The double doors that led to the drawing room were open and we could suddenly see the backs of uniformed staff. As we tiptoed in, the cook – a low-sized rotund woman – turned to us, a finger to her lips.

'It goes without saying how put out we are that this criminality has reached out here and taken someone so close to us.' Lord Barnmere was speaking from the front of the room, beside the piano, hands behind his back. He was dressed in a black frock coat and striped trousers. Lady Barnmere sat to one side, listening attentively. It was several years since I had seen either of them and I was shocked by how frail and old they had become. Lord Barnmere, once a vigorous man with a beard of ink, was now stooped, his beard snowy, his features haggard. Lady Barnmere looked ill.

'Josephine Sinnott was like a sister to you all. Soon after she arrived here as governess, her father died with great valour in the Boer War, which was how Sinnott, her half-brother, a boy at the time, came to live here, in the yard.'

The staff retinue had assembled, including grooms, gardeners and drivers, as well as the household. One of the maids was crying openly.

'When Sinnott left school and expressed a wish to work in government it was rather a pleasure for me to do whatever I could to help his career.'

It was then I saw the man, standing to one side, near the high windows. Very tall, his face ended in a spade-shaped, black beard. Nor had he missed us coming in. As I watched, he stroked his beard as if our arrival had given him cause for reflexion.

'Miss Sinnott will be buoyed up to know that we all share the great blow she has been dealt,' said Lord Barnmere. 'It is a very bad day when a decent chap cannot do his job and walk the streets of Dublin without being murdered by ruffians.'

The sobbing maid was being comforted by the woman who now presided over the linen cupboard.

'I would like to introduce Detective Sergeant Melody of the Dublin Metropolitan Police. Mr Melody is in charge of apprehending Sinnott's assassins and bringing them to the justice that awaits them. I'm sure I speak for us all when I say that such a reckoning cannot come soon enough.'

The peeler walked unhurriedly from the windows to the piano. His heavy-lidded eyes gave the impression that he knew more than we did.

Annie nudged me. 'A Castle man', she whispered, and the cook turned around again, wide-eyed. I wondered if the policeman had also heard her, for he now seemed to be looking directly at us.

'Charlie Sinnott was a dedicated employee of the government of this country.'

The accent was flat, nasal, Dublin.

'As his lordship has just said, Charlie was murdered in cold blood and in full view of the public for no other reason than he was a Castle man. Now I too am a Castle man, and I assure yous – every man and woman here – that Charlie's death will not go unanswered.'

He began to pace the top of the room, his narrow gaze unrelenting, the danger in him manifest.

'Don't be fooled by what you hear. Don't be taken in by the IRA's cowardly courts, their underground government, or their make-believe President of Ireland. There is no President of Ireland, the country is governed from Dublin Castle, and the only legitimate courts of law are those which hand down the justice of His Majesty the King. Would you put a criminal on a pedestal – a man who has spent years in prison – and make him a president? Would you put thugs who murder, steal and burn on the benches of our courts? Are seditionists fit to be our MPs?'

He stared around the room.

'Only a country that had taken leave of its senses would do such things – and I don't think that any of us here are ready for Grangegorman just yet.'

He chuckled at his joke, but his audience was gripped by silence.

'Rest assured, the Union flag will always fly over Bermingham Tower. Even as we speak, troops are landing in Kingstown, Cork and Bantry. An extra twenty thousand men from His Majesty's forces will have landed in the south by next week. Men battle-hardened from Flanders and France. Not to mention the very able police cadets who are now assembling and will soon be sent over to assist in keeping law and order, in keeping decent men and women safe from the criminals who now threaten our way of life. Do you believe a few hooligans with pistols and grenades will defeat such a force? Order will be quickly restored and criminality punished. Let no one tell you otherwise.'

Melody's leather shoes rapped out on the parquet flooring. He walked directly down, into our group, which melted into two. Fear crawled the room. No one could look at him now, nor did Annie and I dare even to look at one another.

'I want you to help me snare those responsible for the murder of your friend, Charlie Sinnott. Who planned this outrage – eh? Who are the two men behind this crime?'

Melody had paused beside us, so close I could hear the ticking of his pocket watch.

'I know that many of you knew Charlie, and that he kept in touch with yous. He liked a tincture out here, now and then, Charlie, am I right? With his old chums? Oh yes, I know where he drank. And who he drank with. I know where he went, where he stopped. So do you. I know his ... arrangements in Dollymount, and so do many of you. But who else knew these facts – eh? Who told these criminals where Charlie would be on the evening he was taken down – eh? Who betrayed this honourable man to his enemies?'

I had never felt fear as I did then.

'I'm not expecting yous to come forward this evening, but come forward you will, because I know that someone in this room has knowledge of these brigands. Knows who they are, where they live. They may be people well liked in this community. Above suspicion. Respectable Mass-goers. But in their hearts a dark stain is spreading and sooner or later it will be seen.'

The policeman walked slowly back to where the Barnmeres were seated, their expressions gripped by anxiety.

'In conclusion, you will be interested to hear that His Excellency the Viceroy has authorised a reward of one hundred guineas to be paid in exchange for information leading to arrests. One. Hundred. Guineas. Think of what you could do with money like that. It would solve many of your problems, I daresay. I look forward to hearing from yous.'

No one of us could move. Lord Barnmere rose to his feet.

'God save His Majesty, the King,' he said.

20

Ultan came home late from work to report that the west of the country had been cut off. No trains were running past Athenry, and the Ballaghadereen Races had been cancelled. Shotguns stolen from farms were being used to assassinate policemen. Three Sinn Féin members had that week been executed – dragged from their homes, driven in lorries to Richmond Barracks and shot the next morning after a sham trial. Their families had the hearses booked from the night before, Ultan reported. The army was now officially on a war footing, and internment of those opposed to British rule was imminent, Ultan said and hiccupped.

'Just one or two after work,' he said when I looked at him. 'Everyone does it.'

I feared for him out after the curfew, even though he had a pass. Everyone was talking about the new militias coming in from England, reinforcements for the police, it was said; but these were no policemen. Nicknamed the Black and Tans because of their mismatched uniforms, they defied their officers and drank on duty. Wagons full of them had been seen going up and down the Hill of Howth.

I took a deep breath. 'Ultan – is Chink Holly in the IRA?'

Ultan's eyes grew round before he laughed noisily.

'Chink Holly? Oh, God, I'm sorry, but that's so funny!'

'Ssssh! You'll wake the parents!'

'I just can't imagine him in a ditch with a rifle, that's all,' Ultan said and wiped his eyes.

'But he could be a sympathiser. I've heard it said that his father gives them money. He doesn't have to be in a ditch with a rifle!'

'You are a tonic!'

'I'm serious, Ultan! Come on!'

He squinted to try and focus the better. 'Look – even if he was, he'd never admit it.'

'At the party . . . I got the impression that he was very much enchanted with the idea of armed rebellion.'

'I'm sure he was just trying to impress you,' Ultan said. 'And who can blame him?'

'He wants to see me again, but I'm afraid of what I might be getting into. He has written to me, but I have yet to reply.'

What I really wanted to tell Ultan, but lacked the courage to do so, was that I had become half mad with want. That my rational side, so commended by the nuns, so admired by my class and valued by my family, had disappeared, as if the sun had turned it to ashes, and I was left with nothing but a deep, agonising need to be with Chink, at whatever cost.

'Say if he is in the IRA,' said Ultan, 'how bad would that be?'

'What do you mean?'

'Someone has to take a stand. This can't go on, we can't continue to be treated like slaves, as if the Brits own us. Even the motormen on the trams are now refusing to go any further when troops come on board. It will get worse.' His expression was almost envious. 'Do you want to see him, Sis?'

'Yes, I think I do.'

'So it boils down to whether you are prepared to take the risk. Things could go very wrong here in the months ahead.'

'You would do it, wouldn't you?' I asked. 'I mean, you don't mind taking risks.'

He looked at me as if I had just appeared.

'Ah,' he said, 'I see.'

I was so relieved that I had at last found the nerve to say it.

'Good night, Sis,' Ultan murmured, on the brink of sleep.

21

On those summer days, when heat rose in clouds from the sandbars and the heat from the Great Northern could be felt as it thundered by the Burrow Road, I knew I was in love. I had written to Chink, saying I would meet him, and asking him to suggest a venue. In the meantime, as I awaited his reply, I tried to behave normally, which meant proceeding with my life along the lines approved by my parents: shelling peas for our supper and taking Freddy for walks on Sutton strand. One morning, Tommy and I went into town and met Mr Barry, Clery's tailor, in his fitting room in the shop's temporary premises, the Metropolitan Hall on Lower Abbey Street. Mr Barry was a talkative little man, with neat hands and darting eyes. Every other word out of him was politics, but in between such remarks, and relaying information about racehorses, he assured Papa that there would soon be a job for me in Clery's.

'I think my reference will count more than a trifle,' he said. 'Rest assured.'

'Hey-ho!' Tommy chuckled as we left the shop and walked back down Lower Abbey Street. 'It's not what you know, it's who you know.'

When Agnes joined me in Clontarf on the garden deck of the Dublin-bound tram she was alight.

'You will never in all your days imagine what he has promised!' she bubbled.

'Tell me.'

'Guess – go on!'

Her aquamarine eyes had never shone more beautifully. A tram passed us going in the opposite direction, its upper deck thronged with families heading for the seaside.

'He says he is going to bring us into the Phoenix Park – in a motorcar!'

'Rudy? Rudy Saddler?'

'That's what I thought! But that's what he said!'

'Where is he going to get a motorcar?'

'He says all will be revealed,' Agnes said. 'There is so much more to my Mr Rudy Saddler than meets the eye!'

Agnes had insisted I come along on this excursion, saying it was only fair since I had introduced her to Rudy Saddler in the first place. As we had sat outside the back door of Nan's Cottage the day before, drinking tea in the sunshine, I had finally told her of my feelings for Chink Holly.

'You mustn't tell anyone,' I said.

'I won't! I promise!'

'I'm serious, Agnes.'

'You have my word, my lips are sealed.'

'It may come to nothing . . .'

'Oh, I can just see you now in that beautiful house!' Agnes had cried. 'Lady Rose, mistress of Howth!'

The tram snaked in from the bay as seagulls kept apace, their wings flexing on the wind. A platoon of shabbily dressed military, some with their caps off, lounged by a derelict house; they spotted us on the top deck and cheered. Agnes had removed her beribboned bonnet and now fluffed out her hair to the breeze. In order to be free on weekends to meet Rudy Saddler, she had left her job in the hotel and was working five days a week in a laundry in Drumcondra.

'He is so talented. He has a lovely tenor voice, you know.'

'Has he sung for you?'

'Indeed, and beautifully. His mother pays for his lessons. She is Italian. There is a strong musical tradition in the family.'

The tip of Nelson's tricorn came into view. My last week had been spent waiting for another letter from Chink, but nothing had arrived. Now Agnes, once the object of my pity, seemed to have everything I desired.

In Sackville Street we changed on to the Inchicore-bound tram. A line of open transporters – maybe ten – crammed with men in khaki, passed us as we crossed the Liffey. Just in off a ship and heading for barracks, I could tell by their kit-bags. Tommy had come home the night before and said that billets in Dublin were running scarce under the weight of reinforcements.

'Where are we going?'

'He's meeting us by the Camac River,' Agnes said happily. 'I've been down there with him. It's where his motor is kept.'

A disturbance had taken place on College Green: troops with rifles held back a group of men by the Bank of Ireland railings while across the road a small number of women remonstrated with the soldiers.

'Look at them and their guns,' Agnes said disdainfully. 'They should be ashamed of themselves.'

I could not tell if war was one big affair or an incremental list of small events. We had always thought of war as pitched battles in faraway lands, and when he had said we were at war here in Ireland I had scorned him. I wanted to tell Agnes of my dilemma, for I had no other woman to talk to, but Agnes

211

seemed to be beyond discussion of anything but herself and Rudy Saddler.

At the junction to Inchicore, as we made to alight, the conductor jumped off first and offered us his arm as we stepped down from the platform.

'*He* was quite a dish,' Agnes said as we walked back uphill, 'couldn't keep his eyes off you!'

'You have men on the brain, Miss Daly,' I said.

'And not just on the brain,' Agnes said slyly and we both shrieked.

A lane veered sharply off the metal road, down by a row of cottages. Dark water sat on one side of a narrow bridge. I could see the looming ramparts of Kilmainham Gaol.

'He's been coming down here with his father since he could walk,' Agnes said, as if long acquainted with the facts. 'He says Mr Potterton is quite taken with me.'

'Mr Potterton?'

'He's the garage owner, an Englishman,' Agnes said. 'Got a roving eye, if you ask me.'

The bridge carried over a weir: water on the city side lay black and still; but on the other plunged white and noisily. Little birds perched on rocks and every so often darted into the waterfall for their needs.

'Hurray!'

Across the river and uphill of it, a stone-built shed with open doors dominated the skyline. Rudy Saddler's gloved hands were at his hips. A white scarf flew from his neck and he wore a helmet and goggles.

'Ladies!' he cried. 'Welcome to paradise!'

22

The black body of the car shone and its wooden-spoked wheels glowed a foxy amber. The roof was folded down leaving two steel-framed and hinged rectangles of glass mounted in front of the foremost leather bench-seat. To the rear, a wicker hamper had been strapped above the spare wheel. I was obliged to sit sideways behind the driver, knees level with my chin. Rudy Saddler's father, who limped, inserted the starting handle below the large, bread-loaf-shaped radiator grille, and cranked it once. The engine came to life with a high-pitched, tinny sound. As we moved out, the garage proprietor, Mr Potterton, removed his fedora for Agnes and swept the ground with its rim.

We climbed the steep hill past Kilmainham Gaol, rattled down on cobblestones into the valley and crossed the Liffey at Islandbridge.

'Isn't she a daisy?' Rudy Saddler shouted.

A flock of ewes with their lambs scattered as we burst into the Phoenix Park. The vastness of it thrilled me as we sped up the die-straight road – the only such vehicle to be seen. I had been here before – with my parents and Ultan – at the Zoological Gardens, but never out in the prairie, as it were, flying effortlessly, the wind tugging at the ribbons of my hat.

In the middle distance horsemen cantered across the wide acres, sunlight glinting from their livery. Rudy Saddler drove fast, arms braced, the tail of his scarf airborne; but suddenly, and alarmingly, he hurled us off to the left, down from the road, across uneven ground and directly into a wood. Agnes yelped as we bumped through vegetation. Deer started from the undergrowth and boughs slapped at the chassis. We tilted side to side on a grassy path before suddenly shooting into a glade and skidding to a halt. The engine barked and sputtered out in a long plume of steam. No one spoke. I could hear the soft beat of contracting metal.

'Are we here?' asked Agnes eventually.

Rudy's helmet and goggles were embroidered with pine needles. Little by little, birdsong was restored and shafts of sunlight lay like golden bars.

'How did you find this place?' Agnes asked.

'By careful reconnoitring,' Rudy said, so seriously that I thought he was joking, but Agnes was spellbound.

'You think of everything,' she said.

He peeled off his headgear and leapt to the ground, then helped us dismount, very carefully instructing us where to place our feet. He lifted down the hamper, set it carefully on the grass and undid the straps. I stared as he began to unpack rugs, linen bouquets filled with bread, fruits, cheese in wax paper, a thermos flask, and, unbelievably to my eyes, a flagon of wine.

'My mother,' he explained to me, 'is Italian.'

'Lucia,' Agnes said with a note of awe. 'That is her name.'

'Make yourselves comfortable,' Rudy said, and offered around cigarettes. 'For the horseflies.'

I marvelled at the perfection of the setting, so complete and

214

self-contained. Rudy poured wine for Agnes and himself, and lemonade for me, while I busied myself laying out plates, a platter, and cutlery. Agnes buttered bread, cut it into squares and began to feed it to Rudy, every so often pausing to drink her wine.

'To health!' Rudy said and we clinked our glasses.

'To love!' Agnes said as her pretty fingers found the buttons of his waistcoat. 'May it live ever more!'

The cheese was yellow, smelly and had all but melted in the heat; I scooped the viscous mess from its wax paper with a spoon, lay back and held the dripping blob above my mouth. My gums and throat melted. Tobacco smoke lay sweetly on the clearing. If I closed my eyes I could imagine Chink beside me. He ran his finger down my face and parted my lips gently. I could taste him. His tongue sought out the sweet melting cheese. A strong need gripped my belly. My breath came short and suddenly I wanted to overflow as Dublin floated beneath me. I looked down and saw all the city there, looking up enviously as we drove across the sky.

I must have dozed off; when I sat up my companions were gazing rapturously at one another.

'Sing for me, Rudy,' Agnes said.

'And disturb the peace?'

'Please! One of Moore's melodies!'

'Which one? There are so many.'

'I will adore any melody you choose.'

Rudy cleared his throat several times, sat up on the rug and joined his hands quite formally.

'Sweet vale of Avoca! how calm could I rest
In thy bosom of shade, with the friends I love best,

Where the storms that we feel in this cold world should cease,

And our hearts, like thy waters, be mingled in peace.'

We applauded and Rudy bowed gracefully. In the days since the party, he had begun to wax his moustaches, probably on Agnes's advice, for they were now a burgeoning appendage to his young face instead of the rather limp attachment I remembered.

'I could die happily listening to you sing,' Agnes said and laid her cheek against his shoulder.

The tops of the trees had begun to creep nearer the sun. Wherever Rudy went, Agnes followed. If he rose to inspect the car, which he felt the need to do from time to time, she was at his elbow; when he put back down on the rug, she did so too. At odd moments I found Rudy looking at me, and I wondered whether Agnes's attentions were making him self-conscious.

'You must tell us more about your Mr Chink Holly,' Agnes said coyly, as if my confidence was public knowledge.

'Agnes?'

'Oh, come on!' she said blithely. 'You're among friends!'

'Mr Holly? Nothing to tell.'

'Now, now, that's not what you told me.'

It amazed me that our pact about such matters was being cast aside so easily.

'I mean, he had eyes for no one else at his party!' Agnes cooed. 'Everyone said so – didn't they, Rudy?'

'I wasn't listening,' Rudy said.

'You're being very quiet about him,' Agnes said craftily. 'You've told me almost nothing.'

'As I said, there's nothing to tell.'

'Don't fib, Rose,' she laughed, 'not to me, please! Have you forgotten our little chat?'

The wine flagon was empty. Rudy looked away.

'I don't want to talk about him, Agnes,' I said as civilly as I could manage.

'We're your friends,' she purred, 'please! Tell!'

There always came a point with Agnes – now draped around Rudy, and giggling – when I found her irritating.

'No! And that's the end of it,' I said, perhaps too firmly.

'Oh,' Agnes said and sat up, 'I do beg your pardon, Rose, I was only showing a friendly interest.' Two little red circles lit her cheeks. 'No need to be like that.'

'Agnes, please,' I said. 'We've had a lovely afternoon.'

'What does that mean?' she asked. 'That our afternoon is now over because you so decide?'

'Please ... let it be.'

'You can't always make the decisions, Rose!'

'All I said was—'

Her eyes seemed huge in their lovely embrasures. 'It's always on your terms, isn't it, Lady Rose? Even in school. Who got to hold the skipping-rope? Lady Rose, Lady Rose. Why should I let you into my life if I'm not let into yours?'

'You're being silly now,' I said.

'Me?' She blinked rapidly. 'Am I being silly? Rudy? Am I?'

Rudy's hands fluttered at his head and he suddenly looked like a man tormented by bees.

'I ... I haven't been following ...' he began.

'You mean you haven't been heeding me?' Agnes said. 'Is that so?'

'Well, not exactly ...'

'You only listen when it suits you,' cried Agnes and got to her feet; but the sudden effort must have tipped the blood in her head since she promptly sat back down again with a soft thump. Rudy and I both laughed outright.

'How dare you!' Agnes cried, scrambling up. 'Both of you!'

'Agnes . . .' Rudy tried to reach for her. 'Please—'

'Don't touch me!'

I could not bring myself to look at her for fear of laughing again.

'And as for you—' She towered over me, enraged. 'I thought you were my friend!'

She bent to the rug, picked up the platter and hurled it into the bushes. Shrieking, she then half stumbled, half ran into the cover of the trees.

We sat there, trying to come to terms with the abrupt change of circumstances.

'She will recover,' I said, 'she always does. I suggest you give her a moment.'

Rudy got up and peered into the darkening wood. I was expecting that he would hasten after Agnes, and when a little time had elapsed, after which he had soothed her with wise and gentle words, the two of them would re-emerge, the scene forgotten. I had known Agnes all my life and this was the procedure. But instead, to my amazement, Rudy approached me, dropped to his knees and removed his boater.

'Miss Raven . . . Rose . . .'

I looked up at him. 'Mr Saddler?'

'I have to say this,' he blurted, 'because if I don't say it now I may never find the courage to do so again. I love you. I have loved you from the moment I first saw you. I will do anything – anything – you want, go anywhere, be your

218

slave, I would die for you. Please give me a chance. Please—'

A scream came from the nearby woods.

'Mr Saddler—'

'I love you and I will always love you, I cannot help it, just tell me you will consider what I have said, I beg you—'

'Mr Saddler,' I said gently, 'I really think you should go after her. She's in there waiting.'

'Am I nothing at all to you?' he asked and I had seldom seen anyone so abruptly distraught. 'Do I not exist?'

'Of course you are not nothing,' I said, 'I admire and like you very much.'

'You do?'

'Yes, of course I do.'

'And so there is a chance you will consider—?'

'You are a fine and generous man,' I said, 'and I hope we can always be friends.'

'But—'

'But now, as a good friend, I'm asking you to please retrieve Miss Daly, and then drive us back to town.'

23

I stepped quickly over the seashells to keep my hem above the rushing tide. Ahead of us, Freddy chased oyster catchers along the shoreline of the Velvet Strand. I had forestalled Annie's opposition to this outing by telling her that Freddy would be my escort, and then ran out to the tram with him before she could object.

'Look at the map,' Chink said. 'We could walk on from here if we had a mind to and in a year we would be back exactly where we started.'

Half a mile earlier, we had left our shoes and stockings on an old oil drum. He had rolled up the legs of his white trousers to below his knees. His light blue blazer was inset with red and white stripes, his shirt and tie were an even lighter blue, and his red hair was flattened to a shine.

'Maybe life is like that,' I said, 'maybe we are always going round in circles.'

He stopped and took some deep breaths as if he had something prepared.

'Miss Raven, I want you to know that I'm very sorry about Mr Charles Sinnott. Ultan told me that he was well known to your family. I'm desperately sorry about what happened. It was awful.'

'Yes, it was.'

'God rest his soul.'

I hadn't expected him to mention Charles Sinnott, but I was now impressed that he had seen fit to bring it up.

'Thank you,' I said, 'but it's happening every day, all over Ireland.'

'It can't be easy for the Barnmeres,' he said, 'at their age.'

I could not believe he had said that. 'A lot you care about Lord and Lady Barnmere,' I laughed. 'Come on!'

'I say!' he said. 'That's unfair!'

'Do they not represent everything you despise?'

'Oh, bother that!' He shook his head and did a little dance of impatience. 'Every pick and shovel in Irrawaddy, every wheelbarrow and lawnmower comes from our shop in Capel Street. My father and Lord Barnmere have been friends for years!'

'Friends? Really?'

He jumped up and down on the spot. 'Daddy sails with Lord Barnmere!'

Some of these contradictions threatened reason, I thought.

'I'm sorry.'

'Oh, no! No! You mustn't apologise!' he cried. 'Politics is such a complicated business I struggle to understand it myself!'

I smiled for his infectious enthusiasm.

'Is he very hot on politics, your father?' I asked innocently, but I could see immediately that he knew the real direction of my question.

'Look, one can be political without being unlawful. One can dream of a free Ireland without being a criminal.' He blew air and was suddenly worried. 'My father is a great man, but his political beliefs have made him old before his time. He is too passionate, you see. He never stops. He now complains of pains in his chest. I fear for his heart.'

I was at once concerned for a man I had never met. 'He's in our club . . . I mean, he's a member in the club where—'

'I know, yes, I know.'

'Where my father works.'

'Yes, of course.'

I looked at him keenly. 'Does the fact that my father is a porter in your father's club make you feel uncomfortable?'

He closed his eyes tight as if to summon enough power to contain himself. 'Before my grandfather built our house in Howth, the neighbours signed a petition urging the vendor of the land to rescind the sale. They could not imagine living beside an Irish Catholic family whose money came from selling hammers. It was as if we were rats moving into the area. But the sale went through. My grandfather remembered that time very well, the shock and hurt of it. The feeling that we were of a lower order. Neither my father nor I would ever look down on another person, least of all someone as well liked as Mr Raven.'

As the heat bent the sand into moving spirals, Chink picked up a flat stone and skimmed it out across the water. 'Ten!' he cried and jumped in the air.

'I counted six.'

'Definitely ten – you must count the little jumps at the end.'

'I did.'

'I may have double counted the last few,' he said.

'Do it again, in that case.'

'Why?'

'Because I bet you can't.'

He pretended to be perplexed. 'What do you bet?'

'I don't gamble.'

'But you said, I bet you.'

'It was an expression.'

'Very well – then, I'll bet you.'

'How does that work if I don't gamble?'

'This is not for money. I'll bet you a kiss I can skip the stone ten times,' he said.

'I don't think . . .'

'The bet is made!' He ran to the water, picked up another stone and arched sideways as he flung it. The stone jigged a few times on the water and disappeared. He sprang up and down on the spot. 'Doubles or quits!'

'Never!'

He spread his arms and hurtled away along the beach, his jacket billowing as if he were a kite about to soar. Freddy ran beside him, yapping madly. I wondered if we could simply live forever in that moment and never turn around. His eyes were radiant when he came back. 'In Italy, the sun shines like this ten months of every year,' he panted. 'Before the Great War my parents travelled by railway from Paris to Rome and were granted a private audience with Pope Pius. My father prays to him every night and says that one day he will be made a saint.'

'Can you do that?' I asked. 'Get on a train in Paris and get off in Rome?'

'Of course – would you like to?'

I laughed. 'Who wouldn't like to?'

'We can do it, you and I! I promise!'

At a sand bar, he took my hand and we waded across.

'We can do anything,' he said and drew me around to face him. 'Do you believe me?'

'Mr Holly—'

'I mean it.'

'Not so fast, remember?'

'Yes, but let us not waste time,' he said.

'Is time not what we have in abundance?' I asked. 'Look at us! We are millionaires!'

'Oh, Rose, I—'

'Sssh.'

He kept my hand in his as the day grew warmer and the sea resounded. Every so often Freddy disappeared into the dunes and minutes later reappeared, his nose black from sand. This was our private world, I thought, this was where we would return to when we were old.

'Let's do it,' he said. 'Let's get on a boat and leave. Come back when all this trouble is over.'

'I have read,' I said, 'that the world will soon have no horizons. That the modern man or woman will be free to travel in a way never known before.'

His eyes stood out, as if I had said something that he had never previously considered. He combed his fingertips through his hair till the gleaming, rusty shell had corrugated into a spiked red bush, and then he stuck out his arms and tore away in gyrating circle, his toes skipping the ground.

'We'll sit in a biplane and fly through the Grand Canyon!' he yelled. 'Did you know until I was twelve I wanted to be a buckaroo? I made a lariat from hemp in the shop and could lasso a calf at ten yards. Yahoo!'

Even Freddy had paused to stare.

'We'll climb the Rockies, sleep in a covered wagon, and

then go to California! The sun is so hot that the earth is white there. Oranges and lemons grow from every tree! No one will stop us to ask our names or by what right we are travelling. Baedeker's our man! All we have to do is pick up a Baedeker and go!'

24

The Velvet Strand ended in a rocky promontory, a stubborn wedge of Neolithic geology that the sea had yet to erase. We climbed across little seaweedy pools and sat on a ledge below the Martello Tower. Over on Lambay Island I could see the field divisions and count the cattle. To the south, the bulk of Ireland's Eye appeared craggy and much more substantial than it did from Sutton.

'I just love it here,' I said.

'Rose.'

'Mmm ... ?'

'May I be candid?'

'It depends ...'

'From the first moment I saw you in the Demesne I was yours. I said to Ultan, look at that ravishing creature! And he said, Steady on, Holly! She's my little sister.'

'Lovely Ultan.'

'You are very close – he told me. He said he loves you more than his life.'

I searched his face for reservations, but his blue eyes were clear and giving.

'When we were small, Ultan used to race me and let me win,' I said. 'I was fast but his legs were so much longer!'

'He's on the rise in his paper, or so he tells me,' Chink said. 'What's he do in there anyway?'

'Well, he used to sweep the floors—'

'Like Saddler! The ticket picker! Ultan introduced me!'

'But recently they've been sending him out to collect scores from the cricket matches and soccer games,' I said. 'He's very good at facts.'

'Good for him.'

'He says he will soon be given more responsibility, that they will allow him write short reports,' I said, 'from the cricket matches.'

'Well, bravo,' Chink said, 'who knows where that might lead?'

High in the vivid blue hawks quivered, in wait for shrews to peep from their burrows. Except for one or two figures in the hazy distance, the strand was deserted. I unpinned my hat and let my hair spill out as he held a lighter to my cigarette.

'He is a rum chap, isn't he?' he said, trailing smoke. 'Ultan.'

'He is . . . very talented, yes. I love him very much.'

'In which case he is not only talented but lucky as any man can be.'

'Why do you call him rum?' I asked lightly, for I could not resist picking at my deepest fear.

'I must apologise . . .'

'No need, I'm just interested, that's all. Do others see him as rum?'

'I have no idea who others are or what they see. Believe me when I say, I am interested only in one person in the world and she has recently removed her hat.'

'Nevertheless—'

'And may have to scamper home in her stockinged feet if

rabbits have eaten her shoes,' he said. 'I know I could not resist a nibble were I a rabbit.'

'But thankfully you're not,' I said, 'and therefore you are able to indulge me, just for a moment, about my big brother.'

He threw away his cigarette.

'All I meant was that he's different,' he said carefully, 'to the other chaps I know.'

'In what way?'

'Can't put my finger on it, but he always was, even when we were at school together. Sometimes when he looks at me I feel he's looking right through me.' Chink frowned. 'I must confess, I felt nonplussed at first.'

'Really?'

'Something in his eyes . . . Look, I've grown used to it. It's just the way he is.'

'I think he's always looking for more than he can see,' I said, and hoped I did not sound too anxious, 'it's why he works in a newspaper. To see around the obvious and tell the world about it.'

'Ah, yes,' Chink said, 'I expect that's it.'

'Ultan is quite normal, believe me.'

'Hmm. But you are not,' he said, 'you are extraordinary.'

'I don't think so, Mr Holly.'

He guided me around rocks to the next strand, where the dunes were altogether tamer. Suddenly he leapt back and clapped.

'Another wager!'

'What?'

'You see that headland?'

I could see through the haze to where the strand and sea appeared to merge.

228

He leapt in the air. 'I bet you all the treasure in the world that if you start now and I stay here for a count of twenty that I can catch you before you reach that headland.'

'I can't run, dressed like this—'

'You just said you were fast!'

'I am but—'

'There's no one here to look!'

'Mr Holly—'

'Very well, I'll count to thirty,' he said.

'Certainly not.'

'Forty, then.'

'Fifty,' I said.

'Forty.'

'Fifty! Fifty!'

'Done!' he said. 'Go!'

All of a sudden I didn't care what he saw or who might be looking on. Throwing my hat at him, my good hat on to which I had sewn cloth roses, I gathered up my skirts in both arms and took off. Because the wet sand was firmer I flew along the tideline with no thought that I would be drenched. Never before had my legs moved so fluently. Ultan had once called me a gazelle! I ran and ran. I came upon gulls almost before they became aware of me. Stones made me veer inland, the softer sand making speed harder. The tide was full, and marking time to the turn, its white foam pushing thickly. I knew if he caught me before the headland that he loved me. Like blowing on a white dandelion. I didn't dare look behind. The beach climbed as the point was reached – I could almost touch it. He tackled me, softly, his arms around me, and we tumbled together on to the rising sand.

'Rose.'

Just feet away the sea roared.

'I'm never going to let you go again.'

I could feel the strong length of him as he put his hand behind my head so my hair would not meet the sand. We kissed, slowly, and even though I had never kissed like that before it was joyfully familiar.

'Rose.' He held my hands. 'Let's do it,' he said. 'Let's go away together.'

'I can't.'

'Why not?'

I sat up. 'I'm going to work in Clery's.'

His face dropped in puzzlement. 'Clery's? *Clery's?*'

'Papá knows someone in there who has promised a position for me in the ladies' department.'

He screwed his eyes shut. 'Listen . . . please don't take this the wrong way from which it is intended. You know how highly I think of you, but . . .'

'Go on.'

He was struggling to get the words right. 'You don't have to work in Clery's.'

'But I want to.'

'And I want for you everything you have ever dreamt of – which is all I could ever wish for myself. Rose Raven, I will always belong to you.'

'Please,' I began. 'Don't say anything you may regret.'

'I will never regret this,' he said and knelt. 'Never.'

'Your clean leggings—'

'I'm begging you. Forget Clery's. Make the journey with me.'

I touched his face. 'People will disapprove.'

'We can lose ourselves, as we just said. Somewhere else.'

'Your family will never allow it.'

'They will rejoice!'

'They may not.'

'If by any chance they didn't I would change my name! It's done the whole time. Thousands of people, starting again.'

'Change your name?' I laughed. 'That's ridiculous!'

'I would jump from the top of Nelson's Pillar into a barrel of water if it made you consider me,' he said. 'I would swim around Lambay—'

I suddenly looked around.

'Oh dear God!'

'What's wrong?' he asked. 'What?'

'Where's Freddy?'

25

We hurried into the flat dunes, calling out. I whistled until my lips were dry. My dread was that he had bustled down a burrow and was stuck. Terriers could not help themselves. Once, years before, in Donabate with my parents, he had done just that. After more than an hour Tommy had heard him barking, way down below his feet. We'd only got him out by breaking the ground with a crowbar.

'Freddy? Freddy!'

'We will find him,' Chink kept saying. 'I know we will.'

I couldn't even begin to think how thoughtless I had been. Every few strides we stopped and listened, but the silence was endless.

'Let's split up,' Chink said.

He ran back the way we had come as I climbed up through the pampas grass towards Malahide.

'Freddy!'

The face of a higher dune poured sand as I scrambled up it. Suddenly the sea looked miles away and the coast stretched into the distance.

'Freddy? Freddy!'

I began to cry as I realised that the chances of finding the dog were hopeless and as the thought of returning home without him overwhelmed me. He was Tommy's best friend, I had often thought. Chink was racing back, peering through cupped hands. The sunlight made his red hair explode.

'Look!'

Where the sea curved around the headland and became an estuary, the tops of two military carriers broke the skyline.

'What are they?' I called.

'Tans, I think,' he said. 'Stay where you are.'

'Where are you going?'

'They may have seen Freddy.'

'Chink! No ...'

'They're not going to hurt me,' he said, 'I'm only looking for a little dog.'

'Well, so am I,' I said and skidded down the dune.

Around the hook, the inlet broadened into a wide body of water. The tide had turned decisively and the estuary was in torrent, sucked back to sea in tight, hectic currents. We had lost sight of the vehicles; I prayed they had driven off. The bluff of sand fell steeply to a narrow path. We rounded a headland and stopped. A group of six or eight men in underclothes stood in a circle. They had been swimming; their hair and cotton-clad bodies dripped water. I smelled tobacco. One of them was making Freddy beg on his hind legs for scraps from a tin.

'Oh, thank God!' I cried. 'Freddy!'

All the faces turned.

'Freddy!' I called. 'Come here!'

But Freddy was glued to his performance. I saw their uniforms, mottled browns and khakis, draped over the bonnets of two armoured cars.

'Freddy! Good boy!' I called.

233

'Freddy's not minded to obey, I'm afraid, my lady,' said one in the accent of some English shire. 'Are you, Freddy?'

The others guffawed. A Lewis gun was mounted high on the back of the nearest wagon.

'It's all right, Rose, leave this to me,' said Chink quietly and stepped forward. 'We thought we'd lost him, thank you for feeding him, men.'

They looked around at one another with disbelieving eyes. A stout, broad-shouldered individual whose wet cottons clung unambiguously to his body reached down and gathered up Freddy.

'Begging you pardon, Captain, we weren't expecting you today, sir,' he said.

The others leered, but the set of their bodies was tense.

'Stand to attention, you low fellows,' the stout man barked, 'respect yer officer!'

Chink, making light of it, advanced.

'That's the boy, Freddy.'

'Want to go to Dandy?' asked the man. He held Freddy out, but at the last moment chucked the dog to his nearest companion. 'Didn't think so!'

The circle widened and as Chink reached once more for Freddy the dog was thrown again, this time to a hairy man, his physique immense. The others howled laughter. Freddy's ears flattened and his teeth were bared.

'Be careful of him!' I called.

The big man launched Freddy, like a ball, high into the air. I could see the dog's terrified expression. A nimble footed Tan with the face of a weasel darted in, hands out.

'Mark!' he cried just as Freddy twisted in his grip and bit him. 'Aagghh! Dirty little bugger!'

'Must be a fuckin' Fenian!' growled the big man. 'Give him back 'ere!'

'With pleasure!'

Freddy was flung once more, but before he could bite again the big man seized his muzzle.

'You see, Freddy, this is the problem with you people,' he said as Freddy squirmed in his grasp. 'We come upon you, lost and wanderin', we take you in, we feed you and give you our water—'

Freddy snarled furiously as he tried to free his head.

'And what do you do? You fucking bite the 'and that feeds you, you ungrateful little cur.'

'Please – he's just frightened!' I said. 'He didn't mean it.'

'That's what you all say,' the man retorted. 'It's just your thankless nature, isn't it, Freddy? You can't help yourselves.'

'If you could please give him to me,' Chink said, and stepped forward. 'He won't bite me.'

'Course not, vermin never bite their own,' said weasel face, sucking blood from his hand. 'Cut his fuckin' 'ead off, Ronnie!'

'No! Please!' I cried. 'My father was a soldier like you! Freddy is his dog!'

'All the more reason to protect your dad from this venomous little bugger,' the big Tan said and reached to a kitbag.

'No! NO!'

Sunlight made the long blade shine. Chink tried to reach for the dog but two of the men stepped into his path and hit hard into his ribs. He went down.

'Beg your pudding, Sir Galahad.'

'Do it, Ronnie!' cried the weasel. 'Be'ead him!'

I screamed. 'Stop!'

235

The Tan called Ronnie wrenched back Freddy's head. I screamed.

'What the 'ell's goin' on here?'

A dressed and booted man, buttoning his trousers, emerged from the higher dunes.

'Nothing, sarge, just dealing with a little local disturbance,' the big Tan said, 'which we 'ave amicably resolved.'

The sergeant glowered. 'I should 'ope so.'

I saw the knife being slipped back into the kit-bag. Chink, winded, was climbing to his feet.

'Get the fuck dressed and prepare to leave,' the sergeant said. 'And get rid of that fuckin' animal – now!'

The men turned to their carriers and began to pull on their fatigues.

'Get rid of 'im, I said!'

'With pleasure, sarge. Cheerio, Freddy.'

The big Tan pivoted and flung Freddy into the midstream of the hurrying tide.

'Freddy!'

Already the dog had been swept out twenty yards .

'Chink!'

He was running so fast he looked airborne. The inlet widened as it neared the sea. Chink bounded in long strides. I couldn't see Freddy. At the point where the bank fell away deeply, Chink flung off his blazer and dived. I was screaming Freddy's name. Suddenly the dog's frantic little head appeared and turned back towards me. Chink was trying to swim, but the power of the water had him in its grip and he was shooting out like a cork.

'CHINK!'

The surface of the sound looked calm, but I could see how

this was a deception and how its hidden currents were surging powerfully. Chink was being carried out at speed, and Freddy was already lost to sight. And then Chink went under. The water where his head had been was smooth as glass. I knew I was screaming. It was as if the ocean had swallowed them both.

'NO!'

I was about to turn back to the revolting men, to beg their help; it didn't matter who they were; but further out, just at that moment, like a miracle, Chink popped up again, and this time he had Freddy by the scruff. He turned on to his back, the dog held, and began to kick across for the sea cliff where I was rooted. Despite the racing currents, now whitely visible, he was carving into them at an angle, defying the tide's strength by small degrees. I could hear his gasps. I leapt into the water and was nearly taken off my feet. They were still twenty yards out.

'It's fine, Freddy,' I could hear him saying. 'We're nearly there.'

His legs thrashed and he could use only one arm to swim; but he was out of the grip of the centre stream. I waded in. Current rushed to undermine my legs. The gap between us narrowed. I went in deeper. I could have been swept to England, for all I cared. As he sensed me there, Freddy began to whimper.

'I'm here!' I cried.

They were almost within reach. I stretched further and grabbed Freddy first, and threw him on to the grass; after which I went back in, struggling to remain upright, caught Chink beneath his armpits and dragged him into the shallows. He turned over, retched at length, then crawled on to the land, where he lay, eyes to heaven, water puddling around him. Freddy panted rapidly, his little eyes wild, his rag tongue hanging out.

237

26

Those days of mid-July, already heavy with pollen, grew ever drowsier. All of Dublin seemed to be on the beaches of Sutton, Portmarnock and Malahide. Chink's shop in Capel Street closed for a week's holiday. Even Tommy's club was all but deserted, he reported, as the members fled the boiling city. The tram stop in Howth was where we mostly met, and walked from there out to the tip of the pier, beyond earshot of the village. Sometimes he did handstands for me on the base of the lighthouse, teetering over the sea, until I begged him to come back in. We often huddled down by the mole with our cigarettes. I saw yachts bending over in good winds as they tacked between the harbour and Lambay, the caps of the sailors dipping between the waves before rebounding as a swell heaved them up again. It was as if the tightening military conflict did not exist out here, as if we lived in a country where harmony and peace were taken for granted.

We picked our way along the shore from Howth and collected scrimshaw. Some days we took the tram up to Balkill Road and went down the narrow, south-facing paths that clung to the cliff faces. Beneath us, the ocean was bright, hard and unfathomable. Every so often a warning gun from the Kish lightship broke the silence and then ebbed away then in cascading reverberations.

Chink showed his love for me in small, attentive details, such as brushing sand dots from my hair, or spreading out his jacket if it appeared I might be inclined to sit, or walking ahead backwards where our path wound through gorse, his arms held wide to deflect any possibility of my face being scarified. He kissed me at every hidden turn, in the lees made by wild broom, in tiny grass valleys that swooped between outcrops, by fields of spangled cattle and behind the tram shelter as we waited to go back down. We talked of how the tracks of our lives were laid out clearly, and laughed at how much more important our happiness was than the opinions of other people. He told me his father had promised him five hundred pounds when he turned twenty-one, which would be the following January, and how when he received it we would go away. That was, he said, if things had not improved – if peace had not broken out. My face must have told of my dismay that his promise was provisional, for he immediately said that we would go no matter what the situation.

'Even if we are a republic by then,' he said, 'you and I are taking that mail boat.'

But I felt I had forced him into an unreasonable pledge, and was ashamed of my own selfishness. The truth was that I just wanted us to be together; whether in Howth or Timbuktu I didn't care as long as we were free from the interference of others.

'They say that in London there are people who have never heard of Ireland,' he said. 'Imagine that! They've never heard of us. To them we may as well be coming from the moon.'

I used to think of that some evenings in Nan's Cottage, when I walked down to the seawall and looked across at Howth bathed in moonlight.

Annie worried, of course, but that was her disposition. I think my new demeanour irritated her, or perhaps she was jealous; but almost every night she recited the latest litany of outrages done in the cause of our so-called emancipation, as she described it. She could speak of nothing else. Society as she knew it was disintegrating, as if the ground beneath her was giving way; and yet she could not move since she had nowhere else to go. Her head was a maelstrom of the battles being fought all over Ireland as the certitude of her generation and class was finally sundered. She felt that my father and she were drowning in the new, chaotic order, and that in such circumstances my dalliance – her word – was most inappropriate. I was deaf to her pleas, for they had been so long rehearsed my mind immediately veered elsewhere as soon as she started. Some days I left home at noon and did not return till just before the curfew. Annie asked Tommy to advance my petition to Clery's urgently, for she knew that if I had a job I could not be out with Chink Holly. Tommy, though, felt that Barry, the tailor, should not be pushed, but would deliver in his own time; and that to show undue eagerness could work against me; and that as these shop jobs were at a premium discretion was called for. Annie's nightly invective was nothing new to Tommy either; he just sat there, appearing to listen, but I knew he was a hundred miles away.

The weather broke quite suddenly as August loomed. Now the upper decks of the trams were empty and washed clean by rain. The wind was in the east and the city filled up again. Chink began to talk about the Horse Show. His parents always reserved a table in the Royal Dublin Society and he wanted to bring me there to meet them. We would go into the jumping pocket where the riders collected before they went out to compete, he said, and he would bet everything he had that I would drink a Pimms.

One afternoon, when my mother was still in Sutton, at Mrs Wilder's, I was working out how best to let her know my plans for the Horse Show, and to then cajole her into lending me the money to buy a new outfit, when the front door shuddered open and Tommy came in, dripping wet, his face the colour of flour. It was too early; he should still have been at work.

'Papa?'

He walked straight past me, into his bedroom, and closed the door.

27

Ultan later told me what had happened. The news was all over Dublin. Papa's club had been raided at lunchtime by detectives from G Division of the DMP, backed up by a contingent of Black and Tans. Four of the club's members, including Mr Jerome Holly, had been arrested and taken away. It was rumoured that one of those arrested – not Mr Holly, thank God – had later died.

'Martial law now prevails,' said Ultan grimly. 'This is war.'

Apparently, the club was just one of a dozen or more locations targeted that day, including private homes, business premises and even the residence of a priest.

'They went into Maison Prost's and lifted two gentlemen still in their shaving foam,' Ultan said.

The political atmosphere, already poisoned with the murder of Charles Sinnott, had darkened far beyond that singular event as the authorities came down with all their expanded force on those opposing them.

'It's like the Somme on Sackville Street,' my brother said, 'that many soldiers.'

Tommy did not emerge until Annie came home, and then looked like an invalid, requiring her arm to lean on. The shock of what he had witnessed had aged him ten years, so much so that my mother, unwell as she was, looked suddenly much the younger.

I sat down immediately and wrote to Chink, saying I was devastated to hear what had taken place, and asking what I could do to help. Ultan said he had heard that many of the men seized in the raids were being detained in Marlborough Barracks, an almost unbearable irony, since my father regarded that barracks with the utmost fondness, as if it were his second home.

When I came back from posting the letter at Sutton Cross, we had our supper; but Tommy left his plate untouched. Annie made him tea and put a good measure of Power's whiskey into the mug. Gradually, he began to come round.

'It was as if they were violating a church,' he said. 'They're not even proper soldiers.'

He'd heard their boots on the club's granite steps. They'd burst into the hall – his domain – rifles at the ready, roaring blue murder. Some of them were almost certainly drunk, Papa said. They must have known who it was they had come for, since Mr Holly and two others were arrested in less than a minute. A fourth club member on their list had tried to get away through the tradesman's entrance but they had shot him in the leg. He was bleeding badly as they dragged him out through the hall and down the steps to an armoured vehicle.

'I cleaned up the blood myself,' Papa said.

The secretary of the club and some of the members, including Dr Bradshaw, the chairman of the members' committee, took a decision to close for the rest of the day, the first time that such a thing had happened. The staff, including Tommy, were sent home.

'I would fear for poor Mr Holly,' Papa said, 'he's not a well man, you know.'

243

'I know, his heart,' I said and they all looked at me. 'Yes – Chink says he suffers from his heart.' I was suddenly in tears. 'It's so awful, the whole thing. I don't understand why we can't just be left alone.'

Ultan put his arm around me. 'It will be all right, Sis, I promise you.'

I looked at my father. 'Papa? Would you be able to visit Mr Holly? To make sure he's being treated properly?'

Annie sat back in astonishment.

'Have you lost your mind, girl?'

'He is my friend's father!' I cried. 'He's not a criminal!'

Tommy did not know what way to turn. He began, 'I suppose I could—'

'You will not!' Annie shouted and the veins in her forehead stood out like leeches. 'It's bad enough you have to work for these people!'

'Mother . . .' I said.

'And as for you—' It seemed that breath eluded her. 'I warned you so many times.'

Ultan cleared his throat and made himself look authoritative. 'Rose's may not be such a bad suggestion,' he said. 'It does no harm to show support at times like these.'

'Are you asking your father to consort with rebels?' asked Annie with her chin thrust out. 'Are you proposing that he goes back into his barracks in front of all the officers he once served, and who know him as a friend, and shows himself to be on the side of the dirt they have collected?'

'Mother!' Her language terrified me. 'Stop! You don't know what you are saying!'

'I think Rose has a point,' said Ultan.

She set her eyes on him. 'Just because you sweep the

244

floors of a newspaper does not give you the right to come back here and tell me what's right and wrong,' she hissed. 'You've had a good upbringing because your father and I have always respected standards. The likes of the people for whom your sister has so much admiration want nothing less than to destroy those standards in the name of their so-called cause. Well, I'm not standing up for their cause and neither is your father. And if you want to continue living in this house – both of you – you won't support it either.'

No one could speak. Although my father and I were often the targets of such invective, to hear Ultan so attacked was a new shock.

'Mother,' Ultan said unsteadily, 'you are talking about our nation!'

Her head was shaking so violently I thought she would fall over. 'This ... this is not a nation!' she shouted. 'This is a ... a province of the Empire!'

Hands clutched to her chest, she fled the kitchen. Ultan went to the sink and poured himself a glass of water. Papa refilled his tea mug and topped it up with whiskey.

'They'll probably keep them in a day or two for questioning,' he said, 'then let them out again. Nothing more will happen unless the situation escalates.'

'That's the problem,' Ultan said, 'every day seems worse than the one before.'

'We're all being torn apart,' I said. 'And for what?'

'Look.' Tommy's face had regained its colour. 'Maybe I can have a look in at the barracks and see—'

'Oh – would you?' I leapt up and kissed him. 'That would be wonderful! It would mean so much to—'

Ultan said, 'Even so, just be very careful, Papa. There are eyes everywhere these days.'

'I often drop by,' Tommy said. 'I was there a few weeks ago.'

'Should we send in some food with you?' I asked.

'Rose!' Ultan shook his head. 'Stop now. That's enough.'

'Why not? Isn't Chink your friend too?'

Tommy was exhausted. 'This will all blow over,' he said, 'just as it did before. And then we can go back to our normal lives.'

28

I was not surprised in the days that followed when no letter came from Chink. I could imagine what he and his family were going through. Ultan had no further news on the fate of the prisoners. Nor did I get a chance to talk on my own to Tommy: he was on a shift that saw him leave in the early morning. At night, when he came home, Annie was always there, so discussion about Mr Holly was impossible. I couldn't sleep for worry and felt ill.

'I shall be seeing our friend Mr Barry day after tomorrow,' Tommy said. He was back to his old chirpy self as if nothing had happened. 'Good news, I hope. Hey-ho, Clery's!'

A sandbag dropped in my chest. How could I tell him that Clery's was the last thing on my mind and that Chink's proposal – for I was sure that is what it had been – meant I would never be going to work there?

'I am in no hurry,' I said and Annie stopped her sewing to stare me down.

The next day Ultan reported that events were changing so fast that the newspapers were struggling to keep up with the news. Even more troops were shipping in, especially to Cork, where law and order no longer existed.

'But they're mostly conscripts, not soldiers!' Ultan said.

'Lloyd George is really scraping the bottom of the barrel.'

'*Mister* Lloyd George,' Annie said.

A week following the arrests in the club, when everyone had left for work, I took the tram to Howth, followed by the train, by way of Howth Junction, to Portmarnock. At the base of the dunes, where the solitary oil drum still stood, I peeled off to my bare feet and set out north, along the Velvet Strand. I wanted this place to possess me again; and part of me believed that Chink would think the same and that he might have come out here to find me. The same warm sand, the same tide in my toes, the same seashells. I climbed across the black rock-scape that separated the two beaches and sooner than I expected came to the mouth of the sea-river in which Chink and Freddy had nearly drowned. The inlet flowed in towards Malahide. I followed it until I came to the little beach from which the Tans had bathed. They had chosen the spot well, for it was hidden and empty, sheltered from the wind, and the water was warm. As if to submerge myself in my memories, I undressed down to my slip and waded in. The beach shelved deeply but the powerful current from the last time was absent. I went deeper and sank until I could sit on the bottom, the water over my head. A lovely peace possessed me. I had no need of air, and despite being underwater I could see.

29

I could always tell Tommy's humour from his step on the gravel path: if tired, or if he had left earlier under a cloud of Annie's bickering, his feet would drag; but today, home from an early shift, he walked with a spring of excellent humour.

'Precious Rose.' He smiled broadly. 'Tea with your old man?'

'Mr Chanticleer must have excelled himself today,' I said, and went about setting the tray.

Annie was still in Sutton, but I knew that that could not exclusively account for my father's happy face.

'Let's take the tea out back,' Tommy said, and when I looked surprised added, 'Such a lovely day, lass, what a shame to sit indoors!'

We sat surrounded by the scent of summer meadow.

'I spoke to Mr Barry today,' Tommy said happily. 'An appointment has been arranged in Clery's for next Wednesday afternoon.'

'Oh.'

'Don't worry, I have taken care of it in the club – I shall be with you. Don't look so aghast! It will be fine! Mr Barry has assured me that he has recommended you in the most celestial terms!'

I tried to smile. Tommy was so radiant I could not bring

myself to break the news to him that I would not be going to Clery's for an interview; that everything had changed; that Chink and I had made plans known to us alone.

'That is . . . very kind of Mr Barry,' I said.

'But that is not all.' Tommy held his teacup in both hands, at his chin. 'There is also news that will please your young man, Mr Holly.'

I stared at my father. Neither of my parents had ever before described Chink as my young man.

'What news?'

'With each nugget of good fortune she looks more like a startled hare!'

'Papa—'

'Well, your old man did as you asked yesterday, after work, and poked his old bugle round the door of Marlborough Barracks,' he said coyly.

'Go on.'

'Following my visit, Mr Holly senior was sent home last night on compassionate grounds.'

'Why, that is . . . oh, you are wonderful!' I cried. 'The most wonderful papa in the world!'

'It may well have happened anyway,' he said deferentially.

'No – I'm sure they think so highly of you, Papa.'

'Well, I do have my old friends there.'

'Of course you do! Thank you!'

'And he's a gentleman who has to watch his health—'

'His heart, yes. Is he . . . is he all right? When you say compassionate grounds—'

'He will recover at home, I have no doubt,' Tommy said. 'While I was there, the captain in charge personally arranged a hackney and saw to it that he was brought out on a litter.'

'A litter?'

'He has been frail of late,' Tommy said, 'Mr Holly.'

'That doesn't sound so good. I mean, it is wonderful that you took the trouble of going there, Papa – thank you, again – but I didn't realise Mr Holly had fallen ill.'

'I did what I could,' said Tommy, 'I did what you asked of me.'

I was deeply worried then, for I knew that however well-intentioned the army might have been in releasing him, the fact of Mr Holly's arrest, probably followed by some rough treatment, was all that would be remembered. As I tried to think what next to do, I could hear the postman at the front of the house with the second delivery.

'You know,' Tommy said, 'at the end of the day no one wants this fight that's going on. The men I soldiered with and those I served under are no different to the lads and lassies I work with in the club, nor to the gentlemen I look after. Deep down we're all chums, you know.'

I thought of the men who had wanted to cut his dog's head off.

'You have done your very best, Papa.'

'Well enough for the teapot to be refilled?' he asked cheekily.

'Right away, sir,' I said and took it inside.

I knew he would hate having to tell the tailor of my decision, but nonetheless it was time to reveal the plans Chink and I had made. I put the kettle on the gas and went to the letter box. A single letter lay there. Soft yellow vellum. I smiled as I picked it up. Addressed to me in a hand I now well knew. From a drawer in the kitchen I took a knife and angled the tip of it. Outside, in the sunshine, my father had started up his pipe. I withdrew the letter from its spongy envelope just as the kettle began to spout.

251

30

My mother said that if I wept as much when she died she would be assured her place in heaven – which made me laugh, even as I cried and cried, for her ability to divert any situation to herself was unbounded. Although she brought me lemonade, which I did not drink, and reluctantly accepted my wish to keep the curtains of my bedroom drawn, her bearing reeked of self-righteousness. In the end, I locked my door, preferring isolation to her overbearing sympathy.

My father did not involve himself, as if this was forbidden ground for a man, but he must have known how raw my wound was. My sickness – an infection of my emotions – was a dull, dark place that stank of despair, like my bedroom.

The curtness of his letter and its chilling formality had shattered me. From the opening – 'Dear Miss Raven' – to the one sentence message that he would be unable to meet me again 'due to circumstances', and the neat signature, 'David Holly', the letter was cold and final. I would prefer to be dead than this, I thought.

Since part of me could not believe that he meant it, I scoured his words for any clues to his true intentions. My cruel hope kept returning to the 'circumstances' he referred to. Clearly the arrest of his father had been a major development since we last met, but that apart, I tried to find a deeper meaning in what he had written. It was likely, I reasoned, that Chink himself was more involved with the IRA than he admitted, and if this were so, then he might reasonably fear that he would be next to be arrested. His father, sick and intimidated, could well have given the Castle information about his son. They had probably tortured the poor man. All of which meant that when Chink said he would be unable to meet me again, it was my safety that was uppermost in his mind. People were being shot resisting arrest all over Ireland. He would not put me in harm's way. He had written his letter not because he no longer loved me, but because he loved me so much.

When Ultan came home he knocked on my door.

'Go away.'

'I have to speak to you, Rose.'

'No.'

'Please,' he said.

He sat on my bed in the dimness. When I heard what he had to say I felt a pain in my chest that I had never thought possible.

'When? When did he . . . ?'

'Shortly after he came home to Howth,' Ultan said. 'They say he would have felt nothing.'

I gasped. 'They killed him.'

'They sent him home, Rose. He died at home surrounded by his family.'

'Yes, but they killed him. The Brits killed him.'

'I know,' Ultan said.

'Papa . . .'

'Papa did his best, he did the right thing,' Ultan said.

31

I could not think of food, despite Annie's attempts to feed me. For two days in my darkened bedroom, alternating between grief and attempts at reason, I became weak and dizzy. The divisions of night and day disappeared. Sometimes I heard the front door grunting open, and voices.

Tommy came to my door.

'Rose?'

'Please go away.'

'Don't forget Wednesday!' he sang out in his best barracks orderly voice. 'Best be thinking how you will present yourself!'

I had completely forgotten about my appointment in Clery's, and now, when I did so, it was like a fresh dagger of pain. I knew Tommy was still outside my door.

'What day is today?' I asked.

'It's Monday evening,' Tommy said. 'I've taken Wednesday afternoon off. The appointment is for four o'clock.'

I went to sleep knowing that I could not disappoint my father after all he had done, and that only a few months ago the job in Clery's had shone like a bright opportunity. I must have sunk into a deep pit of sleep, where I boarded a ship with Chink, and then suddenly we were on a biplane soaring through a canyon, when my mother began to shout.

She had gone to put out the milk bottles and discovered that our front door had been daubed in black paint with the words 'GO HOME'. A line of paint ran from the door down the path to our gate where the posts had also been smeared. The letters that formed the words, as if bleeding, dripped.

'And these are meant to be your friends!' Annie cried, bursting into my bedroom.

'Mother! Stop!' Ultan was in his nightclothes, holding an oil lamp.

'What's going on?' Tommy asked.

Although it was well past ten, the sky was still streaked with fingers of dying light which riddled the sea with phosphorescence.

'Put the kettle on, mother,' Ultan said.

We sat in the kitchen without speaking as Tommy, ever intent on mending, was already trying to wipe paint off the door.

'It's nothing,' he said when he came back in. 'It's just a prank, I know that's all it is.'

Earlier that day in Saint Fintan's, Mr Holly had been laid to rest. If I had gone down to the sea wall I would have been able to make out his funeral in the distant cemetery.

'What are we going to do?' Annie asked as if Papa had not spoken.

'What do you mean?' I asked.

'Oh?' said Annie, suddenly puffed up. 'She can speak!'

'Mother . . .' Ultan began.

'Why shouldn't I?' Annie cried. 'After what we've heard

these last days and all Princess Rose here can do is mope about herself?'

'It will pass,' said Tommy and sat down. He poured himself tea. 'It will all pass.'

'It didn't pass Charlie Sinnott,' Annie said.

'I'm sorry,' I said, 'what is this all about?'

'Sis,' Ultan said, 'Papa has had some threats made to him.' I looked at them. 'What . . .?'

Tommy cleared his throat. 'I put no store in it, it was drink talking. These things happen. And the other members, to a man, were furious – furious! I would not be surprised if the member in question is drummed out.'

'Is our front door drink talking?' Annie demanded. 'Or our gate posts? I wonder what your members have to say about that!'

'Please stop!' I said. 'Very well, I know I have been unavailable – but tell me. Ultan?'

Ultan sighed. He looked suddenly older and for the first time I noticed a run of stubble on his face.

'A member in the club accused Papa of passing information to the Castle,' he said.

'His name is Roche, he's a common sort,' Tommy said, 'not a gentleman.'

'It happened during lunch, when the club was full, isn't that so, Papa?' Ultan said.

'They jumped to their feet, almost to a man, and shouted him down,' Tommy said. 'It was most gratifying.'

'You are a simpleton!' Annie cried.

'Mother!'

'I won't be shushed by you or anyone!' she shouted at Ultan, her face enraged. 'Can you all not see what is happening?'

'It is upsetting,' Tommy said, 'but we have been spared out here up to now. In town they see these outrages, and far worse, every other day.'

'It is what is happening, Mother,' Ultan said. 'Some of them are just common villains.'

'Perhaps they are, but they're right,' Annie said, suddenly deflated, 'we should leave, we don't belong here anymore.'

'Annie, love, don't say that,' Tommy said.

'I want to go,' she said.

'But you've lived here all your life,' Tommy said. 'You were born in this cottage.'

'But then I married you, didn't I?' Annie began to cry. 'People are leaving every week by the boatload. You have family over there, Tom. We won't be any different.'

'We can go if you want, if you want,' he said, 'of course we can go if you want.'

'We're done here,' she sobbed.

I felt ashamed that I had been hiding my head whilst our little world was so convulsed. My father was dabbing at Annie's eyes and speaking softly to her. Why, oh why, I wondered, did we all have to leave our country in order to be happy?

'Papa, what did this Roche person say?' I asked.

Tommy's lovely face was split with bother, but as always, it wasn't for himself.

'He was confused. He never holds his drink.'

'Please, Papa—'

'I expect he was afraid after what happened last week that he will be next,' Tommy said.

'He's a Shinner,' Ultan said grimly. 'His cousin was shot in the GPO, or so he says.'

'So he has a grievance,' Tommy said, 'understandably. No one condones what happened—'

'I've heard that Roche was once a Collins man,' Ultan said, 'but that they had to be shut of him because of his drinking.'

'What exactly did he say?' I asked.

'He said ... he said there was a spy in the club ... and that ...' Tommy faltered. 'That ...'

'He pointed at your father!' Annie cried. 'Someone who's been loading him into hansom cabs and looking after him—'

'Papa?'

Tommy sagged, too weary to go on.

'He more or less accused Papa of being the cause of the arrests last week,' Ultan said. 'Of tipping them off that Mr Holly and the others would be in the club.'

'But surely they knew where Mr Holly lived if they wanted him?' I asked.

'The Castle like to make an example,' Ultan said, 'to send a message. They wanted to humiliate Mr Holly in public.'

'It's all over,' Annie sobbed.

'Mother ...'

As I leaned over to comfort her I saw with a shock that tufts of her hair were missing and her white scalp could be seen.

'This Roche creature also said Papa was a regular visitor to Marlborough Barracks,' Ultan was saying.

Annie sat up. 'But you haven't been in there for at least a year!' she cried. 'How could he say that?'

Ultan and I looked at each other fearfully.

'But then,' said Tommy, as if with a sudden breeze, 'Doctor Bradshaw took the floor and made a speech on my behalf worthy of Gladstone. You should have heard him! Told

Roche he'd be better off in another club. The other members pounded their tables in support. "Tommy Raven is our true friend!" Doctor Bradshaw shouted. "He belongs here!" And do you know what happened next? Every gentleman rose to his feet and applauded me. "To our dear friend, Tommy Raven!" they called out as one.' Tommy smiled brightly. 'I think, apart from my wedding day, it was the happiest moment of my life.'

32

On Tuesday morning, just after breakfast, when Tommy and Ultan had gone to work, as Annie and I were baking in the kitchen and Martha was trying to remove paint from the tiles outside the front door, we heard a car stopping on the road. My mother caught my arm.

'Oh, God.'

I could hear heavy feet on the step. Freddy was emptying his lungs. Annie stood by the range, trembling and wide-eyed.

'It's all right ma'am, it's only Father Shipsey,' said Martha from the hall.

My heart was in my throat.

'Well, well, well. Good morning to you, the ladies Raven, and may God bless this house,' the priest boomed and came in.

I could not recall him ever visiting us before, a fact for which I was grateful. He wore his biretta and black boots with bulbous toecaps. His clever eyes took in my mother standing with her hands clasped either side of her face, and me.

'Father,' Martha said and curtseyed.

Annie was caught between her obligations to hospitality and, as was I, a new fear: that the priest had come to deliver bad news, although his demeanour suggested such an outcome was unlikely. I then saw two men, whose car he must have travelled in, loitering outside.

'I'll put the kettle on,' Martha said.

'Come in, Father,' Annie said, somewhat unnecessarily. She looked outside. 'Will these gentlemen . . . ?'

'Ah, not at all,' Father Shipsey said, 'it's only Kevin Dunne and his son, they're doing a bit of work in the church so when I heard—'

The men, one white headed, one young, smiled and nodded. The older one doffed his cap.

'They've even brought white spirit to clean your gate posts,' said Father Shipsey as if nothing could escape him. His dark hair lay thickly beneath its flat shine.

'That's very kind,' Annie said, although we were both wondering how word had travelled so quickly. 'Now, Father, a cup of tea? Rose and I have just baked some lovely scones.'

'Do you know something?' He glanced towards the kitchen, where we all knew Martha was listening, and inhaled the sweet baking aroma. 'As much as I would go to Purgatory for your baking, ladies, this morning I will resist. You see, it's not often I get to walk along the seafront here – but I'd be honoured if you and Miss Raven would join me. Just until Kevin and his son have fixed things up.' As if we had both accepted the proposal, he turned and walked out. 'You won't be long, will you, Kevin?'

'About half an hour, Father.'

'Very well!' He went to stand outside the front door, face to the sky, inhaling.

We found our hats, and Annie had to change her shoes and fetch her shawl.

'Can I let you into a little secret?' The priest was now over by the sea wall. 'When I was a garsoon and we lived in Killester, my father, God be merciful to him, used bring me down here on his bicycle after school for a swim.'

'That's a good one, right enough, Father,' Annie said.

He began to walk at a good pace towards Clontarf, hands clasped behind him.

'You might well have seen me down here in those times, Mrs Raven. I'll let you into another secret. Sometimes, if my older brother had borrowed the bicycle – to go caddying in Portmarnock – we'd sneak through Irrawaddy for a short cut to get here. Ah dear, oh dear, those were the days.'

Annie was fighting for breath as she tried to keep level, flattered to be seen with the priest in public, still trying to fathom, as was I, the purpose of this excursion. I let them go ahead; I could not bring myself to walk alongside him.

'Dreadfully sad about poor Jerome Holly,' he said with a backward glance to me. 'He wasn't from my parish, of course, but I was at the Mass yesterday. Biggest funeral I can remember. A lovely family.'

I kept looking straight ahead.

'They say he would have been a leading man for Ireland in the coming times,' Father Shipsey said. 'In the new Ireland.'

'What do you think will happen, Father?' Annie asked, deaf to the implication of what she had just heard.

'Hard to know, Mrs Raven, hard to know. All I can say is, this cannot go on. I had Tans in the grounds of the church the day before yesterday and I won't offend your ears by describing their behaviour.'

'Goodness, Father, what did you do?' Annie asked.

'I went back into the church and I prayed to Our Lord to

262

have mercy on their souls,' Father Shipsey said. 'Never forget that the man crucified beside our dear Lord was a thief, and that Jesus promised to meet him that day in Paradise. When I came back out, their tenders were gone.'

The Howth-bound tram passed us, its upper deck flowering with families on their way to the beach.

'I prayed too this morning when I heard the news of what happened to you last night,' Father Shipsey said, 'and I asked the Lord to show you the way forward in your moment of need.'

Annie glanced severely at me, as if I might blurt out what she had said about leaving Ireland.

'That was when the most wonderful idea came to me!' The priest chuckled happily. 'Everyone in Sutton knows that Mr Raven walks as far as the cross to meet you after Mass on Sundays, ma'am. What if, I thought, what if he was to go that extra little bit and come to Mass himself?'

Annie halted, frowned deeply and looked up at Father Shipsey. 'Why?'

'Because,' said the priest, 'if Mr Raven were seen to be a part of our Catholic community, I think it would demonstrate his bona-fides to a certain element. They would start to see him as one of their own, someone on his knees beside them, reciting the Confiteor. It would make all the difference.'

'But . . .' Annie stammered, 'my husband is a Presbyterian.'

'All the more commendable that the lambs who have lost their way return to the fold,' Father Shipsey said genially. 'I can arrange a course of instruction, and although he will not be able to receive Holy Communion until he has satisfied the bishop of his pure intentions, Mr Raven will be perceived by the parish in a completely different light.

He will, I assure you, get the same welcome as the Prodigal Son of whom Our Lord speaks with such affection. He will be embraced as a son, a brother and a father. He will be cherished, Mrs Raven, and you and your family, ever faithful servants of the Lord, will reap the benefits.'

33

I spent that afternoon preparing my mind for the interview next day in Clery's. Annie had gone out to Sutton, to Mrs Wilder's, and Martha had gone home. The priest's intervention had left me with a feeling of deep revulsion. He had made no effort to distinguish between those who had daubed our door and his own parishioners, since the whole thrust of his suggestion had been that if Tommy became a Catholic our troubles would be over. That he could barter a man's long-held faith in such a blatant way made me loathe him deeply. His intervention had left Annie confused and unhappy. Tommy's quiet observance of his own faith, whilst accepting that we, his children, would be brought up in another, was one of the few issues on which my father had seemed to put his opinion first.

I was also confused, for whilst the clergy had spoken out from their pulpits against murder on either side, this move by Father Shipsey sounded as if the church had suddenly recognised where its future lay. The sentiments that Chink had expressed so forcefully to me were the ones now prevailing, or so it seemed.

Freddy lay in shade, asleep, occasionally twitching as he dealt with a dream. Despite what had nearly befallen the dog out in Portmarnock, I would have given anything to relive that day again, Tans or no Tans, and to once more haul Chink from the sea. Although I now accepted that our love was as much victim of the new politics as human life, another part of me knew with certainty that his regard for me was unchanged. I might never be able to prove it, of course, and neither might he, but it did provide me with a little pool of comfort into which to step when desolation tried to overwhelm me.

Our garden that afternoon was abundant in all that nature could provide. Growth burst vigorously and in a rainbow of colours from flowerbeds, the vegetables, gooseberries, the apple tree, the meadow, the grasses and hedges, the distant woods. When I shut my eyes I could hear bees, and the light summer wind, and the sea; and smell lavender, meadow, pine, rosemary, roses and mint.

Freddy woke up and growled. A step on the gravel; the slap of the letterbox. A single white envelope was addressed to me in a hand I did not recognise. I brought a cup of tea and a slice of Martha's apple cake outside. I blinked as I read the letter.

'Dear Miss Raven,

    Excuse my forwardness, but it is essential I see you immediately in order to convey an urgent piece of information. May I please present myself at your house in Sutton when I finish work tomorrow – that is Wednesday?

Your obedient servant,
Rodolfo Saddler.'

34

On Wednesday morning, my mother said, 'Would you like to walk with me as far as Mrs Wilder's?'

Although my head was now full of that afternoon's interview, I agreed. She seldom made such requests of me, but something about her – the way she had looked at me – made me realise this was important. With Freddy in tow we took the tram to Sutton, and then walked towards the railway station, pausing every other minute, as was usual, so that Annie could regain her breath.

I smiled again as I thought of Rudy Saddler on his knees before me in the Phoenix Park; his begging eyes, his almost comical anguish. He had probably heard of my new circumstances from Ultan. He didn't give up easily, Mr Rudy Saddler. The evening before, I had posted a reply to his letter, saying that he would be welcome to pay me a visit, some time in the future, but that Wednesday would not be suitable since I was going to Clery's with my father to be interviewed for a position.

On Wilder's Lane, which crossed the Great Northern line, Freddy was kept on his lead, for he had once chased a rabbit down the railway tracks half way to Howth.

'Today's a big day,' Annie said, 'but remember there are other employers too.'

All at once Clery's seemed the only safe bet in my life.

'I know they look after their staff there wonderfully,' Annie went on, 'but in case today does not meet your expectations, you will always have other choices, Rose.'

'But I will have a pension in Clery's,' I heard myself say.

The gates were closed against us. Freddy whined with impatience to be nearer the burrows across the road. My mother sighed, and for a moment, to my alarm, it looked as if all the wind had left her.

'I want you to know that I have no intention of bothering your poor father with Father Shipsey's nonsense,' she said. 'I know what you think. I saw your face yesterday. You needn't worry.'

She was a curious woman, my mother, for despite all I knew about her, she still had the capacity to surprise me.

'I'm very glad,' I said. 'I thought it was . . .'

'Say it.'

'Repulsive. He wanted to take away Papa's identity. It was cowardly and sly, just like Father Shipsey.'

'Oh, I've heard worse, and the priest may mean well, but you're right,' Annie said. 'Your Papa has very few moments he can truly call his own, and going to his own church is one of them.'

'What will we do?' I asked. 'I mean, if the situation gets worse?'

'That's what I want to talk to you about.' The train suddenly burst upon us, and the air was dense with smoke. The level-crossing man pushed the gates open. 'About what needs to be done,' Annie said and took my arm. 'I've been to see a doctor in Clontarf, someone recommended by Mrs Wilder.'

'Why? Why do you need to see a doctor?'

Her hand tapped her breastbone. 'I've been feeling out of sorts this good while.'

'Mother?'

'More discomfort than pain, but, I've known now for some time ...'

'Known what?'

She stopped and planted her feet the way I so well knew. 'I want you to take your father to his family in England, before something happens to him here. No, Rose! You listen now, please! I've already suggested it to him and he has not dismissed me. He'll do as I ask. I put it to him that it would be a reconnaissance mission, he's a soldier, he understands how these things work. But when you get there I want you to keep him in England, out of harm's way. Until things here blow over.'

My head went dizzy.

'I know this means you will have to delay taking up your new position, but you will always find someone to employ you, whether here or elsewhere. All they have to do is talk to you for two seconds to know how precious you are.'

I could scarcely get the words out. 'And you?'

'I will be fine. You don't need to worry about me.'

'But why won't you go with him?' I asked. 'Mother?'

Her face was small and her eyes had grown distant. 'He was a kind man, the doctor. He didn't want to upset me, but he had little choice, I'm afraid.'

'What?' I shouted.

'Rose—'

'Please,' I said, 'don't do this—'

'He said,' she said slowly, 'that for me Christmas is a very long way off.'

I was conscious, ridiculously so, that Freddy had disappeared, that I must have let go of his lead, but I didn't care. I didn't care if I never saw Freddy again.

'Come here,' she said and hugged me, and for the first time I realised how much she had reduced. 'I want to see it out here, Rose,' she whispered, 'which is why I can't go with him. Everything I know and understand is here. My house, my garden. My church, even my priest, for all his faults. Do you know, I've never in my life been outside the province of Leinster?'

'Does Papa know your . . . diagnosis?'

Her normally sharp face had been softened by her new reality. 'No, and you mustn't tell him, because if you do he will stay and if he stays I fear what will happen. He has many years ahead of him. I can't allow them to take that.'

'He won't go without you.'

'He will if he thinks I'll follow him in a week,' Annie said with all her old authority. 'And if you go with him.'

The scent of woodbine suddenly seemed so insincere.

'Who will look after you?'

'Ultan,' Annie said brightly. 'Ultan will be here.'

I heard the squeak of a gate and saw Mrs Wilder emerge from her front garden and peer up at us, sunlight bouncing from her spectacles.

'I want you to promise me, Rose,' Annie said. 'Promise me you'll take Papa away.'

'Mother, please—'

'You will let me die happy if you promise you will do that,' she said. 'It's all I'm asking.'

I could not stop my tears.

'Your dog, Annie!' Mrs Wilder was calling. 'He's run Poody up a tree!'

'Rose.'

'I . . . I promise.'

'Thank you,' she said. 'But don't waste any time about it.'

'Annie!'

'Coming, Mrs Wilder, I'm coming!' She smiled at me. 'Go on, I'll look after Freddy. You don't want to keep Papa waiting.'

35

I had the notion that if I sat at the front of the tram, on the open, upper deck, and allowed the wind to scour my head, that all my problems would be blown away. I wondered if by remaining on the tram forever I could defeat reality, as if constant motion could defy all the many circumstances whose conclusions were closing in. I had left Martha cleaning out the larder.

'You look lovely! What fools Clery's would be not to snap you up,' she said.

I was wearing my blue dress, with its sprays of white flowers, and I'd decked my hat with red ribbons. 'Thank you, Martha.'

'By the way, when you meet the boss, tell him his lettuce needs picking or it will go to seed,' she said.

I said I would, although much later, when I thought about it, I could not recall telling her I was meeting Papa.

At Dollymount, if I looked back, a heat haze made Howth shimmer, like the biblical apparitions we had been taught in school. I wondered for how much longer I would be able to enjoy that sight, the whitecaps to the horizon, the lovely curve of the bay, or whether in my father's land-bound English county I could grow to love scenery that lacked the sea.

My acceptance of the position was complete. I would never pick oranges or lemons from a tree. I would never pick up a Baedeker and go. My parents, after a lifetime, would be forced apart. All the little signs I had seen in Annie over recent times, when put together, now seemed obvious. I should have been the one to stay at home and nurse her, as would soon be required, whilst Ultan took Tommy to the safety of Leicestershire, but that was not how the affections in our family had fallen. My guilt at the prospect of leaving my mother was now outweighed by my consternation for what might happen to Tommy. He had to get out. Ireland was lost to men like Tommy Raven.

New sandbags for an army post marked a corner in Clontarf. Scruffy, bare-headed troops, the sign of the Black and Tans, lounged by the kerbside. The idea of leaving all this trouble behind, even if that included my unwell mother and my broken dreams, and starting again in England was suddenly appealing. I would have Tommy, the easiest of companions, to myself, and for all I knew, he might even be happier over there.

I would of course go through with the appointment in Clery's, all at once meaningless; but Tommy's heart was set on it, and Sackville Street was not the place to tell him of our new plans. The tram trundled in from Clontarf just as its companion vehicle, in plum and terracotta livery, approached, bound for Howth. As the two upper decks passed each other by, I stared across the moving divide. In the midsection, Rudy Saddler was sitting above an advertisement for Swan Vestas.

'Rudy? Rudy!'

He saw me and leapt to his feet. He waved his arms and shouted something, but we were by then fifty yards apart and with every revolution the gap grew wider.

36

I had taken a limited-stop tram, which arrived with great efficiency in Amiens Street. It was half-past one. I was early. I disembarked and walked up busy Talbot Street. I had no doubt that Rudy Saddler was on his way out to see me in Sutton, despite my letter telling him I would not be there. The sight of him had irritated me, which I knew was unfair, but hearing once more of his undying love for me was the last thing I needed. Soldiers, in this case regular barracks troops with cinched belts and helmets, walked three abreast down the centre of the street.

I made my way with reluctance towards the Pillar. Up ahead, alongside women selling flowers from their barrows, the snout of a machine gun was pointing out at me from sandbags. A wave of weakness swept me, and I wondered how I could go on. I suddenly realised that I needed to bring my father home to Sutton straight away; that he had to be told about Annie's illness; that the charade of an interview was the last thing I needed and that Tommy had to be persuaded of the stark danger of his position.

The flower women were laughing happily when I reached them. Without warning, behind them, from the direction of Sackville Street, Rudy Saddler was hastening towards me, his face distracted.

37

I leaned on one of the flower barrows.

'Miss Raven—' He was out of breath. 'Thank goodness.'

'I thought I just passed you going out to Sutton,' I said weakly.

'Yes, you did, but when I saw you I jumped off at Dollymount and caught the next tram back in,' Rudy said. 'I've already been down to Clery's because I thought that's where you would be.'

'It's where I'm going, Mr Saddler,' I said wearily, 'to meet my father.'

'Listen...' He caught my elbow. 'Excuse us,' he said to flower women and steered me between them, to the inside of the footpath, where, in a miasma of scent, their stocks of flowers were planted in deep buckets. 'Miss Raven, I have an important message for you. From Chink Holly.'

I shook my head. 'I think Mr Holly has already communicated himself to me very clearly.'

'Forget that, he had no choice,' Rudy said. 'His father's death means the people his family consort with are out for revenge. Chink was only protecting you.'

'A strange way he has of showing it,' I said, even though glorious relief surged through me.

'He tracked me down,' Rudy said. 'He has told me to tell you as a matter of the greatest urgency that your dear father must go into hiding.'

I felt my knees give way. He caught me, and then helped me to a doorstep beside the railings.

'Oh, Miss Raven, I know this must come as a shock—'

'It doesn't,' I said and tried to regain my feet, 'it's not a shock.'

One of the flower women approached with a glass of water.

'It's the heat, love,' she said, 'it's never been this bad.'

Rudy dropped to one knee. I wanted nothing more than to close my eyes and sleep.

'What . . . did he say, exactly?' I asked.

'It seems that a certain faction hold your father responsible for what befell Mr Holly senior. I know they're wrong, and so does Chink, but these are men who once decided will not be diverted.'

'Papa was the one who got him released,' I said feebly. 'He went up to the barracks himself . . .'

Rudy winced. 'That is the problem. He was seen going in there.'

'To speak on behalf of Mr Holly!'

'I know, I know. But to some people that proves the opposite,' Rudy said, and looked around nervously, 'and there's no persuading them.'

I knew I had only one big effort left. 'He is meeting me outside Clery's shortly . . .'

'Yes – but Chink says he mustn't go there,' Rudy said.

'How does Chink know where my father is going?'

'I don't know,' Rudy said, 'but you should return to Sutton now. I'll find your dear father and warn him.'

I stared. 'You?'

'Of course.'

'But ... you don't know him,' I said, 'you've never met him.'

'Describe him to me.'

'Oh, please!' I jumped up and began to hasten towards North Earl Street.

'Miss Raven! Rose!'

'Please leave me be.' I was struggling to breathe. 'Please.'

'Walk, don't run,' Rudy said, 'don't draw attention to yourself. Walk as normal.'

I walked, although I could not feel my feet touching the pavement, nor hear the people around me, nor see anything but the sky glaring at me through the gibbets of ruined buildings on Sackville Street.

'If you point him out to me ...' Rudy said.

Scaffolding rose from the street where Clery's had stood before the Rising. We hurried across Sackville Place, with its abandoned buildings, and turned down Lower Abbey Street. The Metropolitan Hall, from which Clery's now traded, was less than a hundred yards away. All the buildings at this end of Lower Abbey Street were smoke-charred, derelict and in ruins. A few carters walked their horses up the centre of the street. To one side, I could see a lad selling newspapers, leaning by a wall.

All would be well, so long as I got to Papa. I tried to compose myself so that when he saw me he would not be startled. I would introduce Rudy, and then the three of us would leave together. Back to the Pillar, where we could get a tram home immediately. Not Rudy, of course, since he would need to return to work. But home, in his house in Sutton, Papa would be safe.

He wasn't there. I looked in both directions. A makeshift sign – Clery & Co – was tacked over the door of the hall. I could see the busy space into which all the commerce of the great store had been squeezed, dozens of people and long tables of boxes overflowing with fabrics.

'He's not here,' I said with a great rush of relief.

Two men walked out of Clery's, both wearing straw boaters. When they saw me they smiled, and one of them tipped the rim of his hat. I felt myself seize on a new assurance. Nothing awry was in motion. This was normal. Perhaps Tommy had received Chink's warning himself, indirectly, from someone in his club, from one of the men who had stood and applauded him. To our dear friend, Tommy Raven! Or perhaps his duties had been such that he had not been able to take the time off to come and meet me.

'He's not here,' I said again, even as I wondered what to do. I would have to walk up to the club and tell him of the threat. Perhaps Rudy would come with me and persuade him. I turned and was about to suggest this, but Rudy was peering down the street.

'Look,' he said.

From the corner of Marlborough Street a shock of bright red hair was approaching. I had to smile. He had stepped out into the thoroughfare. He waved both his arms in the air and I waved back. But he continued to flail rather than to wave. And Rudy said, 'Rose!'

I turned and my father was standing there, a smile of good-mannered interest on his face.

'Good afternoon,' he said.

'Papa!'

'Rose!'

Tommy frowned and looked over my shoulder.

'Rose! Run!' I could not understand why Chink was shouting that. 'Now! Run!'

'What is—' I began and then saw the newspaper lad approaching, his cap pulled low, his arm crooked, as if he was meant to be holding a stack of his papers but they had fallen out. His lopsided walk. He was still a dozen paces off.

I said, 'Eddie?'

Eddie Kidney eyes were enlarged. 'Sorry, Rose.'

'Oh, no—'

The expression on Tommy's face as he stepped around me, towards Eddie Kidney, must have been the face he used so many, many times in the mess in Marlborough Barracks late at night when an officer needed to be reminded gently of his behaviour; likewise in the club, with gentlemen whose need for yet another port was finally outweighed by the necessity to persuade them to go home. It was a face I remembered from my childhood. It had said so many things at once to me. It had said, I will always respect you, just so long as you respect me, but there are certain rules here which I am obliged to enforce; and we can work this through together, if we try, for nothing is to be gained by adversity; if you like I can pick you up, as so, and kiss your forehead, as so, and dry your tears, as so, and so, and we can then go forward into the light.

'Papa!'

Chink was almost there, but Eddie Kidney, his arm now straightening as he threw, was within a few yards of us, and Chink's hair was on fire with the sun, as Tommy said something I never heard, and Rudy Saddler caught me with a charge of his shoulder and hurled me in through the glass

279

door of Clery's as my ears went dead. All I saw was Rudy's full mouth, open as he screamed, and his startled, dark, dark eyes without their spectacles, as all the air behind us became fragmented light.

Epilogue

Transcript of an address by Dr Patrick Lee to a Symposium held at University College Dublin on 6 December 2021 to mark the Centenary of the Signing of the Anglo-Irish Treaty

Thank you all for braving the elements this evening to participate in these centenary events.

My name is Paddy Lee and I'm an associate professor in the School of History here in UCD. In the spring of 1980, long before my time in this eminent department, a package of papers arrived here by post, addressed to the then head of department, the late Arthur O'Reilly. These papers had been sent to UCD by the Dublin auctioneer whose firm, the year before, had overseen the disposal of the convent of the Eternal Sisters of Saint Bernardino in Raheny. We have been unable to ascertain the circumstances surrounding the discovery of these papers in the convent – neither the auctioneering firm nor the convent now exist – but we must assume that whoever came upon the package must have opened it and perused its contents before resealing it and deciding that it belonged in UCD. We are fortunate that they did.

Over the next thirty-five years, these papers remained here in UCD. It has been suggested that Professor O'Reilly took personal charge of the project, but if he did, there is no evidence of this work. Six years ago, in early 2015, Professor John Kiely, head of the School of History, came upon these papers in our archives. He asked me to see what the package contained.

After more than five years of work and research, these papers were published earlier this year under the title 'Freedom Is A Land I Cannot See'. It was a title which everyone on our team felt reflected the core of this most unusual story.

The package was bound with twine and consisted of outer layers of newsprint and a single inner layer of kitchen grease-proof paper which, when removed, revealed loose pages in the form of a typescript. The containing newspaper, the *Irish Independent* dated Monday 17 October 1925, apart from its outer page, was in very good condition, which suggests that the typescript was wrapped in this newspaper on this date in 1925, or if not, then shortly thereafter. The pages themselves, although in reasonable condition, had been assembled haphazardly. As we now know, the author of the typescript, who purports to be a Miss Rose Raven, claims to have been blind, and although this fact could not have been known by us before we started, when it was established it became apparent that blindness may well have accounted for the presentation of the contents.

Large sections of the typescript were indecipherable. On many pages the typewriter ribbon had become stuck, or had just run out, but the typist had continued, as if unaware, leaving mere indentations on the otherwise blank paper. In other cases, the spacing was often irregular where the spacing bar had either not been used or had jammed. Our team was confronted with a typescript that was on over three-quarters of its pages either blank or largely illegible. A sighted person would not, we surmised, have produced a document in this condition. Furthermore, we concluded that the state of the text meant that in all probability Rose Raven had worked alone and had shown her work to no one.

Over a period of twelve months, members of our team used pencils to carefully shade over the indentations on the blank pages and in that way brought most of the words back to life, one by one. Equally challenging was deciphering sentences where the spacing was non-existent. This was achieved by photocopying the original pages and then carefully extracting sentences from the run of letters. These tasks, although extremely time consuming, were nonetheless rewarding. By early 2018 we had completed the first part of our task.

Our attention then turned to the contents of the papers. The fundamental question we posed ourselves was, who was Rose Raven? Our team became a squad of amateur detectives. We set out to find her.

We began in Saint Fintan's cemetery in Sutton, where Rose is so precise about the location of her parents', and later, Ultan's graves. We went there sure of walking right up to the plot described, and believing that her name had most likely joined that of Tommy, Annie and her brother. No such graves exist, either at the so-called denominational corner of the path in the old part of the cemetery, or anywhere else in Saint Fintan's. On no headstone, or indeed anywhere in the burial records of Fingal County Council burial records, is there a mention of anyone by the name of Raven. Rose gives her mother's name as Duffy, but that too was of no help. The name Ultan Raven is not common: but no one of that name is recorded for Saint Fintan's in the years 1910 to 1940.

When I read Rose's story I came away deeply impressed by the intelligence and determination of this young woman. She was someone who defied the most daunting odds at a time of unprecedented upheaval in Ireland's final epic journey to become a sovereign state and in the first two years of that new state's existence. If someone of Rose's acumen and resolve had decided to conceal her identity during an era when it was comparatively easy to disappear then we knew we were engaged in a battle of wits.

We turned to the General Register Office, scrutinising births, marriages and deaths for the period 1875 to 1921. No one matching Rose or any of her family could be found. And it was with a mounting sense of the inevitable that we extended our search to the Saddler family of Curzon Street, the Holly family of Howth, Agnes Daly, Mr and Mrs Barry, a journalist named Harry Deegan and a garage proprietor in Kilmainham by the name of Potterton. No matches were found. Nor could we find an Eddie Kidney. Neither did it greatly surprise us at this stage when neither the records of the Institute of Chartered Accountants in Ireland, nor those of Craig Gardiner & Company, mentioned a Mr Matthew Fleming. The same dead-ends applied to a parish priest in Sutton named Shipsey, Martha Merry of Baldoyle, and a secretary, Miss Doreen Longley. An employee of Dublin Castle named Charles Sinnott was not among the many slain in that employment in 1920; no one called Sinnott had lived in Dartry that we could find.

Further searches of the Land Registry, the Registry of Deeds, the National Archives of Ireland and the records of Dublin Corporation yielded similar results. No trace could be found of a property in Sutton called Nan's Cottage. The same went for records of the Royal Dublin Fusiliers, the Dublin Tram Company and the files of the Queen's Own Cavalry stationed in Marlborough Barracks, Dublin in the period 1900 to 1921.

Although the census of 1911 was not followed by another until 1926 due to political instability in Ireland, we searched both without success for any of the people mentioned. We went through all baptismal and school registers for the Sutton, Howth and Baldoyle areas for the period, and the records for the Church of Ireland. Rose Raven, Tommy, Annie and Ultan, Rudy and Chink had all disappeared, exactly, we presume, as Rose had intended they should.

Notwithstanding these setbacks, there remained details in Rose's story that persuaded us to continue our search. We now narrowed our enquiry to those aspects of her story that she had not tried, or bothered, to hide, or that were otherwise irrefutable.

No question but that a convent and school were established around 1890 in Raheny by the Eternal Sisters of Saint Bernardino, an order of nuns whose mother house can be found in Siena, Italy. Rose claims to have attended school with these nuns in Raheny, and her typescript, as we know, was discovered in the convent during the dispersal in 1979–80. How her papers came to be in the convent is unclear. Rose's antipathy to religion, as stated by her, makes it unlikely in our view that she became a nun. The mother house of the Eternal Sisters of Saint Bernardino in Siena was destroyed by fire during the Allied invasion in 1944 and all records for the worldwide community before this date were lost. Although the details of the sisters in Raheny are recorded in both the census of 1926 and 1936, neither could throw light on our search.

The references to a landowning, titled family by the name of Barnmere, whose daughter is said to have died by drowning in London in 1924, intrigued us. Although no demesne called Irrawaddy existed, Saint Anne's, a manor on five hundred acres situated between Raheny and Clontarf, was the home of the titled Ardilaun family, wealthy descendants of Sir Arthur Guinness, the famous brewer. The original estate, part of which is now a public park, had many of the features attributed by Rose to Irrawaddy, including a magnificent residence, rose gardens and tree-lined walks. It is more than likely that Rose was familiar with Saint Anne's, and lived not far from the estate.

Rose's references to the Tin Church in Sutton are accurate. A chapel-of-ease in Sutton, known locally as the Tin Church, was built in 1912 and was not replaced by the present church until 1973. It is more than likely that the references to the Tin Church were written by someone familiar with the locality.

But what of the alleged famine conditions in the west of Ireland in 1924, a central part of Rose's story? Famine is a word that occupies a particularly sensitive place in the Irish psyche. Famine caused the deaths by starvation in the mid-nineteenth century of at least one million Irish people and the displacement and forced emigration of two and a half million more. This national tragedy ranks alongside the Holocaust as one of the most appalling societal eradications in human history.

Considerable work has been published, not least by distinguished members of this School of History, on the economic and other challenges that faced the new Free State during the Civil War (1922–23) and immediately afterwards. Nonetheless, the threat of famine in 1924 is not something I was aware of. We researched government papers and newspaper reports for the period 1923–26 and were surprised by what we found.

Atrocious weather conditions are recorded for much of 1923–24, especially west of the River Shannon. Widespread flooding led to the abandonment of turf cutting. Animals died for want of fodder and the potato harvest all but failed. In its edition of 20 August 1924 the Meath Chronicle reported *"a famine condition [in the west of Ireland] is imminent as bad as 1847"*. Through the early autumn of 1924, newspapers that published details of the worsening situation included The Freeman's Journal, the Meath Chronicle, The Southern Star and the Connacht Tribune. The Freeman's Journal illustrated the depths of the crisis when reporting from Connemara in late 1924: *"75% of the people had now no potatoes, their chief diet for the last 2 months, and the harvest prospects were never worse in living memory. There is no employment."* By October 1924, people in Connemara were reported to be surviving on seaweed and shellfish.

On 11 February 1925, the Irish cabinet reviewed a telegram received from the editor of the Boston Globe newspaper seeking official clarification on *whether there was a famine in Ireland.* Senator James Douglas, who in 1922 had been appointed by Michael Collins to chair the committee which would draft the Constitution of the Irish Free State, had attached the following note to the Boston Globe telegram: *"The present propaganda in the United States, alleging that there is a famine, will do great harm to our credit in every way unless it is countered".* [Our emphasis]

The crisis facing an impoverished, inexperienced nation struggling to find its feet in the aftermath of a bitter civil war must have seemed overwhelming. Famine, so deeply embedded in the Irish consciousness, would represent the ultimate failure. In Dublin, the instinct of the government was to downplay the impending crisis at all costs while at the same time reacting to it by practical means. £500,000 in direct emergency relief – in today's money more than £30 million – was provided, as coal supplies were shipped into the west of Ireland to replace the saturated turf. At the same time, speaking in the Dáil, the Minister for Agriculture, Mr P.J. Hogan, asserted: *"There is no abnormal distress in the West this year. I say that definitely and deliberately."* In such a dire atmosphere of calamity and the need for secrecy, it is not difficult to understand how a self-appointed protector of the national interest such as the fanatical Detective Sergeant Melody could run amok.

We began to form a hypothesis. In March, 1924, Rudy is killed by Melody while trying to hand over forbidden information about the threatened famine to an American reporter. Rose, grieving, shocked and blind, is terrified that Melody will now turn to her as Rudy's accomplice, and arrest her, perhaps fearing she may be hiding further documents. He has already threatened to have her flogged. She can no longer trust Martha Merry, someone who has betrayed her and whom she must despise. All Rose's loved ones are dead. Who does she turn to? To the sanctuary of the nuns in Raheny, to the Mother Superior who has long admired her. Rose sells her cottage, settles the proceeds on the nuns (a course of action she has already threatened) and moves into the convent, some time in late 1924 or early 1925.

Rose makes no reference to a typewriter in Nan's Cottage, but there must have been one in the convent: she tells us she had been taught to type there as a schoolgirl by Mother Mary Superior. We can thus fairly assume that she did not begin to write her story until she moved to Raheny.

She begins to write, knowing that if she does not record what has happened, and quickly, then no one will. She starts with what is freshest in her mind, the appalling circumstances that led to Rudy's death. And when she has told Rudy's story, she realises she must then tell the story of her love for Chink, which explains why her story is presented in reverse chronological order.

As she writes, feverishly, page after page, showing her work to no one, the spectre of famine in the west is still powerfully present. The danger to Ireland's credit looms large and dictates the actions of government. *And Melody is still out there, trying to stop the secret getting out.* Rose sets down what has happened, unmindful of absent ribbon or jammed typewriter keys. But she must wrap a cloak of secrecy around all the people in her book, herself included, so she changes all the names and places. In this way she cannot be accused of compliance or sedition should Melody come along and discover what she is about.

So who was Detective Sergeant Melody? By now it goes without saying that no one of this name could be found in the records of the time. And yet, some important references crop up in Rose's story when Melody's name is mentioned. The tailor, Mr Barry, for example, when he visits Rose, claims that Melody was "drummed out of Oriel House with blood on his hands". Later on, in Rudy's account to Rose of meeting his father, Sergeant Saddler, in the latter's snow-covered allotment, the sergeant says of Melody, that "[a]fter the Treaty he was part of a gang down in Oriel House that went out and murdered Irregulars". During that same discussion in the allotment, Sergeant Saddler tells Rudy that Melody "has a wife and children in Phibsboro. He owns his house there."

A policeman by the name of Melody may not have existed, but Oriel House certainly did. Much has been written on this subject. Situated on the corner of Westland Row and Fenian Street in central Dublin, between early 1922 and late 1923 Oriel House housed a lethal quasi-police force tasked with eliminating enemies of the new Free State. In the first frantic and chaotic months of the new nation, it is estimated that at least twenty-five men opposed to the Treaty and denying the legitimacy of the elected government were killed extra-judicially by operatives from Oriel House. In November 1923 this murder squad was hastily disbanded. Some members of Oriel House emigrated to escape the retaliation of Republican Irregulars[1], and some were hurried into the Dublin Metropolitan Police. On 15 December 1926, the Freeman's Journal carried a report that a 'well-known DMP detective sergeant was shot dead in his house in Phibsboro' the day before. His killers were thought to be 'Irregulars who harboured a grudge against the officer.' The paper reported that a manhunt was underway. The identity of the deceased was being withheld to 'ensure the safety of the family' whilst his killers remained at large. We could find no further references to this case, despite our extensive searches.

A final word on the threatened famine of 1924. Although a real threat of famine existed, thankfully it never materialised. And while only a small number of people died from lack of food, hundreds of thousands west of the Shannon had to endure hunger and serious malnutrition. Much to the relief of government, a return to the torment of the mid-19th century was averted by a greatly improved harvest in the autumn of 1925. The sun shone, potatoes and turf were harvested, hay was saved. A famine was avoided not by any action of the government or its agents but by the goodness of nature; and the crisis was gratefully forgotten.

---

1. In 1924, 'Irregulars' was still the term used by the government to describe those opposed to the 1920 Treaty that had established the Irish Free State. These Irregulars, who supported an Irish republic, had fought on the losing side in the Irish Civil War (1922–23).

One final avenue of search remained to us. In 1920, a person blinded by a grenade would have almost certainly been brought to the Royal Victoria Eye & Ear Hospital, founded in 1897, on Dublin's Adelaide Road. Rose is not precise on the date of the grenade attack, but puts it in the late summer of 1920, a time when the IRA had dramatically escalated its attacks on British Crown forces and on Irish people it suspected of being spies or collaborators. Between January 1919 and December 1921, over two hundred Irish civilians, including many Protestants, were killed by the IRA for their perceived pro-British allegiances. These IRA targets came from all tiers of Irish society and included farmers, shopkeepers, publicans, judges, civil servants and the professional classes.

We checked the original theatre register for the Eye & Ear Hospital for the year 1920. There were 261 eye operations performed, 34 for trauma. Of the trauma procedures, 16 were enucleations (removal of the eye globe), 12 were for traumatic cataract and 6 were listed as "primary wound repairs/other." Two specific operations resulted from bomb explosions: in April, a 52 year old man from Birmingham, who was likely to have been a soldier; and on 2 September, a Miss Helyett, aged twenty, whose address, in keeping with the very general details entered in the register, is given as 'County Dublin'. The surgeon – described as the "operator" – is listed here, and elsewhere in the register, by his initials, GB, which stand for George Bayliss, one of several prominent surgeons at work in the Eye & Ear Hospital at the time.

Is Miss Helyett Rose Raven? It seems highly likely. The date of Miss Helyett's operation matches Rose's narrative, as does her age and, of course, the cause of her injury. Sensing victory at last, we put the name Helyett through every hoop we could think of: births, marriages and deaths, census returns, archives of the British Army, church records. Alas, we found nothing. We then began to ask ourselves: why, given her subsequent narrative, would Rose Raven have presented to a Dublin hospital in 1920 under a false name? What reason would she have had to hide her true identity? It was her father the IRA had singled out, not her. And given Chink Holly's death in the same attack, Rose would surely have attracted local sympathy rather than vengeance. Four years later, in 1924, living in Nan's Cottage, there is no suggestion that she had to hide. Later, yes, she must hide from Melody, as we have seen, but in 1920 Rose was simply a young woman, robbed of her sight, in urgent need of medical attention.

We were sure Miss Helyett was Rose, the solitary glimpse we have of the real person, yet once again tantalisingly out of reach. She was so close. Before we gave up, we had another look at the medical register. The man who operated on Rose that day in 1920, Surgeon George Bayliss, was a Protestant, living near Balbriggan, County Dublin, a doctor of eminence, in his late-forties, who had served as a medical officer with the rank of captain in the Royal Army Medical Corps during the Anglo-Boer War in 1899. In the frantic atmosphere of Dublin in 1920, Surgeon Bayliss's personal details are suddenly relevant to the events of the day. In June 1920, a police sergeant serving in Malahide but living in Balbriggan was shot dead by the IRA as he left his home. During the same month, the house of a local Protestant farmer, outside Balbriggan, was burned when the farmer refused to subscribe to an IRA collection. Dr Bayliss, an ex-serviceman and a Protestant, living in Balbriggan, would have been keenly aware of these incidents and may well have known the victims. Is it not highly likely that in September 1920 he would have felt it prudent, to say the least, to disguise the fact that he had just attended the wounded daughter of a former British soldier whom the IRA had recently assassinated? He would have known little about Rose, just that the IRA had targeted her family. What if he feared a random IRA squad arriving at the hospital to trump up charges against him, an ex-British Army doctor, based on the evidence of the theatre register? Dr Bayliss would have rightly feared for his life in the rapidly worsening political situation.

We believe that Surgeon Bayliss, knowing the circumstances that gave rise to Rose's injuries, entered a false name in the theatre register for his own protection, unwittingly closing off to history the only clue as to Rose's true identity. He could not take the chance of his medical services being misinterpreted and ending up facing an IRA kangaroo court on charges of collaboration.

But why did he choose the name Miss Helyett? We kept looking. Then one day, a member of our team came up with the following information: in the early years of the twentieth century, a firm of horticulturalists – Laurent Fauke & Fils – from Orleans, France, was well known as a propagator of flowers and shrubs, many of which found their way to the burgeoning Edwardian Gardens of the British Isles. One such creation, an award-winning rambler with carmine-pink outer petals, was described by judges in Paris at the time as "a creation of truly outstanding beauty". The name given to this rose was Miss Helyett, probably called after a popular French opera of the time.

And so, ladies and gentlemen, Rose shines a spotlight into the fledgling Irish nation. She is there, she is not there. Like the butterfly Rudy compared her to, she is translucent, beautiful, ephemeral. In full view of history, she remains hidden. As to what became of her, we cannot say, but we agreed we have an image that might be near the truth.

We see her, alone, striking out north on the flat strand that runs north to the Malahide Estuary. Although blind, the terrain in her mind is perfectly clear. Rose follows the shore as it curves around the headland and becomes an inlet. After the hook, this inlet broadens into a wide body of water. The tide has turned and the estuary is in torrent as it is sucked back to sea in tight, hectic currents. The bluff of sand dives to a narrow path. Rose follows it until she comes to a little beach, a private spot, hidden from the world and sheltered from the wind. She puts down on a grass ridge and removes her shoes, then her stockings. The water kisses her feet warmly. She undresses to her slip and wades in. The beach shelves deeply. She goes in deeper and sinks until she can rest on the ocean floor, the currents running above her head. A peace possesses Rose Raven, and despite being underwater, she can see.

Acknowledgements

I owe sincere thanks to the many people who helped me understand the elusive political situation in Ireland in the period 1920–24, in particular Professor Michael Laffan, Emeritus Professor of History, University College Dublin; Michael Kennedy, National Archives of Ireland; Dr William Murphy, Department of History, Dublin City University; Professor Colm Campbell, Emeritus Professor of Justice, Transitional Justice Institute in the University of Ulster; Peter Costello, Historian, and Fin Dwyer, Irish History Podcast.

Professor Dara Kilmartin, Consultant Ophthalmologist in the Royal Victoria Eye and Ear Hospital, Dublin, provided unstinting advice on the procedures following eye trauma that would have been the norm in 1920.

The Reverend Greg Ryan and Tom Manning of the National Transport Museum guided me through the details of trams, including tram timetables, for the period.

Advice on lepidoptera was gratefully received from the late Dick Warner.

Andrew Healy provided insights into the Rent Restrictions Act, 1915.

Kevin Myers shone a light into barracks life in 1920s Dublin.

The late Tony Farmar gave me valuable information on pensions and insurance cover in the early 20th century.

The people who read the early drafts and who commented so very helpfully include Joe Joyce, Theo Dorgan, Paula Meehan and my agent, Caroline Montgomery of Rupert Crew & Co.

My editor, Moira Forsyth of Sandstone Press, played a central role in shaping the final version of the novel. Bob Davidson and all the team at Sandstone were unfailingly supportive.

Throughout the writing of this story, my mother, Mory Frederick McIntyre, was never far away. Mory was born in 1920 and grew up on the Burrow Road in Sutton, where I spent much of my early childhood. I could not have written this novel without this close connection.

Underlying all the above, Carol Cunningham provided wisdom, unflinching observations, encouragement and love.

www.petercunninghambooks.com

www.sandstonepress.com

facebook.com/SandstonePress/

@SandstonePress